Daddy's Bodyguard: An Age-Gap Protector Ex-Military Romance

Protective Alpha Hero, Forced Proximity, Security/Protection

Forbidden Daddy Steamy Novels

Kathilee Riley[1]

1. *https://www.amazon.com/stores/Kathilee-Riley/author/B0BTCW6HF7*

Published
by Kathilee Riley

Chapter 1

Sofia

"Hey, your dad is on the news again," my best friend and co-worker Carissa says, tapping my shoulder.

I glance at the TV, then stifle a groan. My father is standing on the steps of the courthouse before a cluster of microphones, talking about yet another of his cases. But this time, there's a change to the norm. The grimness in his tone and the hardness in his eyes tells me he's lost. Good. It's a much-needed win for the good guys.

I cut my eyes at the screen before motioning to the stack of paperwork before me. "We need to get on top of this."

"Are you serious?" Carissa asks, staring at me in disbelief. "Your dad just lost a case, Sofia. Aren't you least a little sad for him?"

"Why would I be sad? He defends criminals, Carissa, men who deserve to rot in prison. If it were up to me, he would lose every single case, the old devil."

"Come on, just because he's on the opposite side of the law doesn't mean he's the devil. He's just doing his job. Give him a call, Sofia."

"My answer hasn't changed since the last time you suggested it. It's still no."

Carissa purses her lips while picking up a healthy stack of papers from my desk. "Even if you don't talk *to* him, you're allowed to talk about him."

"I don't want to do that, either. I'd rather talk about this program. It's our job to make charity work look easy, Risa." I tap a folder on my desk. "And to do what we can to make sure everyone gets what they need."

It seems Carissa wants to push me further, but she eventually nods. I don't want anything to distract me from what's actually important: getting the less fortunate what they need to survive, even if the rest of the world would rather forget they exist.

My dad can focus on his life, and I'll focus on mine. It's better that way. I don't approve of his clients or the way he defends them, and he thinks I'm throwing my life away by working at a non-profit organization that pays peanuts—according to him. He would rather I join his legal team, but I would rather climb Mount Everest blindfolded before I succumb to his heinous request. Talking with him is wasting time – time I don't have if I want to fulfil my dream of becoming a congresswoman someday.

"You know, I realize our possible conversation topics just keep getting less," Carissa says, coming back to stand before my desk. "First, I can't talk about setting you up with guys, now we can't discuss your dad. Next, you're going to tell me we can't talk about that wild night in Cancun where you-"

"Nope." I point at her. "We agreed never to bring that up again." That night was an anomaly, the only time I ever lost control. Never again will I get drunk and have random sex with a hot guy in a club. I know how those actions can come back to bite you in the ass later on. And if I'm going to run for congress, my slate needs to be squeaky clean.

Carissa giggles and winks at me. "Fine, you naughty girl. I'll let it go. But final advice; you need to get laid."

"Why don't you pay attention to your sex life?" I ask her. "I don't see you getting laid, either."

"Because I'm waiting for Mr. Right, that's all. But you don't want commitment, so you are free to sleep with whoever you want."

"I'm going to pretend I never told you about my political aspirations because your ignorance is showing just a teeny bit."

Daddy's Bodyguard

Kathilee Riley

Published by Kathilee Riley, 2023.

Table of Contents

"Oh, please," Carissa says, rolling her eyes. "Why should a woman's sex life determine if she's fit to pass legislation?"

"I agree, but we both know that's not how it works. I can't afford to be a sinner, Carissa. I need to be a saint."

"Whatever, saint. I'm going back to work."

I roll out my neck and prepare for another late night. As much as I love my job, it gets exhausting sometimes. Designing and implementing fundraising strategies for a non-profit is no walk in the park, but the work we do helps hundreds of thousands each year, and I know the end result matters more than a few under-eye bags.

So what if I'm not earning a six-figure salary or living in a mansion like my dad? I'm satisfied with the job I'm doing here. There's no way I could relax in a cushiony job while people starve. I'm better than that. I'm definitely not my father's daughter.

I finish a proposal that needs to be emailed by tomorrow morning, then I check the clock. It's already nine, time to shut this down for the night.

Groaning, I peel myself from my chair, step into my heels and make sure all is in place for a successful day tomorrow. Satisfied, I head out, and on my way, I drop off a wireless copier I'd borrowed from the stationery room. As I step through the door on my way out, I run smack into my boss.

Nick grips my arms to keep us both from falling as he apologizes over and over. He's always been clumsy but in a cute, charming way. Backing off, I take in his tousled blond hair, the softness in his grey eyes and the gentle smile on his lips. Nick Arrowell is definitely my type. If he weren't my boss, or if I weren't so hell-bent on being a good girl, I'd give it up to him in a heartbeat.

"You're not teaching tonight?" he asks.

Of course, he remembers my favorite side hustle. I shake my head. "Tuesdays and Thursdays only until we either get more volunteers to teach or more funding."

"Another project." He shakes his head. "How do you make me feel like I don't work enough. *Me*?"

I laugh and shrug. "You work plenty, I just ... can't stop."

"I know the feeling." He motions to the elevator. "But remember that you're young, Sofia."

"That's not an excuse to slack off. I can be productive no matter how old I am. I don't want to wait until I'm physically unable to help."

Nick doesn't reply at first. His body intermittently brushes against mine as we silently walk to my car. I fiddle with my keys as he lingers, his soft eyes taking me in. "You should really take some time off," he says.

"For what?"

"For you. You're one of the best here, and I don't want you burning out before you take my job."

I blink at him, then laugh. "Don't tease."

"With all *your* enthusiasm and promise, I think *I'll* end up promoted, which means finding my own replacement." He inches further, a gentle smile on his lips. "Who better than the one person in the office that works harder than me?"

The compliment makes me want to do a backflip, but instead, I give him a calm nod. I know better than to count my chickens before they hatch. "I'd be honored to fill your shoes."

"I think you're a bit too delicate for mine." He brushes a stray lock of my dark hair from my face. "And I do like seeing you in heels."

A blush warms all the way down to my chest. I lightly touch his chest with a giggle, then lean back against my car. "Power shoes," I mumble.

"Oh, no doubt." He steps back, and I experience an instant flash of disappointment. "I'll see you tomorrow, Sofia."

"Good night, Nick."

Such a tease. I shake my head as Nick turns and walks away, glancing back twice. We have both been involved in this subtle flirting game since my first week at the company. But Nick has never made a solid move, and while I enjoy his teasing, I'm not sure if I want him to make a move. We both have our focus locked on our careers, which leaves no time for a social life, anyway. I don't want a relationship to derail my goals ... again.

Once was enough. Relationships strain my focus, leaving space for people to swoop in and take advantage of me. Even if I know Nick wouldn't do that, I can't afford to get distracted from my dreams. Not for anyone.

So, I put our little moment to the back of my mind, get in my car, and drive home while planning what I can possibly do to provide better homes and hot meals to people less fortunate. Even as I unlock my door and head into my apartment, I'm working out how to get more donations to help the local shelters.

I slide off my shoes and set them on my shoe rack near the door, then head to my fridge to pull out a pre-cooked, oven-ready meal and continue in my routine. It's like clockwork: smooth, predictable, and dependable. It's the reliability that makes it easy and allows my brain to wind down.

With everything else going smoothly, I can focus on other things, like getting through a shower and into comfortable clothes. I haul on cotton shorts and an oversized t-shirt that shows the original poster for *Night of the Living Dead.*

Sitting before my mirror, I remove my thick hair from the trademark bun and watch as it cascades down my shoulder. Reaching for a brush, I spend a few minutes detangling the curls before heading to the kitchen to get my food as well as the folder from my teaching bag.

Teaching English as a second language isn't a difficult task, but I have to ensure my methods are interesting and effective. Half of the class has the attention span of a four-year-old. The rest give me hope to carry on.

Perching on my bar stool, I look over my lesson plan for the week as I eat. A gentle knock on my door soon pulls my attention, and I stare at it with a frown. I wait for another knock, but all is silent. Did I imagine it? Was it a mistake? No one but Carissa knows where I live, and she never drops by unexpectedly. Plus, I only order takeout once a week. Who the hell could it be?

The silence continues. Satisfied, I return to my meal. I'm about to take a bite when another knock comes, then another, each one getting louder than before. I quickly reach for my phone to dial 9-1-1 because those definitely aren't friendly knocking on my door. The phone starts ringing as the door flies open, and I fall off the stool with a cry. I scramble to my feet, my eyes locking on the row of kitchen knives attached to the magnetic strip on the wall. Damn it. They are too far away.

The tall, Viking-looking man standing in the doorway is wearing an amused smile. Hardly the reaction of an intruder, but maybe he's one of those deranged assholes who murder people while smiling from ear to ear. Like the Joker. But he's definitely easier on the eyes.

Fuck. What am I thinking? There's a stranger standing in my foyer! I need to get somewhere safe. Fast!

But as I start backing away, he steps aside, revealing a handsome dark-haired man with greying hair at his temple. His perfect navy suit – never black because it's not a funeral – screams money. Dirty money. Yeah, that's my dad, and he's arguably *worse* than a run-of -the-mill intruder. He seems a little worried at first, but his face clears when he sees me.

"Dad?"

"Buenas tardes, mi amor. Thank God you're okay." He takes a step towards me, but I stop him with a raised palm.

"Why wouldn't I be okay? And why are you—" My head lifts a little as two other guys come up behind him, reducing Dad to hobbit-size next to them. What in the name of active duty is going on here?

Puzzled, I look back at him. "What's going on?"

"We're going to take a trip, princesa."

"A trip? Haha. No thanks." I motion to the door while turning my back to them. "Mind fixing the wall on your way out?"

I pick up my lesson plan and chuck it back into my work bag while listening for their departing footsteps. I don't need him in my life, especially if it means losing my security deposit on my apartment. My landlord will not be pleased about that broken door.

"I'm not leaving without you," Dad insists. "This is a matter of your safety, darling. Your life is in danger. There are people who will try to ruin me by hurting you."

"We don't even share the same last name, so no one knows we're related, anyway." I stop and look up at him, offering my hand. "Hi, I'm Sofia Wilson."

He pushes it aside. "Sofia, you are a Hernandez, like it or not."

"It's only blood. That's hardly anything." I huff. "Keep your problems to yourself instead of sprinkling them around for everyone else."

"It's too late for that." He comes closer, the graveness in his expression making my hair stand on end. "Listen, Sofia, the man I recently represented is about to get sentenced to a lifetime in jail. His family thinks I did little to save him, so they want revenge, which means there will be bad people coming for me, you—my entire family."

"Don't you call that a 'necessary risk' at your firm?"

"Sofia."

"If you would just represent good people, you wouldn't have to worry about murderers being upset when their families go to jail for perfectly acceptable reasons. Like you know ... murder!"

"Sofia! Will you stop acting like a spoiled brat for a second? What part of 'your life is danger' don't you understand? Let's go!"

He might as well have slapped me. My dad has called me plenty of things. He's also spent plenty of time *not* calling me, but that ... that word is unacceptable. I don't let anyone talk to me like that, let alone my *father*.

"First of all, I'm not a spoiled—"

"Now, Sofia!" He booms. "This is not a fucking joke!"

Startled, I take a step back from him. My father has never shouted at me like this before. For the first time ever, I see fear in his eyes.

"You get five minutes to grab a few things. That's the longest I can give you. The longer we linger, the more exposed we'll be when we exit the apartment building. Move your ass, Sofia. I mean it!"

Finally convinced, I grab my work bag from the kitchen counter, then hurry to my bedroom to pack a suitcase with enough clothes and toiletries for... God knows how long. A lone gunshot rings out as I'm grabbing my laptop. I quickly chuck it in my work bag as Dad rushes into the bedroom and pushes me into my closet. I hear muffled fighting as my father glowers at me.

"Yeah, you guessed it, they fucking found us," he whispers, still glaring like it's my fault.

"Why didn't you save yourself, huh? Wouldn't that have been easier?"

"Don't be ridiculous, Sofia. They would kill you in a heartbeat."

"Couldn't have that on your conscience, could you? A failed case *and* a dead daughter?" I hiss. I hear another grunt much closer to my bedroom, and my grip tightens on Dad's arm. Is this the end? Am I really destined to die with a man I can't stand?

I hear a sickening crunch like a bone is being broken. My widened eyes meet my father's as the bedroom door slams against the wall. I curl into Dad as the closet door is flung open, and his relieved sigh makes me pull away. It's just the Viking that kicked down my front door earlier. It seems he has a thing against doors or something. There's an urgent expression on his face as he grips my arm, tugging me out.

"We've managed to subdue the ones who made their way inside the apartment building, but I'm positive there's more coming. We need to move. Now," he says.

I glower at my father as the Viking reaches for my bags. "I'm never forgiving you for this."

"You'll be alive, and that's the point. I'll earn your forgiveness later."

"You mean, go back to ignoring me?" I snort. "I can't wait."

"Stop being dramatic. Let's go!" Dad orders.

My dad heads out one way with the other guys while the Viking takes me in the opposite direction. I don't even want to know who Dad paid to get him. He's probably just some low-level mafia dude, or maybe one of those illegal fighters or something, looking for easy money. Either way, my life is in his hands.

A set of gunshots ring out as we reach the landing on the fourth floor. Before I can react, he jerks me against him, pinning me against a wall just as more shots are fired.

The thunderous barrage makes me whimper with fright. I cover my mouth while leaning against the bodyguard's big frame. I feel his hand soften on my shoulder. "I got you."

"Over here!" Someone else shouts.

"Move!" He drags me towards the end of the hall and through a door.

He pulls me down three flights of stairs to the ground floor, then pauses just inside the door. I can feel my heartbeat fluttering like crazy inside my chest. Taking a deep breath, I try to calm myself. This is just a problem. Another problem with a more ... convincing deadline. I am going to survive this. I have to.

I notice a knife on his hip and slowly rub down his side to claim it. He chuckles, and his blue eyes flick at me. No worry in those eyes. "Gunfire makes you handsy?"

I roll my eyes and grip the handle of the knife, holding it in a ready position. He glances through the window again, then opens the door, keeping me behind him as we move towards the exit. He's huge, really huge. He's as tall as a bear, and it would take four of my hands to wrap around his bicep. I wouldn't be surprised to find out he's bulletproof too.

He turns, looks down at the knife, then at me and gives a slight nod. "Follow me."

"I don't-"

"We're playing red-light green-light. Come on!" He orders.

I sprint after him, trying to keep close, but my short legs are no match for his long strides. We are almost at the exit when I trip over my own fucking feet and faceplant on the floor. There's a sudden grip on my ankle that makes me scream. I feel myself being flipped over, and I come face to face with a guy wearing a bandana around his lower face. His eyes are cold and cruel. Murderous. I slash the knife at him, but he grabs it without effort, leaving me defenseless. But not for long. As he grabs me up by my hair and points a gun at my side, my own personal Hulk doubles back, his gun at the ready. My eyes fly shut as two shots ring out, and the thug's grip loosens on my hair. I hear the sound of a heavy thud beside me, and I open my eyes to see him spread out on the floor. Viking grabs my arm, pulling me with him as he dashes through the front door.

I'm still in a daze when he tosses me on the backseat of a car and hops in beside me. Dad's sitting on the other side, and just like when he entered the front door earlier, he seems relieved to see me.

The Viking slams the car door, and we take off at once. Grimacing, he removes a handkerchief from his pocket and wraps it around his hand. His bleeding hand. My stomach churns from the sight of the blood, and I turn away before I lose my dinner on the floor.

Dad stares at me as I take deep breaths to calm myself, but I keep picturing the guy who almost got me, his lifeless body on the floor. How did a quiet night at home turn into a nightmare? I did everything in my power to cut my association with my father. I changed my name, for God's sake. Still, here I am, being entangled with his shit, having my life completely uprooted. The very thing I've worked so hard to escape.

My father jerks his head towards me. "Get the picture now, princesa?"

I scoff, meeting his eyes with the dirtiest glare I can muster. "Once this is over, we're done. For good. Got that?"

"We'll see," he replies. "For now, my only aim is to keep you alive."

Chapter 2

Jasper

I look between the two subjects, then over to Kingston and Cash, the other two guys on this detail. They shrug and give me a look I know way too well. We all know this isn't going to be a simple in-and-out mission, especially not with these two as our clients.

It's been a few minutes, and they're at each other's throats as much as the asshats that are after them. They might just kill each other before the big, bad guys have the chance.

But it comes with the territory, I guess, and it's what I signed up for when I chose this career. Truly good people rarely require bodyguards, and at some point, you have to prioritize bills over background. Protection, even if you're not protecting the best, is still protection. I'd rather play defense than offense. I would rather be able to save someone, anyone, than end another life to follow through on an order.

I'm trying desperately to leave that old life behind, but it's proving harder than I figured when I was discharged from the military two years ago.

Still, the hellcat beside me doesn't seem to need much protecting. I've watched grown men cower in front of Mr. Hernandez, but this woman didn't miss a beat when she faced off with him earlier in the apartment. Other women would have lost their shit if assassins came after them, but she remained calm throughout most of our escape. She'll never know this, but I was quite impressed when she pulled my knife from my belt to defend herself.

She's determined but probably not the brightest. What is a knife going to do in a gunfight? She would have been better off using those claws. I bet his face would have looked like ribbons when she was done with him.

"Are you ready to behave, Sofia?" Mr. Hernandez says, his hard tone cutting into my thoughts. "We're going to a safehouse with Scarlett. Your mom and brother are still out of the country, so they are safe for now."

"No." She's really fond of *that* word.

"No is not an option."

"Just loan me one of ... these." She motions to us. "But I'm not staying with you and step-mommy."

I cover up a laugh with a fake cough, but Kingston smirks at me.

"I don't think so." Mr. Hernandez growls.

"I have commitments. I'm not upending my life because you couldn't get a bad man back into the streets," Sofia fires back.

"Don't be a child, princesa."

"Then don't call me princess!" She loses her temper, goes off in Spanish, but then takes a deep breath. "I'm not a *child* for having morals."

"You're a child because you'd rather believe this isn't real," Mr. Hernandez growls. "You're staying in a safehouse."

"Not with Scarlett and you," she hisses, sitting back.

They continue arguing while I remind myself this is the life I chose. I guess the two civilians came to an agreement because the car turns left instead of right, and we soon stop at an apartment building we had set up as a plan B safe house, just in case the first option becomes unsafe. Mr. Hernandez waves to the window and to me. "Sofia, your home and your muscle. Jasper Brookes."

Cash shakes his head once while Kingston gives me a look apologizing for my luck. Sofia climbs over me, keeping herself so far from my body that I feel rejected despite not even making a move.

I climb out of the car, and Mr. Hernandez catches me. "I'll be checking in soon."

"Of course."

"And ... you should hurry up." He motions towards his daughter. "She'll run."

I look over and see her doing exactly that. I sigh and take off as I hear a "Good luck" from Kingston. I'll give it to the girl. She's fast. If I didn't have my height or my love of the chase, I'd be royally fucked.

I manage to catch the back of her shirt, and she falls, nearly taking me with her. I hold her in place as she tries to get free.

"Let me go!"

"I have a safehouse to get you to," I remind her. "Plus, we are like sitting ducks out here in the open. We need to move. Now!"

She shoves me again. "I have a life to live! I don't need this."

"Your apartment begs to differ."

"Let me go! I have things to do. I'm not stopping until I'm dead."

"Good to know. Would you like that to be sooner or later?" I ask.

She glares at me, but the longer she looks, the more she softens until I smile. She tugs on her wrist again. "This isn't my fault. My life shouldn't have to stop because of my father's dirty deeds."

"You like having a choice." I nod. "We can work with that. Do you want to walk or be carried?"

"What?" Her eyes go wide. I arch an eyebrow, making my face hard, giving her a stare-down that made violent men shake in their boots. She rolls her eyes and tries to take a step back. "I'm leaving."

"Carried it is," I decide.

"No! Wait!" She yelps as I sling her over my shoulder. "Fuck!"

I wrap an arm around the back of her thighs and clear my throat as I walk us back to the house. "So, I'm Jasper. In case you're worried about my qualifications, I'm a former marine who's done multiple extraction missions during the ten years I've been on tour in the middle east. I've worked in the private sector for about two years since I've been discharged. I take my job seriously, so please, don't make it harder on us both, okay?"

Sofia grunts and tries to push herself up by bracing against my back. "Put me down. I'm an adult!"

"I'll set you down in the apartment. Not a second before then."

She clings to me and wiggles until I steady her with my free hand. She swats at me, Spanish whipping off her tongue. "No me toques!"

"You could have walked, but you chose this," I remind. "I think I like it more."

"Perve."

"Oh yeah. Forgive my imaginary hands on your ass, princess." I snort.

"Sofia." She corrects, giving my back a solid whack as we reach the front door. "Stop carrying me around like a caveman."

"Stop running, then." I pat her thigh.

"Hey! You don't get to touch me like that. This is all business, okay?"

I drop her onto her feet, and she stumbles. I catch her wrist as I grab the key from its space and put it in the door. "And business can't be fun?"

"Business and pleasure are separate."

"That sounds boring." I open the door and push her inside.

She glances at the door behind me and crosses her arms. "If not, the business is compromised, and the pleasure is ... muted."

"I'm starting to think you haven't enjoyed a proper workplace romance, princess." I kick the door shut. "You should get cleaned up and unpacked."

"I'm not staying here. Get it? I can check into a hotel-"

"Under your name, right? Because they didn't find you before?" I ask.

"I can pay cash and check in under another name," she argues.

"Rather than stay here? Where can you still live your life but with a surprise new bestie?"

She shakes her head. "You're not following me. I don't need a babysitter."

"Take a breath. We both have jobs to do, and I want it to be easy." I wait for her to halfheartedly blow out a breath before I continue. "Let's try this beautiful thing called compromise."

"I'm going to both jobs tomorrow. Alone. You have to stay inconspicuous, so you will. By staying here." She gives me a hard face. No negotiation written there.

"Wow, not even trying for charm."

She smiles at me, a slow, dry smile that has me shaking my head. "You'll temporarily live here. And you can do all your normal things ... with me," I say.

Sofia huffs and gets up, grabs her bags from the floor and goes down a hallway. I hear her grumbling to herself, but I'll pay her no mind. I could make her stay here all day, every day, but I'll try to be nice and go easy on her. Just a little.

"What the hell! Jasper!" Sofia yells.

I fly up from the couch, one hand on my gun as I rush towards the sound of her voice. Then I see what she's gawking at. One bedroom, one queen-sized bed. I smirk slightly, deciding between getting under her skin or calming her down. Sofia 's definitely not loving any part of this, but the idea of sharing a bed isn't horrible.

Not horrible at all.

Get your mind out of the gutter, Jasper. This is business, nothing else. Remember, you should never get involved with your clients.

Still, I lean against the door frame and take her in for the first time, her thick dark hair, deep, warm brown eyes, tan skin and full lips. With those curves, her long legs and those thick thighs, she's made to be the little spoon. If she were any other woman, I would definitely take advantage of that.

"I'm not sleeping in this with you," she says furiously as if reading my mind. "No way."

"I'm a pretty good space heater."

She glowers at me, and I grin. Physically, she's definitely my type, but I prefer sweet women who like to laugh. She's the kind of woman who would want to challenge my ass in combat or try to out-bench-press me at the gym. I'm not averse to being with a tough woman, but I'd prefer someone who's warm and loving under the muscle. Sofia isn't warm or loving. The brick wall around her is clear as day.

"This is so far beyond okay." She crosses her arms over her chest and shakes her head at the bed.

"Well, I'm sure you prize feminism, so I'll take the bed, and you can have the couch. Just like I'd deal with any of my male friends," I say.

"Really, you'd just decide *for* them?"

"Fine. Rock, paper scissors."

She looks at me for a long moment, then rolls her eyes. "Just take the fucking bed."

"Later," I reply. "We still have a compromise to make. I'll go to your jobs with you, and I'll give you some privacy, but you can't run."

I go back out to the couch and feel her following me. She shakes her head again. "No. Hell no. I'm not going to have you following me around constantly. What would I tell people?"

"We're dating," I suggest with a shrug.

Her face goes red, and her full lips pull tight as I say it. It takes effort not to smile. I love how she wears every bit of frustration on her face. "No."

"Which is why we're together so often."

"Jasper!"

"It started out as an online thing. But not Tinder. We're too good for that." I rub my chin. "I mean a year of talking, video chats, you being convinced I wouldn't relocate to be with you, and then, just like that, I decided to surprise you."

"You're killing me." She slumps down onto the couch next to me.

I gently nudge her shoulder. "So, what do you say, lover? Do you think our relationship can survive in the real world?"

"You're insane."

"So, you'd rather have me in full uniform, gun out and on display, letting everyone know you have a bodyguard?"

Her head falls against the back of the couch as she releases a conceding breath. "Fine. But you're just a friend. No, a cousin. Absolutely nothing more," she says.

I just smile. Despite how uptight Sofia behaves, I have a feeling she could be fun if she wanted to be. And this assignment could be fun if she'd let it be. I'd prefer that. I'm tired of the brutality of life, of counting the days since my last nightmare and never making an entire week before another one assaults my mind again.

"If you're alive, then fucking live like it." That's what Lieutenant Ryan Jackson had said before he'd gone down in action. I promised him I would, just like I promised I'd tell his wife – my sister – that he loved her. I promised him I'd take care of her and their young daughter. And I'll keep doing it until the day I die.

My sister Daisy will love this story. A willful, spoiled rich daughter who's forced to live with a bodyguard because a mobster wants to take her out. It's just like those romance books she loves to read.

Sofia pulls out a book, dragging my attention to her. She looks at it, then sets it on the coffee table. Before I can even look at the title, she corrects it – lining it up perfectly with the edge of the table.

I tap it out of place, and she bites her lip before pushing it back again. I chuckle, and she glares at me. "Is this really necessary?"

"The book?"

"You."

I turn on the couch to face her. I see dozens of dead men instead of her face. The same men who could only wish for protection, who would have been willing to sit still in a foxhole if it meant they'd get to go home and continue living.

I make myself focus on the moment. "Did you miss the bullets at your house?"

"No, but I-"

"Based on the fact that I've already bled for you, yes." I take her small hands between mine. "It's necessary. Which means you have to put up with me, bad taste in movies and all."

I flash a smile, and she groans, pulling away to slump into the arm of the couch. "Worst. Day. Ever."

I chuckle and get up to order pizza. "Just think of it as an adventure, princess."

"A horror story."

"At least you will be alive."

Chapter 3

Sofia

As we wait for the pizza, I glance over at Jasper again. I've been with him for almost an hour, he rescued me, and yet I haven't really taken him in. It didn't seem important until he was assigned to me. And then there was the fine print to wade through. Now that the adrenaline has worn off, I can take stock of the man I'm stuck with for the foreseeable future.

Jasper's hair is faded at the sides, but I could run my fingers through it at the top. It's dirty blonde and messy. He's clean-shaven, revealing his sharp jawline and his amazing cheekbones that lead to gorgeous blue eyes. A slightly crooked nose, and he's just a hunk with a few scars to prove he's battle ready.

Carissa would already be drooling over him, asking him a million questions. She'd read into those stupid things coming out of his mouth as if it were more than a way to avoid silence.

I don't want to be here. I certainly don't want to be around him. He's not a good guy. Dad doesn't work with people who aren't vicious, who aren't just like him – willing to do whatever it takes to get what they want, no matter who or what it costs. Jasper seems like the kind of man that danger follows, which makes me even more nervous to stay here, even though I said I would.

My eyes flick from Jasper to the door. I need to wait to make a choice. My brain is still on overdrive, and if I show my cards now, he'll have the advantage.

I bite my thumb nail as I look at the TV. It's a rom com ... and he chose it? Is it for me or him? Didn't he say he's a military man?

"Why are we watching this?" I ask, pulling up my leg on the couch.

"We?" Jasper scoffs. "You've barely glanced at the TV since we sat here.

"Wait a minute; you chose this for yourself?"

"I like romance movies, okay? I appreciate the idea of everyone having one true soul mate," Jasper replies. "A lot of them are silly, but they make me feel better."

"How? They remind you of a woman?" It's not hard to imagine a beautiful, leggy blonde waiting for him somewhere. Or maybe two. With a body and face like Jasper's, he could easily be a ladies' man.

"Nope. They make me realize it's almost impossible to find real love, so I shouldn't feel bad that I don't have it," he says.

"You don't have what, a girlfriend?" I ask, puzzled.

He shakes his head.

"Get the heck out of here!"

"Why is that so hard to believe?"

"Because..." I vertically gesture to his body, feeling my face heat as I do so.

Jasper chuckles. "Just say it, Sofia. I promise I won't jump your bones or anything."

I roll my eyes at him but acknowledge another heat wave flooding my face. I do *not* want to think about him jumping my bones. I scoot over a little on the couch and tuck my legs beneath me. "You look like a man who has the women banging on your door all night."

Still grinning, he cocks his head towards the front door, listening. "I don't hear a thing. Do you?"

I give him a whack, and he laughs out loud, and the pleasantness makes me smile. I could listen to him laugh anytime. Oh, gosh. Did that thought really cross my mind?

He leans back and studies my face, making me wonder if he knows what I'm thinking right now.

"Seriously, though. Why don't you have a girlfriend? Don't tell me you're one of those guys who blame the universe for all your fuck-ups that chased a good woman away."

"If I can blame the universe for me not having a girlfriend, you better believe I will."

"Oh, please. The universe doesn't care about us." I cross my arms again. "If the universe cared, bad people wouldn't be able to do the evil, devastating things they do."

"You're probably right. But then, there would be no need for guys like me, huh?"

My eyes run over his solid frame once more. I can't help myself. I can't deny how yummy he is, either. "I'm sure you would find another way to earn a living. Something that doesn't require killing. Doesn't it bother you sometimes?"

"As long as the bad guys lose, I sleep quite sound at night," he casually replies, throwing his arms over the couch. "Can we get back to the movie, please?"

I settle against the couch and tune into the movie for a while. It's not bad, actually. The clumsy heroine makes me laugh out loud a few times, and I love the chemistry between her and the sexy hero. He reminds me of Jasper, tall, chiseled, lips that make me think dirty things—

Stop, Sofia. Don't even go there.

"Seems you're enjoying the movie," Jasper says.

I shrug. "It's alright."

"Good. We can probably watch another after this. You know, to pass the time."

"Oh, no, no, no. I'm working on my lesson plan, then going to bed. You looking for company? Try Tinder. With your face, it shouldn't be hard."

"Are you flirting with me?" He leans towards me and bats his eyelashes. "I'm flattered."

I snort. No. No. I'm squashing that thought before it becomes more than a passing idea. "I'm married to work. I have a plan."

"And how does this arrangement fit into that plan?"

I glower at him. "It's not going to change a damn thing. Universe or not, I have things to do in the world, and I'm going to do them."

"You know, some people say it just because they want to believe it." Jasper leans towards me again, studying my face intently before focusing on my lips. "I might just believe it from your mouth."

"But?"

He arches an eyebrow.

"But? But I'm just a girl? But I should smile more? But if I were nicer, I'd make things happen? What is it? I hear it all the time. Make it original."

Jasper smiles slightly. "You'll learn how to take a compliment around me soon enough." He winks. "Promise."

I narrow my eyes at him. There's always a catch with compliments. Especially from men. I just have to wait, and he'll prove that he's just like all the other men I've known; he's just better at hiding it.

Jasper exhales and rests his arm under his head. His long eyelashes fan his cheeks when he closes his eyes. His big chest gently bounces, making me wonder if he's falling asleep. Either, he's too trusting, or he's testing me. Well, two can play that game. I'd like to know exactly what I'm dealing with. After waiting a few minutes, I slowly rise from the couch. I manage to get to one foot, glance at Jasper – eyes closed, even breathing - then plant my other foot on the ground. I step over him and make a dash towards the door, only to feel his powerful arms around me.

I gasp as he pulls me to the couch, the action leaving me breathless. I can't wiggle free or get my mind to focus, especially when he straddles me on his lap and locks me in with a tight arm around me.

He grins at me, which prompts an urge to wipe that smirk from his beautiful face. "I'm not that easy to distract, Sofia. And I'm a light sleeper. Keep this up, and I'll have to start keeping watch."

"You can't stay awake forever."

"Neither can you." His expression simmers, getting darker by the second. "We made a deal. Keep it, or you're not leaving this house."

"Threats?"

"Compromise doesn't seem to work. And clearly, you don't keep your word." His arm tightens around my waist.

I gasp and try to pull away. Well, I *almost* try to pull away. This is the most someone has touched me in a long time. A very long time. He has me on his lap, his arm around me, our bodies so close I catch a whiff of his scent. The blend of pine needles and sweat makes me want to bury my nose in his neck for a healthy sniff. Those blue eyes are like the bottom of an iceberg, overwhelming and distracting.

No! Focus.

"Sofia." He palms my chin, twisting my head back to him. "Listen. Let's do *one* thing the easy way."

"Easy isn't a good enough reason to do something." I pull my chin from his grip.

"Easy in one area keeps the rest moving. It keeps us easy, so you get to go on living. You want to work? You want to keep your schedule rather than shacking up here? I'm ready to make that happen, but only if I can trust that you're not going to run."

"You won't trust me," I argue.

Jasper looks me over slowly, taking in every inch of me as if he can figure me out with a sure gaze. His perusal pauses at my lips, then finally lift to my eyes. I squirm on his lap, but the heat in my belly spreads in response.

Maybe I should get on Tinder. I need to get laid. I definitely need to get something if just sitting on Jasper's lap is making me horny. I exhale slowly, calming myself.

Jasper leans closer, his gaze dropping to my lips again. I know I should pull back, but my body doesn't want to. There's this crazy desire to know what his lips taste like. But he doesn't kiss me. I lick across my bottom lip, and his eyes darken. Still, he doesn't kiss me.

"Are you going to run?" he murmurs.

His eyes burn into me, scorching my insides. Unable to bear the tension, I try to shimmy off his lap. But his grip tightens, making me release a frustrated groan. Reality sinks in, leaving me aware of how royally fucked I am. I can't escape Jasper. No matter how much I run, he's going to be there. He'll find me, he'll even chain me to the bed if he gets an order to do so. Yeah, I'm fucking trapped, all because my asshole father couldn't resist easy money.

But that's not the worst part of this reality. It's dealing with the unexpected attraction that's making me panic inside. I don't want to feel anything for this man.

"Sofia!" His hand tightens around me again, pulling me against him. I stifle the moan that threatens to leave my mouth as our bodies connect. "Answer me."

"I won't run," I whisper. "As long as you let me work. Let me live."

"No shortage on that. Just don't run," he says evenly. "That's all."

"Deal," I murmur, my lips nearly on his.

He still holds me there, watching me carefully while my heart pounds in my chest. I don't like this sizzle between us, the way his arm feels like it belongs around me, how great our bodies feel together like this. I close my eyes a moment, determined to fight my lust.

I hear the quiver in my voice when I mumble, "I need something to do."

"Look through your bags. Unpack." Another order, sharp, not expecting any compromise.

I feel a gentle pang in my stomach when he lets me go, but I dismiss it right away. No way do I want to remain on his lap, being pressed against his hard chest. What I need is some distance between us. I ease off his lap, and his hand immediately catches my eyes, the blood coming through whatever he wrapped around it. I reach for it, and he jerks it away from me. "You should ... you should fix that."

"He barely clipped me."

"He shot you?" That's enough. I clutch his upper arm, ignoring how deliciously tight his biceps feel. "Get up. I'm taking care of this right away."

Surprisingly he doesn't argue, and I'm glad because there's no way I could get him to the bathroom on my own. He allows me to drag him to the bathroom, and he doesn't say a word when I shove him onto the toilet, then look through the drawers. "There has to be a first aid kit or something."

"I'm fine."

I ignore his response and keep searching until I find one behind the bathroom mirror. He gives me a dark glare when I jerk off his bandage. The wound is on the side of his hand, where his thumb meets his palm. It's a jagged tear right on the edge, bloody and angry but not a hole, like I expected. I swallow the vomit in my throat and clean the wound with alcohol. He doesn't flinch at all.

I try to still my shaky fingers as I wrap his hand carefully. Jasper's eyes on me raise goosebumps, but I refuse to look away from the bandage. I pat the gauze once I tie it, and then I wash my hands twice.

"We need to work on your bedside manner a bit, princess. You could have told me it's going to be okay, that it won't hurt, plenty of things to make that easier."

"I thought it didn't hurt."

"I said it was just a flesh wound, not that it didn't hurt." He snorts. "Thanks for the concern, though."

He stands behind me in the mirror, and I realize I only come up to his chest. It's not too bad, considering how short I always am without my heels, but it doesn't make it any easier to stand up to someone when you're almost half their size.

A sudden knock on the front door makes me tighten my grip around the towel I'm using to dry my hands. There's a déjà vu-like feeling that reminds me of earlier tonight and puts me on edge, but I'm determined not to show it.

Jasper immediately puts me behind him. "Stay here."

"It's just the pizza."

"Yeah, because the pizza man is *so* innocent." He chuckles, then points at the floor in front of me. "Stay."

I roll my eyes but do as he asks. I hear another man's voice respond to his, then the front door softly closes. I peek my head out, then leave the bedroom. Jasper has the pizza box and nothing else. He looks at me and shakes his head. "Patience. We'll have to work on that too."

"This isn't about training me," I huff.

"Why, would you rather do the training?" He teases. "I'm pretty good at following *fun* instructions."

I shake my head at him but join him for pizza before I try to kick him off the couch so I can get some sleep. Jasper shakes his head and points to the bedroom. "Go. I was being a dick."

"No. You take the bed. I can't get in the way of you being a feminist," I insist.

"And give you a clear line to the door? No. Prove I can trust you ... tonight. Then we'll talk about you taking the couch. If not, we can always share a room." He winks at me. "It would be easier on me."

"Don't push your luck." I glower.

"Shouldn't you be doing a happy dance about winning the bed instead of glaring at me?" he asks. "Actually, do you have a setting other than glare?"

"Very funny."

"Most people think I am." He grins and lays back, his big arms crossed under his head. He looks like he got caught doing something he wasn't supposed to and is thrilled at the idea of being punished. Like he could punish me. I shake my head at the thought, and Jasper's grin turns wicked. "I'd pay to see what's going on in your head."

"Learn to read minds," I huff before walking to the bedroom.

"You know life can be fun, right?" he calls after me. "Every day doesn't have to be a battle."

"Says the bodyguard!"

I get into bed and spend the next few minutes trying to get comfortable. I toss, turn, beat the pillows, then groan as sleep continues to evade me. Shimmying from bed, I grab my laptop out of my bag and work on my lesson plan for a while. It's therapeutic. It's almost like sleep.

In fact, it's better. I'm getting things done, which is better than spending another hour trying to sleep. When I'm done with my lesson plan, I open the draft of my proposal and work on the editing for another half hour. Closing the laptop, I crawl back into bed, determined to get some sleep this time.

My mind goes to Jasper as I pull the covers over me. How does he sleep? Is he actually a light sleeper? A heavy sleeper? Does he wear stupid pajamas or just strip down to nothing? Maybe the naked Hulk could scare away some of these people for good and shorten our time together ... Or maybe I should stop thinking about him entirely. Tomorrow will help. I just have to make it to morning.

Chapter 4

Jasper

I make it halfway through the night before I'm brought back to hell itself. It feels so fucking real; the explosion, the shouting and the devastating pain in my leg. I gasp as my body lands on the floor, the impact forcing me out of the bombing incident that changed my life forever. I nearly hit my head on the coffee table, but the crash-landing helps shake me free of the lingering screams in my nightmares.

My lieutenant is gone. The platoon is gone. I don't need to try to fight my way to anyone. If only that knowledge would calm the restlessness buzzing in my body. I take a few deep breaths, glance at the clock, then looked down at how damaged my leg is from war.

I waited an hour after I heard Sofia snoring to take off my pants and get some sleep. It's better if she doesn't know how damaged her protection is.

Sitting back on the couch, I run my hand over my face. I'm not in war. I'm not overseas. I'm safe and sound in a literal *safehouse*. Sofia's in the bedroom, alive, safe, still snoring. Everything is exactly as it should be.

So why the hell is my heart threatening to slingshot itself out of my throat with my stomach's help? I can't tell if I'm going to be sick or if I'm having one of those panic attacks my sister Daisy tries to talk to me about.

It'll only be a few minutes. It'll be fine either way. I'm alive. I'm here, and that's what matters. After three deep, slow breaths, each one reminding me that I'm comfortable and alive, I refocus. It's morning, anyway. No need to go back to sleep.

I decide to raid the kitchen and get some breakfast together. Eggs, bacon, toast, milk. Damn, pre-stocked and everything. I whistle to myself as I start pulling out ingredients. This is shaping up to be a good morning, and after I eat, all of these unpleasant memories will be buried under a plateful of food.

Turning on the radio in the kitchen, I get to work on omelets. I sing along, glancing at the front door every now and again. I have no doubt that Sofia's going to try to head out to work without me. I probably should have done the shower and change thing first.

I set out the plates – omelets included - then slip into the bathroom for the fastest shower ever and jerk on pants before I head to the living room. Sofia is already there, staring at the breakfast as she pulls on a heel.

"You made breakfast?" she asks softly.

It's a rhetorical question, but I answer anyway. "It's my way of starting fresh. It's been a while since I cooked."

Sofia's gaze flows down my body as I finish tugging my t-shirt over my head. A soft blush covers her cheeks as she glances back at the kitchen counter. "I don't normally do breakfast."

"You don't normally deal with me all day either." I sit down around the counter and take a bite. She does the same, then takes another bite. "It's edible, right?"

Shaking her head, Sofia picks up the toast with her fork. We eat in relative silence before I try to get to know her, anything that might help me as we go forward, but after the first question, she rolls her eyes at me.

"So that's what we're doing? Ruining breakfast with conversation?"

"Conversation *makes* breakfast. Who eats in silence?"

She narrows her eyes.

"Only villains and Batman on lonely nights," I reply to my own question. "Last I checked, we're neither."

She shakes her head at me and takes another bite. I swallow my food before continuing. "Personally, I think that eating is the best part of the day. All you have to do is avoid choking. You're doing great in that respect, by the way."

Sofia drops her fork. "Dios mio! I can't even hear myself think!"

"Why not think out loud? All the great geniuses do it."

"You're like ..." her fingers look half broken as she forces her hands together. Like she can make a muzzle manifest between her palms. If only, sweetheart. "You're like an overexcited golden retriever. You're so busy chasing your own tail you wouldn't even notice if I had a ball."

I set my knife down and stare at her with the most serious face I can muster. "Sofia... You had a ball all this time and didn't tell me?"

She shakes her head, but I see the hint of a smile on her face. Maybe there's some human under this robot.

We finish eating, and Sofia takes my plate and silverware without asking. She piles them all in the sink, checks her watch, then gives the plates a wistful look. It's going to bug her; I can already tell.

"We can wash them when we get home," I say.

"Fine. Your rules, right?" Her venom is at full potency again.

"I figured you'd want to get to work faster. Introduce me to all your friends as the guy who almost got away."

"Jasper."

"But it's okay, baby. I'm not going anywhere. How can I resist such a wild minx?" I wink.

She rubs her forehead. "We talked about this. You're my cousin."

"This makes more sense. A cousin wouldn't exactly feel the urge to take you out to dinner."

"We have a car, right, or are we doing a taxi?" She immediately changes the subject, which makes me smirk.

After a short argument about cars, she gives up, and we take a taxi to her job. I know she wants to rent a car, but it'll be in her name, and anyone worth their salt will be able to track that shit down. But maybe I can tweak her limitations a little. It's against my status quo, but this woman makes me want to break every single rule.

Before we go in, I catch her hand. "If you behave, I'll take care of the car later. But only if it's rented in my name." I'm a ghost. These thugs can't track someone they don't know exists.

"I'll behave if you don't drive me insane. How about that?"

"You're big on the give and take, aren't you?"

Sofia eyes me up and down, then moves ahead. "Also, this is job one of two. Just letting you know."

"Fantastic." I grab the door and hold it open for her. She continues to eye me like I can't be trusted, but there's a curious glint in her look. It's progress.

We walk into a flurry of activity. People talking on phones, rushing back and forth, the clicking of keyboards. They're all just jagged streaks of loud voices and muted colors. I fight the urge to drag Sofia against me as a big guy rushes towards her. Reminding myself we're in her office building, a totally safe zone—for now, I focus on my job, turning my attention to the front window of the office.

After checking out the slower-paced world outside, I relax a little. I don't see anyone stopping in vehicles, considering the street parking is full. No one lingers in their car. No loitering with eyes on our building. It's an excellent sign that we weren't followed and that Sofia's place of work hasn't been discovered. Point one for our team.

"Jasper." Sofia tugs my hand and motions to a woman in front of her.

The woman is a little taller than Sofia, curvier, and has the sweetest smile I've ever seen. Her shoulder-length blonde hair, bright green eyes, and the way her blush covers the tip of her nose are all so welcoming that I can't help but grin.

"This is my best friend, Carissa. Carissa, this is Jasper."

I take Carissa's hand in mine, noticing how soft and delicate it feels. "Nice to meet you, Carissa."

"Likewise, Jasper," she replies, her husky tone and traveling eyes making obvious her interest in me.

Sofia opens her mouth to say something, then looks over to where a guy just stepped out of an office. He's taking me in with a slight frown, then he beckons to Sofia. "That's our boss, Nick. Give me a minute, okay?" she says to me.

She walks over to him and follows him into his office without looking back once. I shove my hand in my pocket and refocus on Carissa. Sofia's safe with her boss. No need to worry.

Carissa clears her throat. "So, Jasper, who are you, and why are you here?"

There's no venom in her tone, just a mild curiosity that matches the expression on her face.

I clear my throat. "I'm Sofia's huh... colleague. She invited me to learn a little about what you guys do here." Sofia's backstory has holes, but I wasn't in the mood to prolong the argument. Still, I wonder what people will think if I'm here for longer than a week.

Carissa's face brightens. "That's wonderful. Trust me; you'll enjoy your time here. We reach out to companies and provide incentives to donate to homeless shelters, halfway houses, and foodbanks. A lot of them just send us big checks, which has done a world of good, but we are constantly seeking help in other areas."

"Wow, I'm impressed. You guys are doing a kick-ass job."

"Thanks," Carissa replies, still with that beautiful smile. "But the most impressive person here is Sofia. She's a cut above us all."

Sofia is still locked in the office with her boss, so Carissa offers to give me a brief tour of the office. She shows me Sofia's desk, papers perfectly stacked, calendar covered with sticky notes and clear handwriting. I make a mental note to hide her calendar, so her schedule isn't obvious to everyone who comes in. She has folders in piles in a system only she can figure out.

"Sofia and I go over paperwork most days. She wants to try and get everyone on the streets a place in a shelter or some kind of address so they can apply for jobs. It's her big project of the year."

"I thought she just made phone calls all day," I reply.

"That's just a tiny percent of her job. Other days, she's on the go, meeting with donors, helping with deliveries or making rounds to shelters around town."

"Oh, wow. That's definitely impressive." I glance towards the locked office door where Sofia had disappeared behind earlier. It seems there's a heart beneath that tough exterior, after all.

"It really is," Carissa replies. "And I'm looking forward to having you witness how we do things around here."

Her lingering gaze and the light touch on my arm tell me that's not all she's looking forward to. I shift my attention from her hopeful expression as their boss' office door opens once more. Sofia brushes a loose strand of hair behind her ear as she exits the office with a smile. Hell, she's actually smiling. Her boss is right behind her, and the way he's looking at her makes me edgy, possessive. He gently pats her shoulder, and I suppress the urge to wipe the grin from his face and peel his hand off her. This is crazy. She's not mine to claim or fight over. I'm here to work, nothing else. She flashes a genuine smile that softens every bit of her existence, but as soon as she glances at me, it's gone.

She walks up to us, her gaze directly fixed on Carissa. "I'm about to get the ball rolling. Is there anything you need from me?"

"Well, Mr. Collins sent over the legal documents for the partnership with his company this morning. I need a copy of the initial proposal, but that's it."

Sofia nods and moves towards her desk. I follow behind her and Carissa while checking out every team member we encounter along the way. I want to be on the alert for every new face that enters the office each day. Sofia goes to her desk and scans through a drawer before handing over a file with paperwork.

"It's all there," she says to Carissa.

Carissa rests the file in the crook of her arm as she stops before me. "Good to meet you, Jasper. I'll be seeing you around, right?"

"Definitely." I salute her, making her giggle. I tear my eyes from her retreating form as Sofia clears her throat. I turn to her with a smirk, and she exhales slowly. "You are a reporter. Congratulations on your accomplishment."

"Since when?"

"Since I decided that was the best thing to tell my boss." She closes her eyes a moment and pinches the bridge of her nose. "You're a reporter who is going to share all the hard work we've been doing and how it's helping."

Before I can say anything, she motions to the back of the office, and I follow her through a door to a warehouse. Here, there are people loading huge cardboard boxes with various items. Canned food, blankets, clothes and small bags.

Despite the hard work being done, the workers are in great spirits, laughing and teasing each other. It looks more like fun than a job. Sofia visits with a few people, then returns to my side.

"Put me to work," I say.

"What?"

"Well, I can't report very well if I'm not part of the action. Where do I start?"

"You want to help? Let me do my rounds." She faces me with a plea on her face. "I like delivering. If I split it with Carissa, it'll only be five stops. Please?"

I wish I could tell her yes since she's obviously dying to do it. But I can't justify the risk, especially if it would put us in areas where she'll stand out, where she'll be out in the open. "I'm sorry, Sofia. I really wish I could say yes, but your safety needs to come first."

She seems about to argue, then she bites her bottom lip and takes a slow breath. "Fine, I'll ask Carissa to do it this time, but if we're still in this position in a week, I'm going, even if you tag along."

"I'll agree to that."

Sofia nods once and then motions to the set-up in front of us. "Alright, now that it's settled, let's put you to work."

"Stay where I can see you," I remind her.

She rolls her eyes and explains how to fill the boxes. I'm put on blanket duty while Sofia does a bit of everything. She's often on her phone, but she doesn't stop packing. She's the queen of multitasking. She doesn't miss a beat, just makes all adjustments necessary to get the job done.

By the time noon comes around, everyone starts loading the boxes, Sofia included. She taps boxes, including the ones I carry, and tells us what truck they belong in. Her hands brush mine as she takes a lighter box from me.

Our eyes meet, and she swallows, then she nods once to me, and I assume it's the closest to a thank you that I'm going to get with her. I jump up into the truck to organize the boxes for easier unloading, and she insists on joining me, so I offer my arm to help her up. My arm lingers around her when she joins me, and for a moment, she seems quite contented with not moving at all. But an awareness soon fills her face, and she backs away with a grunt. I stifle my smile and get to work.

By the time the trucks are full, half of the workers are at a pause or missing. Sofia sits on the edge of the truck and looks over me. "You're something else, Jasper."

"Back at you." I smile, acknowledging the warmth spreading through me. This mission will be the most interesting one I ever had. I can already feel it.

Chapter 5

Sofia

Carissa appears when we're done with loading the truck and volunteers to do the deliveries before I can ask her to take over for me. I notice how her eyes keep going to Jasper as she speaks. I'm not surprised. Jasper is... quite a man. Any hot-blooded woman would be attracted to how gorgeous he is. But I can't ignore the flutter of jealousy when I realize he's checking her out too.

What am I doing? I'm not interested in Jasper, am I? Nah. I'm just exhausted, and these heels are killing me. But I can't deny that I'm relieved when she goes back inside. I watch Jasper jump off the back of the truck. I glance at my heels and consider kicking them off when he reaches for me.

I hesitate. I don't know if I want him touching me, really. He rolls his eyes. "Do it for me. If I kept you safe from the bad guys, but you break a leg jumping out of a truck, I'd be just as fucked."

Swallowing, I reach for his shoulders and feel his big hands squeeze my hips. I try to hide my blush as he helps me down to my feet. Jasper watches me as he sets me back onto my heels, and his hands linger on my waist.

"You did your job. I survived," I say, moving away from him.

"I'm proud of you." His lips turn up, just like I've learned to expect. "I get to keep my job another day."

I motion inside, so we can get moving and get some space between us. I don't want to let on how frustrated I am, especially considering he's helped so much today. Still, I hate how easily he's taking all this when having him around is driving me insane, like my adult card is being threatened.

"Compromise," Jasper says to me. "See how pleasant it is? You get to work, and I don't have to toss you around."

I narrow my eyes at him. "Is it that easy for you to lie?"

"I think this is pretty pleasant." His eyes flick to the windows as our trucks take off. He returns his gaze to me and motions to my desk. "But part of being safe is keeping some things secret."

He points out my calendar, and I sigh. I like having it right in front of me so I don't forget things. But he's right. I take off all the sticky notes and organize them by date in my planner, so they're not quite as on display.

I'm trying to buy some trust from Jasper, so I can have a bit more freedom in the long run. It's just a drawn-out agreement. If I think of it that way, then every time I give over something silly and unimportant, he'll have to compromise somewhere else.

"We've had a good day so far." He leans back in the chair in front of me. "Let's call this progress."

"Yeah, well, I still don't appreciate being told what to do, Jasper," I remind him. "I don't like being kept from my normal schedule. This time next week, I'll be doing deliveries again."

He sits up while offering his pinky and a smile. "I'm a man of my word, princess."

"Every time you call me that, you remind me of my dad." I take his pinky anyway. "Just so you know how you're coming off."

"Well, we can't have that. Luckily, I have plenty of alternatives." He winks at me.

I cut my eyes at him and power up my laptop. Eventually, he'll settle for this being professional and stop trying to be my friend. But he rests his elbow on the desk and gives my face a slow-motion scan that leaves me warm and uneasy. "So, *sweetheart*, what are we doing next?"

"I'm not your sweetheart, Goddamnit. *I* have a lunch meeting with a representative from a local deli chain. Mr. Nance wants to talk about donations to our company."

"Great. We can't miss that, now, can we?" He stands and pulls my sunglasses off my desk to cover his face.

"Thanks for stretching my sunglasses." I huff.

"You worry too much, Sofia."

"You don't worry enough. Especially considering... who you are." I cover my slip quickly as Nick goes past my desk. "But you should definitely see the kind of relationship we have with our clients," I say for Nick's benefit, but my boss doesn't seem to hear a word. His eyes are locked to his phone.

I gather the things I need for my meeting, and Jasper follows me to the elevator. It's a perfect day, with the temperature a little above seventy and sparse clouds blocking most of the sun. Usually, I would have taken the opportunity to walk to the bistro instead of taking a cab. I hate that I can't do as I please. I shouldn't have to upend my life because of my father's dirty deeds.

Jasper glances at my face and chuckles softly. "On a scale of one to ten, how mad are you?"

"Six," I grumble.

"Better than I figured." He bumps my hip lightly as we exit the lift. "So, after this lovely lunch date, what are we going to be doing?"

"More paperwork. I thought you'd like a boring day. Doesn't that make your job easy?"

"Nothing about *you* makes my job easy," Jasper says as he hurriedly bundles me in the back of the cab and joins me right away. "But you keep it interesting."

Of course, more of his teasing. That's how he keeps things interesting for himself, not for me. I'd rather him watch from some undisclosed location on the outskirts of my life, so I wouldn't feel half as suffocated.

The bistro is close by, at least. The less time I spend talking to Jasper, the better. I take a table outside since Mr. Nance likes to smoke, and Jasper glowers at my decision. I'm glad when he doesn't argue. I hate smoking, but I need to keep my client happy, so the donations can keep coming in. Jasper's eyes flick around us, never focusing for longer than a few seconds. He adjusts in his seat twice before concentrating on me.

"You look fidgety. You're going to make Mr. Nance nervous." But he ignores me and looks around again, his head swiveling. "Jasper! Seriously. Turn off meerkat mode."

His eyes focus on me. "I noticed someone has been sitting in their car just watching the restaurant."

"Okay, maybe they have a delivery order. Relax." I sigh. "Not everything is life or death, okay? Sometimes, people do things that have nothing at all to do with us. It's just them living their lives."

"Yeah, and that kind of thinking isn't what I'm paid for."

"And it's not letting you blend in either," I hiss. "Come on, Jasper. If we can't fit in and get work done, being out here is pointless."

He glances around again, then adjusts his spot, sitting next to me as if his big body there alone will keep me from being seen or hurt. When there was some distance between us, it was easy for me to forget exactly how big he is, but now that I can't even see around him, I have to admit ... I do feel safe.

Jasper is a wall of muscle and a pretty good human shield. He puts his hand on mine – on the freaking table – when the waitress comes by and offers us menus and a drink. I take an iced tea, and he orders bottled water.

The waitress looks him over and then glances at me. "You guys make such a cute couple," she says with an adorable smile.

"Thank you. Appreciate it," Jasper replies before I open my mouth.

"I see you have a third-place setting. Is this not a date?"

My cheeks must be on fire. Jasper squeezes my hand. "It is. But you know how hard it is to trust someone you've met online. She feels safer out in the open with a work colleague joining us."

"Oh, how did you meet?" she asks.

I fight the urge to kick Jasper's shin as he brings my hand up to his lips and kisses across my knuckles. "I just loved her memes on Instagram. You wouldn't know it, but her sense of humor is amazing. She didn't respond at first when I slid into her DM, but once I turned on my charm, I caught her hook, line and sinker."

"That's such a cute story to tell your kids, am I right?"

"Oh, definitely!" Jasper replies with a grin.

The server winks and walks away, and I shoot Jasper a glare, but he's focusing on the road again, so he doesn't see it. I nudge him. His hand drops to my knee, holding me in place and spreading warmth up my thigh. "Just one second, honey bear."

"Stop with the damn pet names. Especially right now. I'm still working."

"Your person should be heading up now," Jasper says, ignoring me entirely.

The server reappears with our beverages just as Mr. Nance sits down. He smiles and nods to me. "So good to see you again, Miss Wilson."

"Mr. Nance. I'm so glad we could make time to do this today. How long has it been since we've last seen each other?"

Just like that, I focus on business. By the time the food arrives in front of us, Mr. Nance and I have an agreement. He'll make a continuous food donation to three local shelters while making a cash donation to a boys and girls youth club in the projects. I hate that Jasper got involved when Mr. Nance was on the fence about how much money he should donate. But he was able to convince Mr. Nance to raise his offer by ten thousand dollars, which is a lot more than I expected. So, no harm done. But Jasper's forceful manner is a risk I can't afford to take again. Thank God Mr. Nance is a good-natured man who's easily swayed. Next time, we might not be so lucky, and I can't afford to lose a donor, not when there are so many people in need.

I shove Jasper's hand to the side as soon as Mr. Nance is out of sight. "I can handle my job on my own. I don't need your help, got that?"

"Why are you mad when you got what you want?" he asks with a frown.

Another server interrupts my hot reply, offering dessert. Jasper turns his easygoing smile on him. "Oh no. This angel is all the sweetness I need."

"That's sweet. How long have you two been together?" the server asks.

"Oh, it feels like forever." I can already feel the migraine.

"You're so right, love." Jasper squeezes my hand before looking at the server once more. "But really, it's only been a week – in person, I mean. We've been talking on the phone for a year, and she's been begging me for weeks to finally meet in person, how could I say no?"

Biting my lower lip, I give him a hard kick on his ankle. His grip tightens on my hand, but he doesn't stop smiling. Asshole.

"A modern love story. Adorbs. I love it," the server continues. "Okay, so I'll just get your check, and you guys will be all set."

"That was totally unnecessary," I grumble when the server walks away.

Jasper shrugs. "But your face made it worth it. And on that point, what's your love language?"

"No clue."

"You're killing my heart now, gorgeous." He pats his chest. "All I want to do is make this relationship work. Let's be real partners and work together."

"We are not partners, Jasper, nor are we in a relationship. You were hired by my father to keep me safe." I make air quotes with my fingers. "Although I think it's a complete waste of time."

"Whatever you say, baby girl," he says, whipping out his credit card to pay for the meal. "I'm just doing the job your father paid me to do. And if it means pretending that we're a couple to blend in, I don't see the problem."

"Of course, you wouldn't because you get off on getting under my skin. And for the last time, I'm not your baby girl."

But his devilish grin tells me he won't stop. He keeps up the teasing until we get back to the office. Then, as if a switch flips, he gets serious again, his head darting left and right as we head into my office building.

"So far, so good, Sofia," he says when we get inside. "No signs of trouble."

"Because they're not interested in me, just like I said before. So how about we call it a day, and you go home," I reply.

"How about you stop fighting and let me do my job?"

After glancing around, I spot Carissa standing by the water cooler, talking to Trina, a college student who volunteers a few hours each week. Maybe I can push Jasper in her direction. They are obviously attracted to each other, and I know she'll love his company. I wave my hands to get her attention, and she immediately scurries over to us, her gaze locked on Jasper. Again, there's that stupid twinge in my chest, but I ignore it.

"Carissa, do you mind giving Jasper a run-through of your daily functions? I have a batch of phone calls to make."

"Of course!" Carissa's face lights up at once, and she slips her arm into Jasper's. "The pleasure's all mine."

I ignore his frown and meet Carissa's smile with my own. "Have fun!"

"You know what? I think I will," Jasper replies, cutting his eyes at me. "It would be a pleasure to hang out with you, Carissa," Jasper nearly purrs. "I'd really like to pick your brain."

Carissa's giggling carries down the hall as she and Jasper walk away. I'm relieved. I really am. Now, I can refocus on work and hope that he clings to her for the rest of the day, using her as a point of distraction from me and a cover for himself.

But within five minutes, he's back at my desk. Exasperated, I rub my temple to soothe the headache that's been plaguing me all day. "Why the hell are you back already?"

Jasper shrugs. "Carissa's a sweet girl, but she doesn't raise my temperature like you do. Plus, her desk is too far away. I can't see you from all the way over there."

Of course, I'm not going to read too much into what he just said, although my tripping pulse seems to have its own mind. My racing heart, too.

He moves his chair next to me and glances at the time. "What time are we going to tackle job two?"

"You sound a little eager, almost like my life isn't boring."

"I never said it was, darling." He sighs. "I said it was an unnecessary risk."

"Say it with me: Sofia. So-fia."

"Sofia." His velvety voice caresses my name and sends a shiver down my spine.

I sit a little taller. "At five thirty, we have to head over to the community college where I teach the English language three days a week."

"One more hour here, then to another open, unfamiliar space while crossing our fingers."

"Just call it an adventure," I tease.

"Don't forget who's doing who the favor here."

I roll my eyes but avoid his. I know he's right. He doesn't have to let me out of the safehouse, but he also knows that I would have made life impossible for him. Not that it matters either way since I'm *sure* that whoever is after my dad just followed him to my place and doesn't actually care about me.

"Soon enough, we'll get to go our separate ways and get back to our lives. Let's not kill each other until then," I say.

"Killing each other would be counterproductive to my mission." He flashes a grin. "Let's just keep up the compromise and easy living."

"This *isn't* easy."

"It's easier than it could be." His face hardens. "Trust me on that."

Chapter 6

Jasper

By the time we get back to the safehouse from Sofia's second job – teaching English to adults – I'm beat. My leg aches, and I swear I feel every single year of combat weighing on me. Every injury re-opened, and every bit of my body was exhausted. Even my *eyes* ache.

I must be getting old. Fuck.

I flop down on the couch and groan. When I open my eyes, I see Sofia slipping out of her heels. She toes them in line with the other shoes and continues into the apartment. She makes a beeline for the dishes from this morning and knocks those out within a few minutes. Then she changes into pajamas and goes to the fridge. From my seat on the couch, I watch her every move, each action leaving me more turned on by the minute.

She spent the whole day looking like some kind of corporate wet dream – a woman that can do it all and then some, with a smile - and now, in her lounge pants and oversized t-shirt, she looks real, tangible, warm. Totally fuckable.

I take my mind out of the gutter when she sits next to me with a soft groan. "I usually prepare my meals for the entire week, you know. Now, there's nothing ready-made in the fridge."

"Ordering pizza was already a risk. Just like getting a rental car." I stretch my arms high above my head and roll out my neck. "It's safer to cook. There's plenty of stuff in the fridge."

She sighs. "I don't think I have it in me to cook."

Honestly, I believe it. All I did was watch her today, and that was enough to exhaust me. I rub my forehead. "Pizza leftovers are in the oven."

"They belong in the fridge."

"Why the hell would I put bread in the fridge? It heats up better when its room temp." I let my eyes close. "Como se dice "fridge"?"

She shoves me lightly. "It's dairy. You have to put it in the fridge for it to stay good."

"Yes, dear. Now I know for the future." I slide my arm over her shoulders.

Sofia surprises me by leaning into me, taking a deep breath before yawning. "Give me five minutes, and I'll heat it up."

"Take ten."

"It's the best thing you've said since we met," she murmurs, giggling when I pinch her side.

Corporate work shouldn't have me this ready to sleep. Honestly, my exhaustion and Sofia being sweet seems like a trap. An easy way for her to get me knocked out, so she can run. But she adjusts on me, her head on my chest as she presses against my side, one hand resting on my opposite hip. Each movement sends a flare of desire running through me that I desperately try to ignore, but my hardening cock tells me it's not working at all. I put my hand on my lap so she doesn't accidentally brush against it. The last thing I want to do is alarm her or ruin this moment between us.

Again, Sofia adjusts herself against me until she's comfortable. "These are my tiring days," she says with a deep yawn.

"I'm sure last night didn't help." I adjust, letting my head fall back on the couch. "A lot of action and adrenaline."

"Shhh. You're cutting into my ten-minute break. After that, we have to do dinner, and then I have some lesson plans to adjust."

"Jesus, woman, you just never stop. What do you have to lose by taking *one night* off?"

"Why waste the available time?"

"Because resting is just as important as working. If you don't rest, studies show your brain doesn't operate at its highest capability." I let my hand stroke over her arm. "Maybe take just one night off. Call it ... recalibration."

"Sounds like procrastination to me."

I chuckle and shake my head. She's stubborn, but I have to admit her ability to argue, to plan out the rest of the day, to go this hard constantly is amazing. A little energizer bunny who knows what needs her attention, where to focus and exactly how to get a job done. She's a freaking powerhouse, this woman.

Sofia would kick ass in the military. She'd have soldiers ready to follow every command, and I bet she'd still take on other projects. She's really something else, a woman who's ready to make the life she's dreamed of, whether it comes easy or takes constant effort.

I chill with her for a while, almost shocked that she's sticking to the idea of rest for even this long. With the energy of a four-year-old and the drive of someone with a legacy to protect, Sofia doesn't seem like the kind to give herself any relaxation, but here she is proving me wrong – like she has been over and over today.

More than some corporate hard ass, she's the kind who rolls up her sleeves to get the job done and never asks for more than what someone can do. When she's in her element, her stubborn, persistent, and pissy attitude gets shit done. Her determination is kind of ... sexy. Not that I can possibly tell her that.

Sofia takes a deep breath, then exhales across my chest. Slowly, I open my eyes and look her over. Her dark hair sweeps across her face, hiding a bit of her beauty. She's quite small and soft and fits perfectly against my side. I could get used to this, having her here against me because she wants to be. She didn't hesitate to take this spot; I didn't have to force her. But I'm sure it's temporary. Once she's back at full battery strength, she's going to find a way to brush off this moment and turn it into nothing at all.

Which makes me all the more eager to save what I can. Cuddling Sofia on the couch isn't exactly the white picket fence and happy family I want, but it's a huge step closer to a normal civilian existence. It's nine at night, but we're comfortable, home and safe.

I'm not on the battlefield or trying to put a fire together to keep my team warm on a cold night, not assigning two men to stand watch as we hunker down in the desert. I can just enjoy the plush couch under me, the woman pressed to my side, and the fact I don't have to worry about some late-night hellfire to interrupt my sleep.

Sofia stays in place for another minute before her eyes open and meet mine. She clears her throat and sits back, pushing her hair out of her face. "So ... that pizza."

"I need to check the windows and door along with the security feed," I murmur.

Sofia gets up with a yawn, then stretches and walks quietly to the kitchen. Her feet barely make a sound across the wood floors. I hear her go to the kitchen, then she starts grumbling again about me leaving the pizza in the oven.

Shaking my head, I get up, check all the windows and walk around outside to note any changes, any shoe prints, anything that might hint that we're not as safe as we think. Nothing. The windows are latched. The home security is in place. The cameras aren't obvious.

We should be alerted to any kind of breach before it becomes a problem. Honestly, I don't see an easy way for anyone to get in the safehouse, which means if they do come for Sofia, they'll go for her while she's at work or commuting.

I return to the apartment, intending to talk to Sofia about that possibility. Before I can bring this potential attack to light, Sofia's cell phone rings. Her eyes flick to me, and she picks it up. "Qué quieres?"

It must be her father. She minimizes her Spanish use around me, but I'd rather her think I don't know what she's saying. It's a good way to ensure that I'll have a heads-up if she decides to voice a plan to leave.

Leaning against the wall that separates the kitchen from the living room, I watch her as she paces the kitchen floor, obviously agitated. She complains about the restrictions, makes it clear that she's not enjoying being here with me and reminds her father that no one actually wants her; they want him. Soon she sighs, then closes the distance between us to hand me the phone.

"He wants to talk to you."

I pick up the phone. "Hello, Mr. Hernandez."

"Mr. Brookes. How are things going with my daughter? We're nearing the twenty-four-hour mark, and I want to be sure she doesn't have you hog-tied."

"We've reached a compromise that ensures I'm doing the most effective work possible." I slip into my normal reporting mode. "No targets have been spotted, and no boogies have made contact."

"Excellent. Let's keep it that way," Mr. Hernandez replies. "And don't be afraid to put her in line. Nothing is more important than her safety ... including her comfort."

"Of course, sir." My eyes flick to Sofia, and the scowl on her face lets me know she heard every word of what her father just said. Damn it. The last thing I need is to take two steps back with her.

"I'd like to speak to my daughter, please. Thank you, Brookes." Mr. Hernandez keeps his even tone.

I hand her the phone, and Sofia hangs it up at once, then tosses it on the kitchen counter. She has the pizza warming in the oven rather than the microwave, and I shake my head at her. She puts her hand on her hip, giving me a glare.

"Do you have something against doing things the right way?" she asks.

"I could ask you the same, darling," I tease. "Don't approve of breakfast? Don't approve of naps? Making life hard by ignoring the magic of the microwave."

"Okay, the right way and the easy way are two different things. Why are you determined to disagree with me?" she demands. "Think that if you admit I'm right once, I'll take advantage of it and take control?"

"I'd love you to take control, baby. Just give me the outline of what that looks like. Are we talking about wearing the pants in the relationship, holding the flogger, or full-on pegging?"

Her eyes narrow despite the fact she's blushing all the way to her neck. She sputters, then reels off a line of unintelligible Spanish before stomping back to the kitchen. There go our few minutes of friendship. But maybe it's better this way. Better for us to be at odds so I can focus on her safety rather than thinking about fucking her on the living room carpet.

I lay back on the couch, staring at the ceiling. We'll be fine. This *should* be the easiest assignment yet. If I can keep finding compromise with this woman, and she stays in line to allow me to do my job, we shouldn't have any issues at all.

That's the goal.

The easier, the more boring, the better. Also, I want to limit our out time. The office has me thinking about the tightly packed, crowded markets in Brazil. Those weekend art and farmer markets that turned an entire block into a crowd with no rush, plenty of conversations, and no way to pick out someone stalking over someone exploring.

I'm not looking forward to doing the same tomorrow, so instead, I'll focus on the end goal. If I get through this assignment, I'll have enough to put a good down-payment on a house. Even after that, I'll have some savings, which means I can look for a normal forty-hour a week job. Maybe I can teach a self-defense class or something.

Exhaling, I push myself up and get off the couch. “Sofia, what do you want to do with this long life I’m making sure you have?”

She looks over her shoulder at me. “I’m going to get on congress and balance shit out.”

It’s so simple on her tongue. As if the journey doesn’t contain a thousand steps and a million obstacles for her to jump over, hurdles that only get higher and uglier the closer she gets to her goal. She meets my eyes, then leans back. “Why do you ask?

I shrug. “Just curious, I guess. I’m trying to get to know the woman beneath that tough exterior.”

“I’m going to take that as a compliment.”

“Whatever you want to do, baby girl.”

Her jawline tightens, then she takes a deep breath. I’m waiting for her backlash against my term of endearment, but she just asks, “How about you? What are your plans for the future?”

“I don’t really know job wise, but I know I want a good, normal life. A one-story house with a nice yard, a dog, a family, and a job that pays the bills without taking over every second of my life.”

“Really? You want to be ... boring?”

“Normal.”

“Same thing.” Sofia shakes her head. “What’s the point of living if you’re not going to grab life and take the opportunity to change the world?”

“What’s the point of living if you’re not going to stop and enjoy the life you have?” I argue.

We stare at each other for a long moment, then the timer beeps. Sofia doesn’t move. She crosses her arms, shaking her head at me. “I think you’re in the wrong business, Jasper.”

“Eh, I’m pretty good at keeping people alive.” I take a step towards her. “Which means you’ll get to fight all those other people who want to take your spot in congress and change the country just like you want.”

Her eyes study me for a moment, then she arches an eyebrow. "Is that your fancy way of getting to choose your slice first?"

My lips turn up. It wasn't, but it's a good enough excuse. "You see right through me."

Chapter 7

Sofia

It's almost midnight when I slip into bed, bracing for another long, restless night. After getting my lesson plans done and taking a shower, I thought my body would get the message that it's time to rest. It was a long, exhaustive day, even more than before. Sure, my daily tasks hadn't increased, but having to deal with Jasper all day was an added burden that took its toll on me.

Lying alone in bed, with nothing but my thoughts, I'm not afraid to deny how much I'm attracted to him. My body wants him, even if my mind thinks it's the most ridiculous thing ever. And he's not making it any easier by flirting with me.

Right now, all I'm thinking about is how his body felt against mine each time we touch or how I'm aching to taste his lips. I was aware of his arousal while we snuggled on the couch earlier, and I'm sure he wouldn't have resisted if I had made a move. And that's a problem. I don't want Jasper to want me. I don't want to want him either. Being attracted to a man like this will only distract me from what I'm trying to achieve, and I can't have that.

I need to redirect his attention elsewhere. I'm sure my attraction will go away if he stops flirting with me.

Turning on my side, I make a clear plan to push Jasper onto Carissa, and when I'm done, my mind feels at peace. Mostly. As long as I don't think about the distraction sleeping on the couch. I should have offered the bed, but he didn't even ask. He just started preparing the couch to sleep, and I let him deal with it.

JASPER AND I GET THROUGH half of the day at work, but it's not as pleasant as yesterday. By noon, I'm ready to kill him. He's stepped in between me and three different clients, not trusting their approach to me at all. I've lost count of the 'I'm sorrys' I had to give to keep them to stay.

Relief floods me when the elevator opens, and Carissa steps out, back from her dental appointment. Taking Jasper's hand, I lead him over to her desk.

"Carissa, do you mind showing Jasper how you create the spreadsheet for our deliveries each week?"

"She might not, but I do mind," Jasper mumbles. "I'm not leaving your side, Sofia."

Carissa's mouth gapes a bit as she looks between us. The questions are clear as day on her face.

Jasper treats her to a charming smile. "It's not you, Carissa, I promise."

"Well, that's a relief," Carissa says with a scoff. She tugs me to the side and palms her hips. "Spill. Is there something going on between you and Jasper?"

I shake my head. "Of course not!" My response comes out louder than I intend. Jasper frowns at me from his place at Carissa's desk, and I cut my eyes at him. "He's driving me up the wall all day, and I need a break. Besides, I think you two would be really good together. It's the perfect opportunity for you to get to know him."

She laughs and looks him over slowly. "Well... he *is* dreamy and funny."

"Cocky, frustrating, and pushy," I grumble.

Carissa looks between us again. "You sure? Because honestly ... I'm sensing some vibes here."

"That's my frustration." I give her a pout. "Please. Take him off my hands."

"Fine. Good looking out, by the way."

"Don't mention it," I reply.

Carissa walks over to Jasper, shy but determined, and Jasper is almost immediately won over. Carissa has that effect on people. Even when she doesn't recognize it, people soften around her. They adore her, and it's because of who she is. Smart, funny, so genuinely sweet. If I could trade personalities with anyone for ten minutes, it would be her – hands down.

I manage to get a solid hour and a half of work done before Jasper sits his ass on my desk. I take a sobering breath. He doesn't get to throw me off my game. I can get around him. Once he's off-limits per Carissa, the curiosity will be *gone,* and soon enough, Dad will bribe whoever he has to bribe to remove the hit. And Jasper will be a thing of the past.

I'll give it a few more days. I made it through college – frat boys and all – and I made it through high school, Mom and Dad's divorce, practically raising my little brother. I can handle a few days of Jasper and his tempting body.

"I missed you, baby," Jasper says, coming up beside me, giving me a start.

"Jasper, seriously. Stop," I hiss at him. "Not while I'm at work. Actually, how about not *ever*."

"Don't say that. You're breaking my heart." He glances out the window. "Also, I noticed the same car parked in the same spot as yesterday."

"You're paranoid."

"I'm observant. That's why I'm a specialized hire, Sofia. Don't try to distract me with Carissa. That's not what I'm here for."

"You sure?" I narrow my eyes. "Because you seem to need an outlet for all your ... frustration or flirting or your shit."

Jasper blinks at me a few times, then sighs. "We're going straight home."

I glance around quickly, but Carissa is out of earshot. "Don't say that so loudly."

"Look, Carissa's nice, but that's not my speed."

"Then what is your speed, Jasper? Believe me, I have plenty of friends."

"Why are you so hell-bent on getting me laid, Sofia?" he asks, leaning closer. "Are you afraid of your attraction to me?"

My face heats at Jasper's shot in the dark that found its mark. But I'm good at poker. He doesn't need to know what my thoughts are. "Not even close."

"If you say so..."

"Carissa is a great girl, that's all. I'm sure you two would enjoy being with each other."

"I already told you, she's not the girl I want."

"Maybe you should step outside your comfort zone like you're forcing me to." I rub my temple. "Leave me alone for the rest of today. Sit in the waiting area."

"Ruins the reporter angle you chose."

We end up arguing for most of the day. Whenever I can, I pawn him off on Carissa. She loves it, his attention, his flirting, his everything. And he actually seems to enjoy their conversations as the day goes on. The more they hang out together, the more intense their conversations seem to be. For some reason, I'm bothered by them getting along.

But Jasper's just a blip in our lives, not a permanent fixture. A homeless cat you try to bring in but wanders away at the first sign of an open door. He'll be gone soon enough.

I still feel super bummed while heading home with Jasper after work, and I don't know if I'm madder at him or myself. I refuse to answer when he tries to talk to me, but that seems to be just fine since he can have a conversation with himself, no problem. When we get back to the house, though, he stops me before I can open the door.

"Sofia—"

"Don't fucking start. I've dealt with you all day. I'm taking a shower, locking myself in that bedroom and ignoring your existence for the rest of the night," I hiss.

A sudden sound behind us makes him pull me close. His big hand strokes over my hip, and I fight my body's reaction. I don't like him. I don't like his touch. I *do not* want more.

The flutter in my stomach, the ache in my pussy, the urge to fuck him out of my system... that's nothing but lust. There's no substance. A cold shower and it will disappear in a heartbeat.

Turns out it's just a neighbor's dog fucking with a delivery box on a doorstep. I breathe a sigh of relief when Jasper opens the door and hustles me inside.

"Sofia, you can't just pass me off to your friend because you don't like me doing my job. It defeats the purpose of keeping you safe. I'm getting concerned with you being at work."

"Without reason."

"Take tomorrow off. Please." He keeps his voice low, gazing deep into my eyes. "I'm asking, not telling."

"And *when* I say no, are you going to put me over your shoulder? Tie me to the bed like a hostage? What?" I shove him. I know it's childish, I know his job will be easier if I obey, but I can't just give in that easily.

I won't. I refuse.

Jasper sighs, braces his forearm against the door and leans down to me. My breath catches in my throat. It's the opposite of what I've expected. I thought he'd yell, but instead ... he's just staring at me with those damn earnest, beautiful eyes.

"I want to keep you safe, Sofia, and that's damn hard when you refuse to trust me." He snaps his fingers. "We need a trust game."

"Trust falling? Fuck no."

"How about two truths and a lie? That way we can get to know each other."

"Sounds like torture."

"Guantanamo Bay. The best kind of torture for you." That devilish smile turns the corner of his lips up, and I have to remind myself I hate him for the fifth time today. Because he's relentless. A boulder I'm constantly pushing uphill. "Say yes, and I won't ask you to stay home tomorrow."

Fuck, his bartering system is too well-tuned. I grab his shirt and jerk him closer. "If I even *think* you're messing with me, I'll make you pay."

"Ooh, sounds dirty."

"Not even close, you perv."

Chuckling, Jasper drops the keys on the side table, but when he turns to me again, the smile slowly melts from his face. I take in the way his Adam's apple moves as he swallows, my gaze drifting upwards to his lips.

"Seriously, I need you to try harder for me, Sofia. You have to put in the effort, or this is going to be hell on both of us."

I give him a brief nod in response, and he returns to the door. I take a seat on the couch, not sure where else to go, as Jasper double-checks the lock on the door and pulls the chain across it. He returns to the couch and sits beside me, tossing his gun and knife on the coffee table.

"So, first things first. We need each other's cell phone numbers." Without waiting for my response, he tosses me his phone.

I hand him mine, then enter my number in his phone under the name: Hostage. Jasper returns mine, and when I check his contact, there are cute little hearts beside his name. I shake my head and roll my eyes, but he smirks when he looks at his phone.

"You're funny when you want to be, you know." He leans back and looks me over slowly. "Want to get comfortable before we get started?"

I don't know what he has in mind, which is slightly more discomfiting. Not in the mood to argue, I nod in response, then head to the bedroom and change into cotton shorts and a t-shirt. When I return, Jasper is still reclining in the same position, but his shoes are off, leaving him in socks that have a hole on the heel of the right one.

He's so big, such a huge presence. I should feel safe around him, more protected than ever. But I don't know what I feel. Jasper is either way too open or way too good at lying, and I'm not sure which I prefer.

"What are we doing?" I ask.

"Two truths and a lie. We can learn each other's tells. Or we can play a game where we ask a question and have to give a convincing lie as an answer. Either one."

I narrow my eyes at him. Why is he giving me a choice? Why is lying in both of these options? "Or we could just tell each other the truth."

"We can always end it with the truth. How about that? You need to be a good liar, good enough to convince me. And you need to be able to see through my lies."

"Again, the truth ... really handy." I huff.

He chuckles. "Choose a game, buttercup."

"Two truths and a lie. I go first." I point at him. "My favorite ice cream is vanilla. I wanted to be a CSI growing up. I had my first kiss at fourteen."

Jasper rubs his jaw and starts to answer, but then a peel of thunder does on his behalf. He glances up and nods. "Alright, Thor. Thanks for joining."

I watch him, waiting. He studies my face for a while. "Your first kiss. That's the lie."

Nodding once, I sigh. "I was fifteen. Truth or dare at a party. A girl that hated me got dared to kiss me."

"How was it?"

"It was a peck. Nothing else." I shrug.

"Then it wasn't your first kiss. A real first kiss has tongue." He leans back and thinks for a moment. "I'm terrified of snakes. I tried witchcraft for a while. I've got more than twelve tattoos."

There's no change on his face. He lists them out the same way someone would list what groceries they're getting. I bite my bottom lip. The first two seem insane. But the third one. Well, I can already see at least six tattoos.

"The snake one." I guess.

"Oof, nope." He shakes his head, then chuckles. "Do I seem like the witchcraft type to you?"

"Maybe you're hiding some kind of goth phase. I don't know." I roll my eyes but feel a smile tug at the corner of my mouth.

Jasper motions for me to continue, and we go back and forth until I notice that his eyes flick to the left when he lies. I try exploiting it a few times, and he smirks. The next time around, he leans towards me. Tiny flutters appear in my stomach, and a soft warmth settles over me. I realize I'm leaning towards him as well, drawn in like he's a magnet and I'm metal. Hopeless, unthinking metal.

"I've never gotten off from a blowjob," he starts, eyes focusing entirely on me. "I haven't fucked in two years." No tell. His fingers brush across my jaw. "I'm really into Carissa."

"The last one," I breathe.

He sighs. "The tell?"

"You touched me. Your eyes didn't move, but you did," I whisper. "You should give Carissa a chance. She could make you really happy. She's the sweetest person in the world, the one person who will see the best in everyone."

Why am I pushing him towards my best friend when it's obvious I'm attracted to him? Am I crazy? Or is it still the right thing to do?

Of course, it is. My goals haven't changed because of an insane attraction to a guy. I'm still focused on my endgame. There's no time to get distracted by whatever this is I'm feeling right now.

"I don't doubt that for a second. Any man would be lucky to have Carissa in his life," Jasper agrees.

Including you. A breath scrapes along my throat as I exhale, and I fight the envy that threatens to display itself on my face. A part of me wishes I had to freedom to fall in love like Carissa. Maybe then I could— no. I'm not going to think of a possible relationship with Jasper. It's not worth it.

"Your turn," Jasper says, eyeing me curiously.

I clear my throat. "My last relationship ended badly. Masturbation got boring. I ..." I swallow and try to lean away. "I hate not being in control."

He leans his head to the side and hums low in his throat. "Masturbation never gets boring, sweetheart. Keep to solid lies."

"I forgot to lie," I admit.

Japer's eyes search my face, his tongue teasing his lower lip, the action triggering an ache within my pussy. There's something bothering me about this whole conversation, about how close we are, all of it. I tuck my leg from under me and inch a little further down the couch. Time to put some distance between us.

"I know you well enough now, Jasper," I say, pushing to stand. "No need to continue. Let's end this game right now."

He catches my wrist. "Not quite yet."

Chapter 8

Jasper

Sofia stares at my hand around her wrist, and I expect her to jerk away. She doesn't. She doesn't sit either, but she watches me like she's waiting for me to jerk her into my lap. I clear my throat. "Tell me something about you that no one knows."

"Why?"

"In case you're in trouble, or you need to check in with me to confirm that you're okay. Tell me something no one else knows."

Sofia sits back down, and I slowly release her. I don't want to play this game anymore than she does. I prefer lying games. I know how to deal with those. I don't know how to deal with being completely open. I don't know how to handle vulnerability.

"Um ..." Sofia pushes her hair behind her ear. "I'm ... I don't know what to say, Jasper. Why don't you go first?"

"I have nightmares every night. The only way I've found to get rid of them is to keep myself up until I physically can't sleep. Then my brain goes quiet." It's the easier secret to admit. It's something my sister doesn't know. Not when it comes to the method I use.

Sofia bites her bottom lip and looks up at me from under her lashes. How could I possibly go for her best friend when she's here, looking at me like that? Heck, I shouldn't want her. She's so complex, confusing, frustrating, but yet so... unforgettable. It's only been a few days, and she's in every other thought I have. Which is ridiculous.

But that look right there ... it goes right to my—

"I'm afraid of becoming my mom," she finally whispers.

"Why?"

"She put her whole life on hold to let my dad live his dream. She chose to do it – she loved him – but I saw how hard it was on her. She took care of us, wore a smile all day, but she never had time to tackle her goals. Worse, she got nothing in return for her sacrifice. My dad did nothing but lie and cheat, then traded her for a younger model. I don't want to end up like her."

"Is that why you're still single, or is it solely about your career?"

She shrugs. "A little of both, I guess. It's safer this way, trust me."

The way she said it makes me suspect there's something else she's not telling me. Did someone else break her heart?

Deciding not to push her, I settle for the silence that descends between us. Sofia seems lost in her thoughts, and there's a lot on my mind, too, like the layer I peeled off Sofia just now. It's amazing how my opinion of her has altered within the last five minutes. I still think she's a cold, stubborn woman, but now I understand why. The question is, do I want the job of tearing down her walls, or is it too much to handle?

Carissa is the total opposite; sweet, laidback and definitely no walls. Being with her would be so easy. But she doesn't set me on fire like Sofia does. I'm not yearning for her touch. Only Sofia's.

I lean back against the couch with a soft sigh. Sofia sighs, too, then adjusts so she's leaning into me. I clear my throat and gently ease her off, and she stares up at me with a questioning frown.

"What?"

"We should make food or something." Anything to escape the torture of having her body pressed against mine.

"Eating does sound good," she says, getting up from the couch. "What's your least favorite food, by the way?"

"Brussel sprouts." I let her see how disgusted I am. "Shouldn't even be considered a food."

"I don't like sour candy," she says before heading to the kitchen. "Or fried chicken."

"What? You don't like fried chicken?" I can't resist the urge to follow her. Especially not with that bit of knowledge dropped on my shoulders.

She doesn't reply at first. Her hands get busy pulling something out of the fridge. I realize it's mushroom caps. Then she reaches for some chicken, eggs, cheese, butter and goes to the spices. After organizing everything together, she looks up at me.

"It's all fried food really. The only thing I tolerate is actual fries. I love them. Extra salty, with cheese."

I'm not sure what to do with Sofia being open and not actively insulting me. So, I help her cook. Cooking makes sense. We talk about basic stuff as we work together.

But with every passing second, I feel Sofia pull away. By the time she shuts the stuffed mushroom caps in the oven, the old Sofia has returned. The pensive Sofia. Distant. But I won't let it deter me. I've gotten a glimpse of her softness beneath the tough surface, and I want more. I need more.

Somehow, there's a spot of seasoning on her forehead. I reach up to wipe it off. She tries to duck away from my touch, but I move my thumb over the garlic salt anyway.

"You're like baby Simba," she mumbles.

I suck my thumb and grin at her. "Kind of cute, right?"

"Always back to teasing with you." She removes her apron and hangs it on the rack.

Is that what she thinks? That I'm just teasing her? She clearly has no clue how much I want her. I move towards her, blocking her path. "Want to play Uno or Scrabble or Monopoly? There are ways to spice them up."

"Board games?"

"Something to do." I wink. "Other than each other."

"Work is something to do," she argues. "And work helps people. Games just distract from reality."

"Then we should donate games. Help people get some bit of joy in their lives." I lean my head to the side. "Or are you unfamiliar with the concept of fun?"

"I can have fun." Of course, she takes it like a challenge. Sofia is just that predictable. "And I could kick your ass in Scrabble."

"How about we play without a dictionary? We just have to remember words. I'm thinking ten tiles per person. We can play diagonal as well as the normal way."

"So we break the rules?" She tries to step around me, but I block her way. She sighs. "I thought military men were all about rules."

"Rules are important. But I can't talk about what I did and didn't do in the military." I smirk at her. "Confidential."

"Are you telling me you were a spy? Well, I'd better hop on Facebook and let the world know."

"Very funny." I roll my eyes. "No one wants real war stories."

"Maybe if they heard the real stories, things would change. Have you considered that?"

"Tell that to the author of Catch-22. Slaughterhouse 5 ... All Quiet on the Western Front," I murmur. "Didn't do shit."

"That wasn't the real story. That was absurdism," she argues.

"War is absurd in a lot of ways. But it's a lot like that. It doesn't make sense in the moment. It's a sadistic game of chess in some ways."

"Is it?"

For the first time, I think she's actually asking me. She wants a real answer, not bullshit. Not just asking to ask. Sofia's dark eyes drink me in, and I'm powerless to stop my tongue. "Sadistic and unforgiving. One wrong move by a pawn can doom an entire unit."

"I'm sorry."

"War is older than democracy." I shrug. "It'll outlive us all."

"I thought vets were normally proud Americans."

"Depends on the Vet. Depends on where they served, what division, what unit, what rank," I murmur, thinking of all the proud men who never got to come home. I exhale slowly as I push down the craving for a cigarette. I left that habit overseas. "I've met people on all sides of the fence."

"There are more than two?"

"Yup." But I try to say that like the conclusion to an essay. I'm not allowed to say more. As much as I have issue with my life, I know some people choose it happily. Others like the benefits. It's not my place to judge their choices.

And the military can do some good in the world. They can do a lot of good, in all honesty. If used for the right reason, by the right people, it can change the world. Or it can waste a lot of valuable lives that could stand to be more than they actually are.

Pushing the thoughts of war to the back of my mind, I turn and head to the couch. But then I start thinking about Sofia and my unrelenting attraction to her. Is it real or am I just drawn to the danger she represents? Is she just an itch I want to scratch, or is there substance to what I feel?

I should just let her be. Get this job done and move on. Hell, I could focus entirely on Carissa when I'm not worrying about Sofia's safety. Sofia's best friend is definitely more interested in me than she is. It's a simple choice, right? I should focus on the woman who's a better fit for me.

"Jasper?"

I glance up at Sofia standing before me, looking as close to nervous as I think she can get. Her eyes are on the floor, her back straight, her hands fidgeting at her sides. She meets my gaze when I remain quiet.

"It's unfair for you having to deal with me and this stupid task. It's unnecessary and a waste of your skills. So, on behalf of my father, I'm sorry."

"I chose this job, Sofia, and I'm not wasting my skills. You may not think it's necessary, but I have a purpose here. I'd hate to prove you wrong, so just pretend you believe I'm right."

"Look, I know I'm not making it any easier, but I need you to see my side as well." She sits on the table in front of me and folds her hands together. "This is your job, but it's fucking with my life. My life is the only thing I control."

"It's not your life that's being bothered, it's your job. You should know the difference," I grumble.

"My job helps other people. That's my life. I want to make sure the people forgotten by society get a second chance in life. You can relate to that, can't you?"

"Of course, I can, Sofia." I sigh. "But you being alive will ensure you can keep helping people who need you."

"And I don't think anyone wants to kill me!" She stands up, obviously exasperated. "We can play nice all day long, but that doesn't change the facts! The facts are, these bad guys want my *dad* dead. The dad I haven't talked to in four years!"

"Doesn't stop them from using you to get to him," I growl back.

"You don't know shit about my life, about my dad, about anything where we're concerned." It's a hiss on her tongue.

"Sofia."

"I promised you a week, and that's all you're getting from me. I'm not hanging out with Carissa, having dinner, hitting the club—"

"Do you normally?" I interrupt with disbelief. Sofia doesn't strike me as the clubbing type.

"I'm not hooking up with random people," she continues, ignoring my outburst.

"*I'm* killing your weekends?"

"And I'm not trying to shake free of you. I'm keeping up my end."

I stand up, frustrated as hell. How did I lose control over tonight? I had her where I needed her, right where I wanted her. We were getting along, bonding, talking, but just like that, she's back at my throat, trying to bully me into getting her way.

"And so am I!" I stand closer to her.

She nearly falls back over the table, but I catch her and pull her close so she can't ignore me. "For the last time: my priority is your life, not your comfort. You don't have to like me. If you want this to be hard, fine. Don't be pissy with me because you don't like what your father does for a living or because you can't get a pat on the back for all you do."

Sofia's eyes widen, and I know I've hit a nerve. A very tender, raw one at that. Her eyes water, but she hits me. She actually hits me. I know I deserve it, but her fury is something else. It's sharp and venomous, a snake you only see when it's too late.

"I don't do *shit* for a pat on the back." After that, she dives into Spanish. She insults me with every word that flicks off her tongue, calling me small, pathetic, a lying bastard who wouldn't recognize the taste of the truth, no better than her pig of a father.

Still, I don't let her go. She pushes against my chest, hits my shoulder and fights me while I hold her in place until she's left panting. Her face is red, eyes nearly spilling over with tears, passion vibrating from her.

Something else is between us. Other than every punch she wants to throw, other than the actual air between us. There's tension, so thick and hot, it's like summer in Louisiana. But it makes my spine weak.

"Then we'll do this in silence. No more attempts to make this easy on you."

Her eyes narrow. "I'm still working."

"Fucking hell, Sofia. You don't listen to a goddamn thing anyone says unless you agree with it." I snarl. "Enjoy your dinner. I'm doing a quick patrol. We'll go to work together again, and then you can chaperone a fucking date between me and Carissa since you're so eager to get me laid."

Her eyes widen. "What? I never said-"

"You want to compromise? That's my offer. If you want to go back to work, then I'm asking her out. Let me know what you decide."

"Jasper."

I let her go and head to the door. I'm afraid of my temper. She might be afraid of becoming her mother, but damn if I don't have my father's genes, his temper, his crave for control.

But I fight it. I'm not going to hurt Sofia. I'm going to strangle my temper until it's where it belongs and deal with the fallout myself.

I'M ALMOST DONE WITH my shower when Sofia enters the bathroom, clad in a towel that barely covers her thighs. She gasps when she sees me, then rushes back through the door. Luckily, the steam from the shower fogged the glass, and she was in and out so fast, she didn't see how damaged my leg was. After rinsing off completely, I leave the stall and stand before the mirror while drying myself, staring at my reflection.

I can't let Sofia see me like this. Scarred, burned, broken, with damaged parts. If she saw what's left of me, I'd become another project. She'd stay in line, but it would be pity, not respect. So, I'll find another way. I'll cope.

I'll finish this assignment, date a sweet girl like Carissa and settle down into a life that lets me forget about war, bullets and nightmares.

And Sofia.

Chapter 9

Sofia

The next few days feel like the calm before the storm. Jasper has been quiet all weekend. There's no teasing, no trying to piss me off with his attempts to control me. But then again, we've been locked in the house for two days with nowhere to go. He plays Scrabble alone, and I get busy with work on my laptop. When I'm sick of working on my lesson plan or drafting my fundraising schedule, I clean the entire apartment. But I'm still not exhausted when I'm done. I'm restless. Horny as hell.

This is torture. Living in an apartment with a man I'm aching to fuck, a man I *shouldn't want to fuck* is worse than purgatory. I'm losing a piece of my mind with each passing minute.

I steal a glance at Jasper reclining on the couch, swiping through his phone. His quiet side is worse than his flirting or bugging me with silly games and advice. But I'm not going to break the silence. Not until he apologizes. What he said to me was so ... wrong. I don't care about being recognized, and if he can say that after seeing me work, seeing everything I do, then ...

No. He's just wrong. I'm not going to think about the implications. He's just pissy that I'm not obedient. That's all. I'm just a punching bag for him since I refuse to fall in line. But I'd be lying if I said I didn't like the night we spent together talking, at least until I actually confronted him about his controlling ways.

I was trying to be rational and clear. I was trying to tell him where my mind was at. I wanted him to understand my need to remain in control of my life. But that opened a can of worms because it always will. All we have are our lies.

I'm almost done with wiping off the dining table when my cell phone rings. I pick it up after seeing Dad's name on the screen. Ignoring him was my first thought, but I'm hoping he's calling with news I'm desperate to hear. Wanting some privacy, I switch to Spanish.

"Are we done with this yet?"

"No, princess. I'm sorry." Dad actually sounds apologetic this time. My stomach falls, and I drop my butt to the chair. Jasper sits up on the couch, his eyes narrowing as he watches me. "I know it's not easy on you, but we have to wait this out."

"I promise to have dinner with you and Scarlett every Sunday, whatever else you want. Please, just let me go."

"I'm not holding you hostage, Sofia. I'm keeping you safe. There's a big difference here," he says. "Just keep doing what you're doing. Behave for Jasper, do what he says, and you'll be just fine."

"I'm not a dog," I huff.

"No, or this wouldn't be half as problematic. A few more weeks, and you'll be back to your normal life with no problems."

"A few more weeks!"

"Yes, darling. At least until the sentencing is done. Hopefully, they give up afterwards."

I don't answer. I'm fighting the urge to stomp my foot. It would be easier to throw a full temper tantrum than to deal with this, and I'm tempted to do just that. I just want to scream, want to cry, want to take life by the cojones and castrate it.

I hang up the phone and toss it to the table. Ignoring Jasper's questioning stare, I storm into the bedroom and plop down on the bed. I scream into the pillow, punch the bed, then lay there as I absorb what I have to deal with. I can't handle a few more weeks of living like this. Jasper isn't the worst thing to look at, but he's casually throwing himself where he doesn't belong in my life, and I'm already sick of it.

He's always around. Not just in the physical spaces I inhabit, but in my head, too. How will I survive being around him when I want him so much? Taking a deep breath, I rub my temple. I'm sure there's nothing in this apartment to cure a headache. What are we going to do when we run out of groceries? We don't have a list. Are we allowed to go shopping? Will Major Pain in My Ass tie me down in the house and do the shopping on his own?

He'll need a list. And maybe I can agree to stay put for an hour to let him get some things. Soap, razors, decent food, tissues, paper towels.

I don't know when I fell asleep, but when I awake, it's almost nightfall. I can see the orange-grey sky and the streetlights through the bedroom window. I remake my bed, then return to the living room. Jasper's nowhere in sight. Assuming he's outside doing his daily checks, I grab a pad and a pen and start making the grocery list. With any luck, we can grab a few items before the grocery stores close tonight.

When I'm halfway through, I hear the front door open. Lifting my gaze, I watch as Jasper heads to the fridge and removes a bottled water. Miffed, I return to the list. I can't believe the asshole is icing me out after insulting me. I'm the only one who should be giving a cold shoulder. I furiously scribble the remaining items on the list.

"What are you doing?"

I look up, and Jasper's leaning against the wall that separates the living room from the kitchen, his hand tucked in the pocket of his jeans, the other holding the water bottle. I tear my eyes from his yummy frame and focus on the sheet of paper before me.

"I'm creating a grocery list. We're running out of food."

I expect him to argue, but he nods in agreement. "Did you add coffee and creamer?"

Shaking my head, I add them to the list. He comes up to me with his hand outstretched, and I set the list within his palm. He takes a long drink of water, then gives me a stern look. "Can I trust you to stay here, Sofia?"

"Not going to tie me up?"

"That's a reward for good girls when they behave." He finally looks at me, pinning me in that icy blue gaze. "You're a disobedient brat."

Why does his response make my pussy clench so hard? Why does it make me want to flick him off and obey at the same time? Jasper tucks the list in the back pocket of his jeans while looking me over. I don't flinch. I know I look perfect. My jeans and top match and are wrinkle-free, my hair loose and flirty, running over my shoulders like a waterfall.

"There's still a question hanging, Sofia. Can I trust you to stay?" He takes another step forward. "Or would you *like* me to tie you to the bed until I come back home to collect you?"

I shiver from the thought of being restrained in bed, naked, waiting for him to return. "I'll stay."

"Inside."

"Inside," I repeat, looking up at him. "I can't tell if you're full of shit or not."

"Want to find out?" He cocks an eyebrow, then that slow wolfish smile spreads over his face.

How stupid is it that I've missed that smile? That I've missed his stupid sense of humor, the way he can turn anything into a joke and his voice. I must really be going insane.

"I'll stay inside just so I can enjoy some peace and quiet," I reply, unwilling to let him have even one win. If he gets one win for himself, I feel like he'll start closing in on a second one as soon as possible.

Jasper smiles. "Do I get a kiss for luck?"

"No."

"A kiss in case I die on a mission for groceries?"

"If I liked you ... maybe. But I don't. So, I won't."

"Ah, so you're a masochist." He chuckles. "I see it now. Shame. A relationship can't work with *two* masochists."

"But you're a sadist, tap dancing on every one of my nerves," I say.

Still chuckling, he turns and heads towards the door. He pauses with his hand on the knob, suddenly all serious again. "For what it's worth, Sofia, I'm sorry about what I said. I know you do your job because you value others, not for recognition."

Jasper doesn't wait for me to answer, he just leaves.

But his apology is enough to make me stay and behave. And when he returns, we unload the groceries together, arguing about where things go until Jasper sets me on the counter to get me out of the way. I glare at him, still feeling his hands on me despite the fact he's piling things in the fridge.

"No! Bread doesn't go in the fridge. Dios mio."

"Well, I assumed because of the pizza conversation..."

"No. That goes in the fridge because of the cheese. How many times do I have to tell you?"

"Always one more time, darling." He stands up and sets the loaf in my lap before kissing my cheek. "You're going to make a wonderful wife someday."

Shocked, I blink at him, then poke his chest. "No PDA."

"We're not in public."

"No affection!"

"Does it break your rules? Welcome to being in your presence, breaking all my rules." He snorts.

We manage not to fight all night. I even offer him the bed because I'm still feeling so pleased from his apology, but I'm shocked when he says yes. I'm even more shocked when he goes. I hear a low groan and smile slightly. My bit of niceness should pay off later. Because I'm trying. I'm making an effort to earn a more relaxed detail, so I can enjoy my life a little more.

THE TRUCE BETWEEN JASPER and I comes to a halt on Monday. He tags along to work like always, but by mid-morning, I spot him flirting with Carissa by the water cooler, his hand resting on top, his eyes focused on her.

Just her.

It's fine. I'm fine. This is exactly what I want. Jasper is a decent guy, and my best friend's quite a catch. They belong together. I'm happy for them.

But why does it feel like I can't breathe?

Grabbing my purse, I take the back door and head across the street to the convenience store that serves kick-ass coffee. I need a caffeine rush. My energy level suddenly gauging on empty. I order a cup of Frappuccino, then wander around the store while it's being prepared, trying not to think about what Jasper and Carissa are doing right now. Are they exchanging numbers? Is he asking her out on a date? Are they making plans to hook up when he's done protecting me?

Sighing, I pick up a basket and start filling it with snacks. I haven't had junk food in ages, but they are my comfort food when I'm depressed.

As I fill my basket, I feel goosebumps crawling up my neck, and there's a sudden feeling like I'm being watched. Glancing around, I don't notice anyone who looks like they're doing anything other than shopping. There's a tall, elderly woman wearing an expensive-looking scarf, a kid who looks like he's still in high school, and a middle-aged man wearing a shirt two sizes small. They all seem normal. Harmless. I exhale, check out, and leave the store.

As I step onto the pavement, I spot Jasper sprinting towards me with Carissa jogging behind him. He stops before me, looking like he wants to put me over his knee and spank me. I'm surprised when he pulls me in for a hug.

"You fucking scared me, Sofia," he says when he pulls away. "And I don't usually get scared." He's looking pissed now, and I open my mouth to argue when Carissa comes up to us, panting like she's just run a mile.

Jasper immediately moves us forward, his head swiveling as he checks our surroundings. His left hand shadows the spot at his side where he tucked his gun this morning before we left the apartment. Carissa slips her arm through mine and picks up the pace to create some distance between us and Jasper.

"What the hell's going on?" she whispers. "One minute Jasper's laughing and talking with me; the next he's getting all flustered when he notices you're gone from your desk. I almost burst a lung trying to keep up with him."

Damn it. How do I tell my best friend the truth without alarming her? I can't. I don't want to get her upset for no reason, especially when I still doubt there's someone out to get me.

"I have no clue. He probably thinks I left for my meeting without him. I promised him I'd take him with me."

Carissa doesn't look convinced, but she doesn't push it, and I'm glad. We enter the office building, Jasper coming in backwards, still scanning the street. He seems satisfied when he closes the door. We walk over to the elevator, and as we wait for the car, he seizes my arm, twisting me to face him.

"I'm serious, Sofia," he growls. "Don't you ever pull that shit again. I almost lost my fucking mind."

I glance at Carissa. She meets my eyes, then looks away, the confusion clear on her face. I ignore Jasper and follow her into the lift, and we ride in silence to the top floor. The minute-long ride feels like a long, awkward two-hour trip. Carissa will need answers, especially after what Jasper said just now. I don't know what the fuck to tell her. Anything but the truth.

Finally, we arrive on our floor, and Jasper immediately moves to a window, checking out the street. I dip into my bag and offer a bag of Doritos to Carissa.

"Hey, you want this?" I say to her.

"Thanks." She takes the snack, her eyes flicking to Jasper. She exhales, looking back at me. "Are you sure there's nothing going on with you and Jasper?"

"There's nothing between us," I assure her. "He's all yours, Carissa."

Her smile returns, but it's hesitant. "I don't know..."

"Look, I'm not forcing you to date him. I'm just letting you know we're nothing but... friends."

"If you're sure."

"I am sure."

I have to be. I have no room in my life for Jasper. Carissa seems a little cheerful as she goes back to work, while I feel like shit. I know this is wrong. I shouldn't instigate an affair with Carissa when I'm battling with my feelings for him. What if they never go away? How will I cope if Jasper and Carissa start a relationship?

I can't think about that now. Besides, I'm sure my feelings will subside once Jasper gets discharged from my life.

I've barely rested my butt on my chair when Jasper grabs my arm and pulls me up. Luckily, there's no one around my section to witness his rough handling as he drags me outside. I try to shake him off, but I'm no match for his strength, especially when he's so pissed. He braces me against the wall, his arms barring me in from both sides.

"Is there a reason you chose to disobey my orders, Sofia?"

He's seething. I can tell. The violent fury in his eyes sends a confusing thrill running through me. "I'm not your child, Jasper," I reply, sounding surprisingly calm, considering the heat wave I'm experiencing from his stare. "I don't take orders from you. I wanted coffee. You were talking with Carissa. It took five minutes. There's no problem."

Jasper hits the wall beside me, and I jump. Fuck, he's really, really pissed.

"There is a fucking problem, Sofia. A massive one." He snarls. "You are too fucking rebellious for your own good. What if something had happened to you out there? How the fuck would I face your father?"

"But it didn't. We both know it wouldn't have. I keep telling you, there's no one out to get me."

Jasper closes his eyes with a sigh, pinching the skin above his nose bridge. "It's not in my nature to give leeway, Sofia, but I've been doing so since we met. I've tried respecting you and your time. I've tried showing you how I'd *like* our relationship to go."

"We don't have a relationship."

"But you clearly don't respect me, my time, or what I'm trying to do. My goal is to keep you alive. I can't do that if you're not beside me."

"If you weren't so busy, you probably would have seen me go," I say with a shrug.

"Fucking hell. You just told me not to treat you like a child, yet here you are, acting like one. Perhaps I should let your father know how this is going. How you keep playing me and disobeying me, running from me. What do you think he'd do?"

"I don't fucking care, Jasper!" I try to dip under his arm, but he holds me back.

"Do you even hear yourself?" He takes a slow breath. "What part of life or death don't you get? Are you just that ready to spit in your father's face? Or do you think you're fucking invincible?"

"Don't try to get in my head." Again, I try to get past him, but he braces me against the wall again.

"Fall in line, Sofia."

"I'm not a fucking soldier," I argue.

"Oh, that's clear. Because a real soldier, a good one, does what they can to help their partners. They see others as their equals at minimum. They recognize that everyone has to make sacrifices to achieve a goal. What are you sacrificing, Sofia? Because I'm expected to sacrifice my life to keep you safe."

I take a deep breath to calm the volatile emotions swirling inside me. This isn't the time or place to give him the hell I want to, even though he's being a condescending ass, treating me like I'm some terrible kid. But I don't have to stand here and take this. I push at his chest, and this time he lets me go.

"I don't need you. I'll take this risk all on my own. I don't need you in my life."

"Sofia." He follows me, but I ignore him, picking up the pace when I hear his footsteps getting closer. "Sofia!"

The urgency in his tone makes me turn around just as he barrels into me, and we land with a hard thud on the pavement. The sound of an explosion above my head makes me curl into him. It's a fucking gunshot. Did someone just fire a gun at us?

Oh, my God. My father was right, wasn't he? So was Jasper. Someone's trying to kill me!

Another gunshot rings out. I whimper with fright. This isn't my time. I can't go out like this.

Jasper raises up on his elbows, with half of his bulk protecting me. My ears ring as he returns fire, the sound ripping through the commercial district. I'm aware of screaming and shouting and the sound of running feet. A bullet flies to my right, chipping away the concrete on the wall where it hit. Panicking, I try to move, but Jasper pins me down.

"For God's sake, Sofia. Stay still!"

His hand jerks as he fires again, then he suddenly recoils with a curse. "Fuck."

My heart flies in my throat when he bites his lower lip, the screeching tires competing with his groan. "Don't play with me, Jasper," I say, but it comes out strangled. "You're fine."

Jasper slumps to the side, and I gasp, rolling over and pulling his head in my lap as red blooms across his side. No. No. He can't be hurt. Fuck! No. "Jasper! Fuck. Fuck! Get help! Someone help!"

I put my hand on him and press down hard, like I've seen in movies. I fight my tears and focus on the problem at hand. "You'd better fucking live so I can apologize."

"Apologize first, so I reject that nice white light," he groans, his hand coming down on mine. Even with the joke hanging between us, I can see the pain etched into every feature of his face.

His fingers lace through mine, pressing harder as he moans. I brush my fingers through his hair and swallow. I can feel my own heart thudding in my throat and his pounding in my arm. Jasper smiles slightly as he looks up at me.

"Now what, buttercup?"

"Just don't fucking die, you hear me? Please..." I drop my head as a sob flies from my lips.

Chapter 10

Jasper

Fuck. I've forgotten how painful a gunshot wound can be. It feels like my insides are being ripped apart. I summon a smile to ease the panic on Sofia's face. She's on the verge of losing it, I can tell.

"Don't you fucking die on me," she mumbles between her desperate moans.

"Not a chance, buttercup. Not when I know you really care," I murmur, chuckling when she scoffs through her tears.

Sofia takes out my cell phone and dials 911 and gives them the address, her hand never leaving my wound. She tucks the phone in her bosom and returns her free hand to my side. "Okay, so I just keep applying pressure?"

"You're going great," I assure, then pull her hands down on me harder. "Just like that."

"Doesn't it hurt?" She gasps when I wince.

My leg twitches, and I force a laugh. "I've had worse, baby doll."

"You ... you took a bullet for me." Her eyes spear mine. They're watery, soft, but there's something else there too. Something warm and gentle. She swallows and shakes her head. "I've been nothing but awful to you, yet—"

Her head lifts as running footsteps comes towards us, and a man says, "How's he doing? I just called 911."

Sofia looks down at me with a sniffle. "He's hanging on."

Well, I'm trying. The pain pulses through me, triggering a chill that starts in my feet and spreads through my body. But it's not as bad as when I damaged my leg at the bombing. This is a walk in the park compared to the hell I went through then. So, I'm sure I'll make it. I have to.

I groan when she applies extra pressure, and she groans. "Where the hell is that fucking ambulance?"

There are more people gathering around us, some on their phones trying to speed up the EMT's response time. I hear a loud gasp just as Carissa drops to her knees beside me. I watch the horror bloom on her face, and my chest tightens at her concern.

"Oh, my god! What happened?"

"It's just a flesh wound," I assure her, and I hope I'm right. I mean, if it's not, then who cares if I'm wrong. Well ... Daisy. Daisy would care. "I'll be fine, gorgeous."

"What happened?" she asks again, looking between us.

"Just the wrong place, wrong time," I reply through gritted teeth.

Sofia has gone quiet. When I look at her, I swear she's green. Shit. I forgot she couldn't handle the sight of blood. It's amazing how she lasted this long. She closes her eyes and takes a breath.

"Here, sweetie," Carissa says, gently touching her shoulder. "Your arms must be tired. Let me take over until the ambulance gets here."

"No," Sofia replies at once. "I can do this."

The sirens get closer, but Sofia doesn't move. I actually feel her fingers in my hair, stroking softly despite the fact she can't look at me. Carissa glances between us again, and I see the hurt on her face.

I think about our conversation earlier, the one that now feels like it happened hours ago. The way she looked at me, hanging on to my every word, I know she's into me. I don't want to jerk her around. If I were another man, I wouldn't be so stupid. I'd sweep her up off her feet. I can almost see it. Can almost see her leaning towards me with a gentle smile and eager eyes before kissing me softly, the kind of soft that leads to actual lovemaking, not sex.

The wailing of an incoming ambulance fills the air, and within a minute, the EMTs are resting me on a gurney and placing me in the back of the ambulance. Sofia insists on coming with me, and as she sits on the bench beside me, I notice the blood on her shirt.

"Fuck. You're hurt, Sofia."

She glances down, then shakes her head. "No. This is all you."

I glance back at the area, but it's hard to tell if she's right. I drop my head to the gurney as a wave of dizziness takes over. Fuck. I hate feeling helpless.

Sophia's voice sounds raw and shaky as she asks the paramedic, "Is he going to be okay?"

"It's a through and through and missed anything vital. That's a good sign. He'll probably be patched up and released quickly," he replies. His chin jerks towards her. "Your shirt looks a little more bloodied than a minute ago. Your friend's right. You've been injured."

"No, I'm not," she replies, lifting her shirt. "I'm sure I'd know if—" She stops, her mouth flying open as she stares at the wound on her side. She's been grazed. It's not terrible, but it needs treatment.

"Why don't I feel anything?" she asks.

"The adrenaline, no doubt," the paramedic says, peering at it. He dabs it with cotton containing something that makes her wince, then he instructs her to keep pressure on it.

We get to the hospital, and I'm immediately taken into surgery. Sofia's waiting for me in the hospital room when they wheel me back in. I'm still a little drowsy from the drugs, but I'm alert enough to check if Sofia has gotten her wound looked after. Satisfied, I get out of bed and reach for my clothes.

"What are you doing?" Sofia hisses.

"What does it look like?" I reply, groaning as I try to get my shirt over my head. I can't keep you here. We're sitting ducks, and that's a risk I refuse to allow."

And if they know Sophia lived, they're going to try again, no doubt. In a hospital filled with hundreds of people, it will be hard to tell if the bad boys decide to strike. I barely saw the face of the asshole who fired after us. I only caught a glimpse of his tan skin, dark hair, a tattoo on the neck that I couldn't make out. A skull tattooed on the hand with a gun. One missing finger.

Not exactly going to help me in a crowd, especially at a hospital.

The doctor tries to stop us when we're leaving, but one dark scowl from me, and he backs down. Luckily, our Uber came on time, so we didn't have to linger outside the hospital. I keep watch on the ride back to the safehouse, satisfied when nothing stands out. Sofia supports my body all the way up to our apartment. She doesn't release me until I'm in bed. She disappears for a moment, then returns wearing a t-shirt that slips over one shoulder and is cropped, so I can see the shorts underneath and a sliver of her hip. And that sliver of skin is probably the best thing I've seen today.

Her hands shake as she looks at my gauze. "I'm not good with blood."

"Truth." I nod.

"You're scary." She sits next to me and swallows. "Acting so calm like it's a bruise and not a bullet wound."

"I've had worse."

"You keep saying that," she whispers. "Like it matters. It doesn't. You got hurt – shot – because of me. I can't ..."

"You got shot, too," I remind her, pushing her hair back from her face. "How does it feel? Are you okay, Sofia?"

Her eyes meet mine, and she nods, but her hands are still shaking. I'm tempted to tell her to get into bed with me, so I can comfort her and tell her it's okay. But she wouldn't tolerate that. And I have a feeling that she's the type who deals with shit like this by working through it, staying busy, pushing it down until it's small and digestible.

"You should call your dad and give him an update."

"No."

"Do it, or I'll get up and do it myself," I threaten, starting to get up.

"Fine, I'll do it. You're not only scary but crazy," she says, moving from the bed. I hear her on the phone a minute later, and I relax. Good. She doesn't need to be in the room with me. It'll make it easier to avoid doting on her. Maybe I can get over how she makes me feel by keeping her busy.

I can ask her to make dinner or something. I don't know if she'll actually do it, but it will go over better than asking her to sing for me. Especially since her father puts her in a shit mood. I should tell her to work or ask about her lesson plans for her English class.

Despite this snag in our plans, I can't see her putting her life on hold, not even because she was shot at. She values everyone above herself. I've seen that proof every single day since we've met.

"You should get comfortable," she says, her return to the room pulling me from my thoughts. "I can lay out clothes. Do you need help changing?"

"Trying to see me naked?" I tease. "I thought I belonged to Carissa now."

Her face scrunches with a frown. "I'm not. You do." She takes a step back. "You do. She would love to be here and take care of you. She's better at it."

"Sofia."

"I'll get you something to eat. If you need help, just yell for me, okay?"

I roll my eyes. "This is fine. I'm fine. Stop worrying about me."

"I'm not worried. It's just ..." She shakes her head. "If you die or quit, I'll be stuck in this safe house with one of the other guys, who I'm sure are worse than you were. I may not like you or your puns, but I like my freedom."

"I'm not quitting."

She nods. "You'd better not, or I'm going to kick your butt."

I can't help but chuckle, and she soon joins in. Our eyes meet and linger. She's the first one to look away, her eyes watching her fingers fiddle with the hem of her shirt.

"Thanks again," she mumbles. She briefly glances at me, then returns her attention to her shirt. "I know you're just doing your job, but I appreciate what you did for me today."

"Anytime."

THE NEXT FEW DAYS PASS like a blur. I don't know it's because I'm injured, but Sofia has been quiet, compliant even. She didn't argue when I told her we had to lay low for the rest of the week. Granted, she wasn't pleased about it, but all I got was a flip of her middle finger before she made the phone calls to her team to let them know. She even had a cordial conversation with her dad—a short one, but at least she didn't hang up on him this time. Is the ice queen finally thawing out? I guess time will tell. For now, she's been keeping her distance, only coming into the room to check on me. By Friday, I feel better, good enough to change my own bandages which is great, considering I'm tired of watching Sofia heave as she changes them.

"So... Carissa called me last night," I begin, as she drops the used bandages into the small trash can at her feet.

Her eyes flick to me, then back down. "Oh? What did you guys talk about?"

I'm watching her face. She's giving nothing away. There's no way to tell how she really feels. "We got to know each other a bit, that's all. But I... I'm going to ask her out on a date."

"Oh. Good for you."

"Well, not good, really. There's a bit of a problem."

An expression flashes across her face so fast I don't get to identify it. "What problem?"

"I can't leave you unsupervised. If something were to happen—"

"I'm not a child, Jasper. I won't wander away."

"What if the bad guys strike while I'm out? How will I explain if something bad happens to you?"

"What are the odds of that? We've been laying low all week, and there's been no activity outside. You little buddies have been experiencing the same thing, too."

"That doesn't mean—"

"Ask her out, Jasper. Go have fun on your date. I can take care of myself for one night."

I can't help being disappointed in her response. A part of me had hoped she would try to convince me not to go out. But here she is doing the total opposite, and I'm finally convinced she's not into me. I need to take the hint and move on.

It's a risk going out on a date and leaving her all alone, but she's right. We haven't had any activity all week. What are the odds of an attack while I'm out? The house will be secured anyway.

"Ok, fine. I'll ask her out."

A coolness slips into her eyes, but then she looks down at my side. "And try not to do much on your first date. Have fun with Carissa. She likes flowers. Pink ones."

"Of course."

"And make sure you compliment her outfit. It will matter to her," she lists.

She continues telling me all about Carissa's likes and dislikes as she cleans up around the bedroom, but there's an edge to her voice.

She's frustrated but trying not to show it. I don't understand why. She's getting what she wants twice over. She gets some time to herself, and I'm leaving her alone.

"Is something wrong?" I ask, sitting up in bed.

“No.” She shakes her head while adjusting the duvet over my lower half, her lips pursed.

I grip her wrist, pulling her towards me. “If you don’t want me to go out with Carissa, just say it. You want all my attention on keeping you safe and alive? You want me to focus on you, sweet cheeks?”

“No. Take her out. You’ve been flirting with her, and it’s the right thing to do. You’re both interested in each other.”

“That’s not what I asked,” I argue.

Again, she purses her lips, her eyes searching my face. I can smell her scent, feel the heat coming off her body in waves. Is she burning for me? Is her racing pulse a sign that she wants me? Her lips slowly part, and she leans in, I almost think she’s going to kiss me, but she just gives me a retail smile. “I want you to go out with Carissa.”

“Okay.” I nod, quickly releasing her wrist.

“Good.” She picks up the trash can and sails from the room, her hair bouncing against her shoulders. I drop back to the pillows with a disappointed sigh.

It’s official. Sofia does not want to be with me. It’s a blow to my ego and a strike at my heart, but I’m man enough to handle rejection. There’s a first time for everything, anyway.

Chapter 11

Sofia

My eyes flick over to Jasper and Carissa. I can tell he's asked her out since she's glowing and can't stop smiling. My best friend filled with butterflies and all the damn sweet things a girl feels when a hunk shows he's into her. This is what I wanted, Jasper focused on Carissa, done with teasing me.

Then why do I feel so... weird?

Jasper pushes Carissa's hair back behind her ear, and something pulls at my stomach. I take a deep breath and look away.

I need to focus on work. It's right in front of me, the proposal for an emergency meeting I need to prepare for. There are five company representatives coming in for a discussion about a gala we're hosting later this month to help raise funds for a new shelter we want to build by the end of the year. It's the only reason Jasper backed down when I told him I had to come in today.

But I can't focus on the proposal I've been trying to memorize for the last twenty minutes. My eyes keep flicking to Carissa and Jasper. She's touching his chest now, her smile more illuminating than a fricking Christmas tree. And he's clearly enjoying the attention. They didn't even notice when Robbie from accounts faceplanted on the floor a few feet away. They are so into each other; it makes me sick. I swear I'm half insane by the time Jasper returns to my desk. But it's not jealousy. It can't be. Because I don't like him. I'm just ...

"So, tomorrow night, Carissa and I are going out." He flashes a smile as he leans back in the chair.

"Sounds nice," I reply, swallowing whatever frustration is eating at me.

"I think you should come with us," he says, surprising me.

Oh, hell no. Seeing them just now almost drove me crazy. Sitting through a date with Jasper and Carissa sounds like the worst torture ever. "No, thanks. I'm not interested in being your third wheel. I'll stay home, that way you can focus on Carissa," I say. "Besides, I have work I can do and-"

"You know what? I'm going to postpone, just until I'm sure the coast is clear."

"Don't you dare. Carissa will be crushed, Jasper," she hissed. "You can't do that to her. If you postpone, I swear to God, I'll give you hell."

"Sofia ..." He trails off and rubs his chin. "This is a bad idea. What if someone breaks in? What if something happens, and I'm not there?"

"I just die and never have to think about this moment again." I assure with a smile. "Or I fight them off."

He rolls his eyes. "The attitude isn't called for."

"We already discussed this, Jasper. It's called a safehouse for a reason. It's quite secure, and I promise I won't leave the apartment while you're gone. Just trust me, please."

His eyes narrow at me. "Why are you so hell bent on hooking me up with Carissa?"

My eyes flick down to his side. I had to change his gauze for the entire week, had to clean up the blood, make sure he wasn't infected, and deal with him flinching each time I got too rough. A part of me—most of me feels guilty for putting us in harm's way. If I hadn't gone out for coffee, I wouldn't have been spotted, and we wouldn't have gotten attacked.

"It's my fault you got shot, so consider this my way of saying thank you. Carissa's a really great person, just like you. I'm sure you two will be great together."

"I'm still not comfortable with you being alone."

"I'm not as helpless as you think, Jasper. Believe me, I can handle myself."

"And you feel qualified to fight off people who have a tendency to have guns?" Jasper keeps his voice low as he leans towards me. "If you have a hidden talent, please let me know."

"I've seen *Home Alone*. I can fuck them up."

Jasper smiles, his whole face softening. Shaking my head, I look away, trying to suppress the grin that wants to answer his. I focus on the computer, but Jasper taps a pen on my desk, steadily driving me insane.

"Oh, my god." I put my hand on his. "Stop."

"So that's how to get your attention." He chuckles. "Annoying sounds."

"What do you want?"

"Talk to me. I'm bored." He pouts.

"Do your protection stuff. You're good at it," I remind him.

"Yeah, that's how I know that car I was worried about isn't here today," Jasper says.

"Do you think there's a connection between the car and the person who attacked us?"

"There has to be."

"Do you think their absence means they've given up?"

"I doubt it. Which means we still need to tread carefully, got it?"

"Loud and clear," I reply, relaxing in my chair. "But you're still going on that date."

"We'll see."

The day passes by so quickly, and for the first time ever, I can't wait to get home. But when Jasper ushers me into the apartment and secures the door, it occurs to me that I'm about to spend another slew of endless days being cooped up in the apartment with this annoying lust for him. I thought hooking him up with Carissa would make it go away, but it's worse than ever, so strong that I can almost taste it on my tongue.

Jasper's cell phone rings, the shrilling sound pulling me back from the edge. He picks it up after looking at it. His mouth opens to say something, but I can actually hear the woman shouting on the phone. He shakes his head at me and rolls his eyes like we have some inside joke.

We absolutely don't. In fact, laughing is the last thing I feel like doing right now.

"Daisy. Daisy!" He yells. He chuckles. "Listen, work has certain hazards, but I'm fine."

He listens again, then sighs. "It was just a bullet graze, Daisy. Kingston had no right to alarm you like that."

After a moment, he looks to me. "Okay, fine. If that's my punishment for scaring you, then yes, I'll come. But I'm bringing someone with me. See you on Sunday, okay?"

I shake my head. Hell no. I'm not going anywhere with him, although the stare he's giving says I am, whether I want to or not. He hangs up and smiles. "We're visiting my sister on Sunday."

"What happened to staying away from family because it's dangerous for them?" I demand.

"Daisy's stronger than the average bear." He points to his side. "Would you let your brother off the hook if he got shot and didn't tell you?"

No. I wouldn't. I'd fly across the ocean and rip him a new one and make sure he's okay. Which means if we don't go, she's going to try and track us down.

"It will be easy. Promise. My niece is cute too." He rubs my shoulder, leaving a warmth and longing for him to touch me more. "You'll love her. She'll take your mind off everything going on."

"Maybe I'm not fond of kids."

"That's perfect for Ellie. She'll change you. She's, hands down, the coolest three-year-old in the world. I keep waiting for her to turn twenty-one because she's going to be the most entertaining drunk in the world."

I roll my eyes. "Just ... fine. But no pretending. No backstories about dating."

"Aww. It's almost like you don't like my stories," he teases. "What about... we met while on vacation? You, a rich amazing girl eager to get back at daddy. Me, as me, giving you an amazing night that made you fall for me right then and there."

I narrow my eyes. "No more romcoms."

"Come on, snickerdoodle, I'll be there." He offers. "Am I suddenly not capable of conversation?"

"We're capable of arguing."

"You either hate me, or you like me so much that you think you hate me." He steps closer to me. "Are you mad about going to see my sister or because I'm going out with Carissa instead of you?"

"I don't care who you date or what else you do with your life. I just want you out of mine." I cross my fingers behind my back.

But Jasper looks me over slowly, and his expression tells me he didn't believe what I just said. He takes his shirt off, and my mouth falls open. "What are you doing!?"

"Well, if you hate me and aren't interested, this shouldn't bother you." He shrugs, undoing the top button on his jeans. "Just don't look."

Like that's an option. Jasper is damn attractive, and he knows it. He's not bodybuilder ripped, but his muscular frame, his tattoos and scars draw my attention to the fact that he's solid hunk of a man. I remember feeling his body on mine when he had me over his shoulder. Seeing is different, in the damning, tempting, mouthwatering way.

I can't look away. Not even from his back. I've never really been into backs, but his is sexy, with two obvious bullet wounds other than the one from our time together. Damn, I see the appeal of being a nurse now. I'd give him a sponge bath and - No!

Fuck. I make myself look away and shake my head. "Get dressed, cave man."

"Aw, that's a cute nickname, Sofia. We're taking this to the next level."

"If you drop your pants, I swear my foot is going up your ass."

"You and your dirty talk." He groans.

Huffing, I go to the room and get changed into an oversized t-shirt and a pair of biker tights. I let my hair down, give it a quick brush, telling myself I'm not doing this for Jasper— then I head to the kitchen. I'm not really a drinker, but fuck it. Tonight, I think I need alcohol. I pour myself a few fingers of tequila – because what safe house is complete without it – and then fill the rest with cranberry juice.

Not exactly my normal drink, but it's Friday, I survived an attempt on my life, and I deserve it, right? Just one drink.

"Ooh... looks like tonight will be fun," Jasper says from behind me. "Ready for Scrabble?"

"I'll kick your ass in drunk Scrabble," I say, taking a long drink.

But as I turn around, I nearly spit it out. Jasper stands there in a pair of pajama pants that leaves nothing to my imagination. Fuck, he's huge. His cock—holy fuck, I'm literally drooling right now. It's like a small plantain, and it's not even erect. No. No. He's Carissa's. They're basically dating. I can't keep staring at him like this.

Jasper moves into the kitchen, his eyes on me. I take another drink, and he wraps his hand around my cup. He steals it from me, takes a drink, then hands it back to me. "I'll take that bet. If I win, you're coming with me to Daisy's without complaint."

"Only if you win." I huff.

"I plan to, babe." He winks.

Thankfully, he puts on a shirt that covers his front before pulling out the Scrabble game, although the image of his cock still stains my mind. He points at me. "Fake words only."

"That's bullshit! Then it's just the luck of the letters."

"You have to give a plausible definition."

I narrow my eyes, but I already accepted the challenge, so what is there to do but follow through? I take a drink every time I play a word and Jasper does the same, not bothering to get his own cup. Sharing is caring, I guess.

We get towards the end, and I play all ten tiles in my hand. "Hellicious."

"Definition?"

"Delicious hell, the kind of torture a person enjoys." I sit back victoriously.

"Ah, the kinky masochistic kind?" He chuckles, giving me a wink.

"Sure." I snort. "Let's just add that to our new dictionary."

"I think it would do really well in bookstores."

"Considering you have the ability to make everything sassy or sexual, I'd say yes."

"Don't forget funny."

"You're not that funny. I wouldn't watch a Netflix special starring you," I tease.

Jasper chuckles. "I can't say the same. You have some zingers."

"I'm not sure that's a compliment coming from you."

He rolls his eyes and starts playing off my word: Sycholoic. When I arch an eyebrow," he chuckles. "An obviously faked supernatural event, adjective I think."

"That's ..." But a cough interrupts me, and I choke on my own saliva, laughing and sputtering until Jasper is so worried, he rubs my back.

"Sofia? You can't die mid game. That's not how I want to win. I won't get to rub it in your face."

That sends me into a fit of giggles. I shake my head, and we somehow end up laughing together on the floor. Jasper grins at me and stupidly, I smile back. "That was terrible."

"You laughed."

"Apparently, I'm starved for entertainment."

"You love murdering my ego, don't you?"

"Well, the damn thing just keeps growing back." I shove his shoulder. "You'll survive."

We lay there for a moment, and Jasper sighs. "Tell me something real, Sofia. What's with the obsessive neatness?"

"Everything has a place. It belongs in that place," I reply with a shrug.

"Bullshit."

"It's true. And things are simpler when everything is where it belongs. Organization, planning, all of that makes the bigger stuff, the abstract stuff easier. And it has to be done anyway, so why wait?"

"I think you're just obsessed with keeping things in place, that's all."

"You take that back." I shove his shoulder again, and he chuckles.

"Admit it, if I moved your shoes from the front door, you'd lose your shit."

"Would not." I roll my eyes.

"Testing this theory!" He jumps up and tosses one of my shoes on the couch and drops the other in front of me.

I want to fix it, to put them back where they belong, in line with the others. But at the same time, I don't want to prove him right. The war rages for a moment, but my fingers itch to correct the issue. I bite my lip, then go for my shoes. Jasper catches me on the couch, and I smack him with my shoe. "Knock it off."

"O.C.D., huh?"

"Okay, I admit it. So what? Plenty of people have it. The people around them should be happy because everything's always clean and ... and..."

His eyes drink me in, boring deep into me and stealing my trail of thought. I want to look away from his magnetic stare, but I can't. Hell, I'm in trouble. Big, big trouble.

"I have PTSD," he suddenly murmurs, his face serious. "There are nights when I don't sleep because there's no other way to keep the nightmares at bay."

"Oh, Jasper," I whisper, clutching my shoe tighter, so I don't touch him. I don't think there would be any coming back from it. But damn, he's giving me all the feels right now. I just want to erase that sadness in his eyes.

He takes a deep breath, his mouth slightly parted like he's about to say something, but then it seems he's changed his mind. The transformation on his face happens so quickly, it's like the sun moving from behind a dark cloud. But the smile he's giving me isn't real.

"We're both screwed in the head, aren't we?" I say, when he tightens his arms around me.

"That's why we're here, hot stuff." He brushes his fingers through my hair, and for half a second, I'm sure he's going to kiss me. "And why we're going to survive this shit without killing each other. Right?"

The last thing on my mind is killing you, Jasper. If only you knew. Out loud I reply, "Right."

Chapter 12

Jasper

"You're sure about this?" I ask Sofia again as I button my shirt. I'm not a fan of any item of clothing that takes over ten seconds to haul on, but for tonight I'll make an effort.

"Yes. I'm sure. For the final fucking time," Sofia says, and I look up to find her palming her eyes like she does anytime I walk around shirtless. I smirk slightly. She's been sweet the last few days, overly sweet, but she got back to her normal self last night with the help of some alcohol and terrible scrabble.

And we almost got into trouble. On the couch, before we somehow got untangled, I nearly kissed her, nearly tried to take my shot ... and would have shot myself in the foot based on the fact I'm going out on a date with her best friend tonight, and she's been talking about it all day.

She spreads her fingers to look at me, then drops her hand. I arch an eyebrow. It feels wrong. Like I should find an excuse to stay here, keep her safe, or drag her along with me. My job says I should. This tug in my chest says I should. But Sofia ... she says no. She pulls out her laptop and a few folders.

"Seriously? Are you really going to work on a Saturday night?"

She rolls her eyes. "What are my options? There isn't much to do here, so I'm going to be productive."

"You could come and tell me all the ways to get Carissa to fall for me." I shrug.

She looks up at me and arches an eyebrow. After shaking her head, she tucks her feet under her. "I'm good. Thanks."

"Sarcasm hurts."

"You'll live." She refocuses on her laptop screen, an obvious sign of dismissal. I decide to leave her to it. I'm already late, anyway.

I check my phone, making sure I have alerts from the security system going there and access to the cameras. Even if I'm not here, I can keep an eye on her. Plus, the restaurant is only five minutes away.

The cab pulls up to the restaurant a short while later, and I immediately scan the area, check my phone, and see Sofia in the exact same spot I left her. I smile slightly as she bites the tip of her pen. She holds it between her lips as her fingers glide over the keyboard.

"Ahem."

Looking up, I see Carissa strolling towards me. She's wearing a cute, deep blue, knee-length dress that accentuates her figure beautifully. Wetting my lips, I stuff my phone in my pants. "Wow."

"Wow good or just a basic wow?" she asks, running her hands over her hips.

"Wow very good. Great." Jeeze, it sounds like I've never given a compliment. "You brought your appetite, right?"

She grins and accept my kiss on her cheek. "Absolutely."

Dinner goes well. Carissa is so open and sweet. She asks about my past, and I give her a selective reply, avoiding everything related to war or anything that would bring down the mood. Meaning I make up a lot of fun stories instead.

She laughs the entire time, which makes me feel like the coolest date ever. But as fun as this is, my mind keeps going back to the feisty woman in the apartment we share. I check my phone when Carissa goes to the bathroom. The perimeter is clear, Sofia's still working away, and everything seems quiet. It's a nice break honestly. Maybe Sofia was right about us needing some time apart. It could be just what we need.

Carissa comes back and gives me a sly face as she sits down. "So... you and Sofia. What's going on with you two?"

I shake my head. "We're here to talk about you and me."

"Well, I'm just curious." She shrugs. "I mean, you came out of nowhere, and you and Sofia seems awfully close."

"I-"

"She told me you're a reporter doing research on our company. But I can't help feeling there's more between you two. So, is there anything I need to know?"

"I wish I could tell you everything, Carissa. But I can assure you, Sofia and I aren't dating." She made it perfectly clear she's not interested in going down that road.

"Because Sofia doesn't date." She shrugs but looks away. "I get it."

"You're not a second choice," I reply, taking her hand. "And anyone who meets you would know that right away."

"I know what I am, Jasper. But I mean, you took a bullet for Sofia, and she wouldn't leave your side even though blood makes her nauseous. It's hard not to wonder if you two have a thing going on."

"Carissa. It's not what you think. I can't tell you anything more. But Sofia and I aren't like that."

She leans her head to the side and smiles slightly. "Look, I like things to be clear from the start. As hot as I think you are, as funny as you are, I can't be with you if there are secrets between us."

"I..." I hesitate, but I have to go with my gut. "I'm sorry."

It feels like I'm missing out on an opportunity, especially considering that look on her face. I'd love to explore things with her, to see what we could have, but I can't tell her about my job. I can't tell her why I'm around Sofia like I am.

"I wish things were different so we could explore this," I admit.

Her face falls a little, then she smiles again. "I get it. Nothing serious can happen right now."

"Right now," I agree.

Despite that uncomfortable moment between us, the date ends on a high note. Carissa goes back to talking about herself, dropping in things she likes, namely things that sound awful to me: working, cleaning, shopping, and dancing when she's drunk.

The last one is something I'll remember.

Before we part ways, Carissa plays with her keys in front of her, then bites her bottom lip. I smile and slip my hand over her cheek. She looks up at me, and I lean towards her. "Am I allowed to kiss you?"

"Well, since you asked ... yes." She tugs the front of my shirt, pulling me towards her.

I grin, then kiss her softly. Her lips mold to mine, but I feel nothing. I want to. I want this to be a great first kiss, but my heart just isn't in it. No sparks at all. What I'd give to have sparks fly, for this to be the romance that pushes my feelings for Sofia to the back burner. When I draw back, Carissa giggles a little and touches her bottom lip.

"Wow."

"I'm glad to hear it." I wink at her. "Nothing serious but..."

"Exactly." She nods, but there's a darker look in her eyes. She's turned on. Fuck.

There's a reluctant expression on her face when we part ways. Safely in the back seat of the cab, I check my phone again, bracing for any issues, but there's nothing unusual on the security footage. Well... except Sofia is missing though. She's not in her usual spot. I ignore the tightness in my chest as I flick through the internal cameras. Sofia's fine. She's still in the apartment somewhere. Relief melts the tension when I spot her in the kitchen, dancing as she stirs something in a saucepan. I can't help smiling as I watch her. Hell, I can't help wanting her, either. God help me. What the fuck am I going to do about these feelings for her?

Once I get home, I stow my phone away and unlock the door, enter the security code, and re-arm everything. Sofia emerges from the kitchen with more color in her cheeks than normal.

She sets her bowl on the center table, then looks me over slowly. "How was the date?"

"It went well. Carissa is a sweet woman, just as you said," I reply, leaving out everything else. She doesn't need to know Carissa and I—"

"She says you're a good kisser."

Fuck.

Damn it, Carissa's quick. I imagine she made that phone call the second she pulled away from the parking lot. Well, Sofia's her best friend, so I guess that's unavoidable. I move to sit on the couch. Sofia crosses her arms and stares down at me.

"Something you want to say about that?" I ask when she keeps staring.

"No."

"Are you sure? I can practically see the gears turning in your brain. What's going on in there?"

She glowers at me, but I see wrinkles between her eyebrows. I smile and lean my head to the side. "You want to know if she's right? If I'm a good kisser?"

"Oh, fuck off." But her blush gives her away.

"So you want to, but you don't want to hurt Carissa. Got it," I tease.

She rolls her eyes. "Why are you like this?"

"Wonderful, charming?"

"Yeah. That's clearly what I mean." She huffs.

I glance at the food on the center table, and my stomach growls. Chili and rice. I hadn't eaten a huge dinner, and now my appetite's gone through the roof. "How much of that did you make?"

"Have some." She sighs. "Maybe you'll stay quiet, so I can work."

I eat it and relax a moment, letting Sofia work until she lets out a frustrated sigh. It can't be me; I'm not doing anything. She runs her fingers through her hair with a groan. "We were just rejected."

"What do you mean?"

"My proposal. It was just rejected by a fortune 500 company we've been after for months. The assholes don't see the value in treating people like people. Fucking shit."

"Sofia." I turn her chin to face me. "Hey."

"Go ahead. Give me some bullshit 'it'll be okay' thing or how I shouldn't expect different."

"I'm sorry." I say. "Not everyone sees the world like you do, and if they can't profit off it, they don't see the worth."

Sofia looks at me for a long time, then swallows. "Thanks for that. I'll just try harder next time."

"It's not about how much you try. Some people just suck, and I'm sorry about that. You do a lot, and I know that it's recognized by the people who matter."

She narrows her eyes, then pokes my chest. "If you're teasing me."

"Why would I be teasing you?"

"Because every second thing out of your mouth is a lie. I know that. Telling Carissa you were in Greenpeace?"

"I didn't want to tell her I was in the military. It would lead to too many questions that I don't want to answer. You only get to know that because I'm protecting you," I point out. "I don't lie to you, Sofia."

"But you lie to everyone else. Got it."

"Trust me, lies are a mercy."

"They're a cop-out, and you know it."

I glower at her. "You want real shit?"

"No, please lie to me more."

"I lost my entire team on my last mission, including my sister's husband. I watched him die just after he asked me to protect her and their daughter at all costs. I was badly injured and failed my psych eval, so I was discharged from the military, which is why I do *this* now. This is all after I lost my kid brother under similar circumstances. Oh, and my father hates me because he thinks I'm weak, that I failed my psych eval on purpose. But that's about enough of my messed-up life. Happy?"

Sofia looks at me for a long moment, then leans in to hug me. Sighing, I slowly wrap my arms around her. I'm not sure what to do with her affection, how to take it, or if I even should. She rubs my back with soothing sounds that relaxes me.

"I'm sorry for what you went through, Jasper. I can't imagine how horrific it must have been. And I'm sorry I let my temper get the best of me."

"Don't worry about it. Shit happens. That's life in a nutshell."

Her warmth spreads through me until I'm tempted to let everything spill out. Instead, I press my face to her hair and try to accept her affection, as gentle and sweet as it is. She smells like peaches and vanilla, warm and gentle and everything she isn't.

I kiss her temple. "Thank you."

"For what?" she asks. "Being a decent human?"

"Yeah," I nod. "For that."

When Sofia finally draws back, she stares down at her hands. "What's your love language? You asked me that once."

"Uh, quality time and words of affirmation according to this online test I took." I clear my throat, shifting over on the couch. "Physical stuff isn't high priority."

"So you're asexual?"

"No." I chuckle. "It just scored lowest on the test. What about you?"

"Not important. But you got all tense when I hugged you, and I was worried I made you uncomfortable."

"It was okay," I assure her, minimizing to keep myself in check. "I've been more uncomfortable in worse situations."

She nods, then makes an excuse about needing to shower. Which is fine. I did just go on a date with her best friend. I don't need to pour my soul out to Sofia, tell her all the details I spared Carissa about my father, about war, about anything in my past. I shake my head and go change, taking the moment to rub my damaged leg. I still worry about the shit hitting the fan at night and me getting my leg into action fast enough.

And Sofia can't know about this. Her faith in me is the most important thing. It's the only way I can keep her safe. We made progress with the whole saving her thing, but if she knows I'm like this ... it will kill any potential for her trusting me. I'll just be the broken guy that she pities.

Been there. Done that. Not interested in a repeat.

Exhaling, I pull myself together. I need to focus on tomorrow, not anything else.

Chapter 13

Sofia

I stare out the window, watching the city disappear as we head to Daisy's house in the suburbs. I still can't believe I said yes to meeting Jasper's sister. It feels too official, like we're a couple or something. I don't want to give my emotions ammunition to use against me later on. Meeting his family could put him in a new light and make me want him more.

I haven't exactly processed what he said last night. He's a military man, so death and destruction are familiar figures in his life. But to see someone important to you die in front of you? That's a lot to endure. My heart keeps going out to him.

But he's still hedging. There's something he still hasn't told me. He mentioned an injury, and I doubt it's any of the scars I've seen. I figured it would have to be potentially lethal for a discharge. Why do I care that he's keeping secrets anyway? I don't know him, nor do I want that honor. He'll be gone from my life soon enough. Soon, I won't think about him anymore.

We're still basically strangers. Even though we're living together, have only spent a few hours apart since we met, and he knows more about what I do than most. He's a huge question mark, and I'd rather it stays that way. That's the way it *should* be.

"Cupcake, you alive over there? It's been a solid thirty minutes since you've given me sass."

"Yeah. Just processing."

"Like a computer?"

I roll my eyes and finally look over at him. "How much longer?"

"Another thirty minutes. She's not far," Jasper says. "Why, you impatient?"

"Something like that."

He reaches over and rubs my knee after hesitating once. For someone who doesn't think of physical relationships, he certainly doesn't have a problem touching me. Maybe it's being touched that's harder for him.

I've seen that in some of the kids we help out. They hate hugs, flinch when someone reaches out, they don't think about giving hugs or high fives or anything else. But here he is, touching me like he's done it a hundred times.

"It'll be fine, Sofia. My sister knows what I do, so I'll spare you another excellent backstory."

"The same one you told me last time?"

"Oh no. A brand new one."

"Dios mio." I shake my head.

"How we bumped into each other at the bookstore while reaching for the last copy of Twilight. And then we got to arguing about who Bella should be with. After that, I realized that I wanted to see what would happen if we were on the same page. So I asked you out by buying you the book, and you said yes."

I stare at him. He laughs at my face and puts both hands back on the wheel. "Speechless just like you were when I kissed your cheek and told you I was a better bet than Edward, huh?"

"You've read the books?"

"That's what you're taking from the story?"

"It's what I asked."

"Yes," he answers. "My sister really liked the books, so I read them with her. Edward's a creepy fucker by the way. Watching someone sleep? When you haven't even taken them on a date?"

"Oh, but after the date it's fine."

"Well obviously, you have to look through the window to see if they're actually laughing when they type LOL."

I smirk and shake my head. "You're severely fucked up."

When he finally stops, we're in the driveway of a beautiful town house. I glance at him, and he pulls the keys out. "Ready to drop the pretenses?"

"Beyond ready."

He knocks on the door, and I hear a squeal inside. The door flies open, and a little girl stands there, bouncing with a wide smile. "Jazzy!"

"Hey, Ellie!" He offers her a high five that she has to jump to get. "Where's Mommy?"

"What did I tell you about answering the door?" A woman comes rushing in to claim the child.

The woman has thick brown hair and wears sweatpants and a t-shirt. I don't miss the bags under her blue eyes that are just like Jasper's. She looks Jasper over, then hugs him tightly, the little one smooshed between them.

"You're alive."

"I still have seven lives left." He sighs, patting her back twice. "Like a cat."

"Cats have nine lives." I correct.

"Yeah, and he's down two now." The woman huffs, slugging Jasper.

The little girl clings to him, and he takes her despite the wince. The woman looks at me, to Jasper, then smiles. "You must be the assignment."

I nod. "Sofia."

"Daisy." She takes my hand, shakes it, then motions to the house. "Come in. Please don't mind the mess."

"Oh, she'll mind." Jasper chuckles.

I elbow him, and he flinches. I put my hands over my mouth, then realize I elbowed his good side, and I shove him as he laughs. "You're too easy, dumpling."

Daisy's house *is* a mess. There's stuff everywhere, toys all over the floor, dishes in the sink, laundry piled in a computer chair that's seen better days. There are stains on the couch and on the rug. The table is covered in a whole lot of things, but it's not gross.

Jasper leans over after setting the child down. "Single mom life."

I nod, remembering the moments of chaos when I was growing up, before I was expected to help out.

"Ellie, how old are you now?" Jasper asks.

She holds up three fingers and grins. "Soon, I'll be four."

"You know what happens when you get to five, right?" He bends over and whispers in her ear.

She squeals and runs towards her mom. Daisy shakes her head. "What did you tell her?"

"It's a secret." He winks at the little girl.

They keep talking and catching up, but I don't really know what to do with myself. Do I get some work done from my phone? Do I entertain Ellie? I drop my butt on the empty side of the couch as Daisy calls to me. "Sofia, are you thirsty or anything?"

"I'm okay."

"It's no trouble. I have all kinds. Apple juice-"

"Juice! Juice, mommy!" Ellie bounces on her toes.

"Well, she sold me." Jasper tickles Ellie. "I'll take a juice too."

I follow the family into the kitchen while Jasper and Ellie have a very serious conversation about elephants and that the blue ones need the most love because they're sad. Jasper treats every one of her 'facts' as if it's the most important thing he's ever heard.

It's kind of sweet. He's so gentle with her but really treats her like a person, like everything she says deserves consideration rather than a correction or brush off. Not to mention that warm, genuine smile.

It's the kind of expression any girl could get lost in. I bite my bottom lip and remind myself again that this is the same shameless Jasper I know.

Daisy bumps my hip. When I flinch, she arches an eyebrow, then glowers at Jasper. "Did you let her get hurt?"

"It's nothing," I insist.

"Yeah. She got grazed. How does it feel, baby doll?" His eyes shift to me immediately, and there's something fierce in them that makes it hard to take a breath.

"It's fine." I drop my gaze to Ellie bouncing on her toes, begging Jasper to take her outside.

Daisy shakes her head as Ellie drags him to the backyard. "He's a hot mess."

"He kept me from getting shot twice, so I can't really complain," I admit. "Other than the puns."

"Yeah, can't break him of that." She laughs, then slides me a beer. I lift it to my lips at once and take a healthy drink.

"Whoa, easy there. It's alcohol, not water," she says with another chuckle.

I rest the half-empty bottle on the counter, welcoming the warmth that's flooding my system. "Trust me, I needed that."

Her face fills with concern, and she moves closer to me. "Jasper told me a bit about what happened. But you don't look like the type to piss someone off enough to kill you. So, what gives?"

"You'd get some arguments there," I grumble. "My dad got himself and the family into trouble."

"That sucks. I'm sure it will be done soon enough though." She glances out back while taking a swig of her drink. "We can forget about all that today and just relax like adults ... with a three-year-old."

"So ... poker," I tease.

She grins. "I don't know about poker, but she's pretty good at Go Fish. It's her favorite way to learn numbers and counting."

We end up on the patio, playing Go Fish. It's oddly intense for a friendly game. Probably because Jasper decided to involve poker chips. But, as promised, Ellie cleans house. I don't know if it's because Jasper's helping her cheat, or what, but that little girl has a radar for who's got what.

Jasper tries to bullshit her. I don't even see his tell, but she holds his gaze, looking deeper and deeper, then puts her hand out. Jasper groans, then hands over two threes. Ellie happily bounces and puts them down with the card in her hand.

"How did you know he was lying, Ellie?" I ask.

"His face." She shrugs, then grins at me. "Any fours?"

I shake my head, and she sighs before drawing a card. The game continues with Ellie coming out as the winner and me taking a close second. She leans towards me and whispers in my ear. "Mommy lets me win and thinks I don't notice."

"Oh yeah?" I whisper back.

"I caught her." She nods with the conviction of someone who's been betrayed before.

I laugh softly, and we put the cards back together. Ellie goes to play, and Jasper chases her around the backyard. Whenever he catches her, he tips her upside down and asks her for her lunch money as she squeals and giggles.

Daisy shakes her head. "I wish he would be more careful sometimes."

"With Ellie?" I ask with a frown. "It seems like he's handling her fine. Plus, she looks like she's enjoying it."

"It's not that. Yeah, Jasper's my strong older brother, but I keep worrying about him since his leg got blasted. He's not the same. It's like he's trying to compensate for the injury or something, the way he keeps pushing himself harder than he should. I wish he would take care of himself. Hell, he would have stopped going to physical therapy altogether if I didn't treat him here."

I blink at her, unable to process anything she said beyond the first two lines. He what? He blasted *what*? I look over at Jasper again. I notice he has a little bit more trouble getting up once he goes down. He avoids getting on his knees, and there's the slightest limp there. How come I hadn't noticed that before?

Daisy nudges me. "You didn't know, did you?"

"No." I shake my head. "He never told me." But it does explain why he's always wearing pants. When he got shot, he refused to let me take them off. He made me stand outside the bedroom door while he handled it himself. I thought he was being modest, but knowing Jasper like I do, I should have realized something was off.

"Well, then don't mention it. He gets bothered about it. Like —" She shakes her head, taking a step forward, her focus on the two playing on the lawn. "Ellie! Be careful!"

Ellie looks over from where she's climbing just before Jasper grabs her and tosses her in the air. He shouldn't be doing that, considering he was in the hospital less than a week ago. I sigh. "I hope to God he doesn't open that wound."

"So do I," Daisy says, leaning towards me as I take another drink. "Now that he's out of earshot, tell me the real stuff. Is there something going on between you two?"

A thin spray of beer flies from my mouth. "Wha— no! No. He's just doing his job. That's all."

Daisy looks me over, and her wicked smile reaches her eyes. "Sure, *Baby-doll*."

I groan, remembering Jasper's term of endearment he used for me earlier. Of course, his sister would read into it. Anyone would. But I need to set the record straight, so she doesn't get any ideas. "I'm Jasper's client, that's it. There's nothing going on between us and there never will."

Daisy gives me an if-you-say-so smile. "Will you guys stay for dinner? I want to check the wound and make sure he's good. A little outside my area of expertise, but it's better than nothing, right?"

It's hard to say no to her, so I give her a nod. She takes Ellie inside to get her cleaned up, and Jasper sits down next to me. He blows out a breath and puts a hand to his chest. "Damn. They need to bottle the energy kids have and sell it."

"Well, this is the life you want, isn't it? A lovely home with big backyard for your kids."

His eyes flick to me, and he takes a long drink of water before nodding, suddenly serious. "I know it's not much to a future congresswoman, but it's comfortable, real, and very far away from battle."

"It could be worse. Your goal could be world domination."

"Everyone should be happy it isn't. I think I could rope you into that future." He gives me a slight smile. "You'd make it happen too."

"Your confidence in me is astounding."

"I learn pretty fast." He taps his head. "There's more than stuffing up here."

"But there is stuffing. Is that what I'm hearing?" I shift in the seat, so I'm facing him. "So that's why you and Carissa are 'just having fun' and not dating?"

He takes another drink before replying. "You're very worried about me and Carissa. Is there a reason why?"

"She's my best friend. I want to make sure you're not going to break her heart," I reply before searching for a different topic.

No, I don't want him to break her heart, but I wouldn't be devastated if they didn't go out again. Not because I like him, no. Just because ... because it would be awkward once I'm free of this house arrest bullshit. That's all.

My eyes flick to Jasper again, and I see his slight smile. He takes another drink and nods. “I think I’m starting to rub off on you, Sofia. Lying gets easier when it protects you.”

For the first time, I silently agree with how right he is.

Chapter 14

Jasper

After a long awkward silence, Sofia gets up to go play with Ellie. Daisy comes to sit beside me as I rub at my leg. As much as I love my niece, she's a struggle to keep up with.

"I like her, Jasper," Daisy says. "She's not like those spineless bimbos you brought home when you were younger. This one, she has substance."

"Hey!" I nudge her side with a chuckle. "I never dated any bimbos, you twit."

"Right... so I imagined the one who slept with half the town—what's her name..."

"Anna."

"Haha! So I was right."

"Oh, whatever. That's only one."

When our laughing subsides, she takes my hand. "I'm serious, though. Sofia's a keeper. You should hold on to her."

"I don't even have a grip, Daisy. Sofia and I aren't an item."

"Sofia said the same thing, but I'm not fooled. I see the way you two look at each other."

I sigh. "It's time for you to get those eyes checked, little sis. I'm sure you're seeing things. Sofia doesn't want me like that."

My attention shifts to where Sofia and Ellie are racing on the lawn. Sofia's barely jogging, giving Ellie a head start, and my niece releases a triumphant howl when she crosses the makeshift finish line.

"I beg to differ, but—" Daisy raises a palm when I attempt to argue, "I'll say no more, just watch the inevitable unfold."

Ellie comes running up to us, her arms outstretched. "I won, Uncle Jasper, I won!"

"Good for you, bug." I ruffle her hair while giving Sofia a glance. Her skin looks flushed, which makes her even more beautiful to me. I'm trying not to keep staring, but it would be easier to walk without my leg. Damn it, this woman is getting under my skin.

"Mommy, can Sofia and I play with your makeup?" Ellie asks, bouncing.

"Ellie." Daisy captures her daughter. "That's up to Sofia."

"She said yes!" Ellie shouts. "I'm going to make her pretty."

Sofia's smile is so hesitant and halting it looks more like a grimace. She gives me a look that says, "Save me" and I shake my head once. She made this choice; she has to live with it. Daisy approves, and they head inside, Sofia's hand held captive by Ellie's.

"It's fine," Daisy says when I ask if it's a good idea. "Makeup isn't permanent. If she asks to play hair stylist, we'll have a problem," she ends with a laugh.

I nod, then drum my fingers on the table. Daisy sighs, and the smile on her face slowly fades. She didn't just invite me over here because I'm injured. I know that. It's an odd week if I don't end up hurt. I just have to wait her out, and she'll spill.

"Ellie's started asking about her dad," she finally mumbles.

"Damn." I suck in a harsh breath. "I guess it's time for the pics to come out."

"She's too young to know everything. I just tell her he was a hero and a good man, but I'm worried that won't be enough for much longer."

"I'll be here if you decide to tell her everything," I promise. "You don't have to do it alone, Daisy."

"Thanks, Jaz."

I roll my eyes at the nickname. "I don't like when Ellie calls me that, but she gets a pass. You don't."

She pouts, giving me puppy dog eyes that have always worked and probably always will. Then she glances behind her as Ellie giggles from inside. "And how are *you*?"

"Eager to make this my last job before I settle down. I'm not sure what I want to do, though. I'm not sure what I'm qualified to do. I could be a recruiter, but ..."

"But." Her eyes fall to her lap. "You'd think of Rick the whole time."

I look down at my drink. My brother is pretty high on the list of things we don't talk about. His first tour, his first week, and he became a victim of a bomb attack. There was barely enough of him to send home. He'd wanted to uphold dad's legacy with me, and it got him killed.

"Yeah." I nod.

"Speaking of family ..."

"No."

"Dad's been wondering when you're going to visit. He knows you're around, as in ... in state, and he's hurt you haven't tried to get in touch."

"You mean angry."

"If you'd just listen to him, you'd see how much you matter to him." She takes my hand. "He's just bad at expressing how he feels."

"And it's not my job to be a therapist or deal with his shitty attitude, Daze. If he's going to be an asshole, he can, but not to me. I won't tolerate it."

She slumps back in her chair. "You're a lot like him, you know. So stubborn."

"I'm nothing like that man. I make people laugh."

"Of course, you do." She rolls her eyes. "And you avoid your problems, ignore what's right in front of you, and plow forward as if the past won't catch up with you."

"Not if I'm fast enough."

She continues to stare at me until I roll my eyes. "Look, some stuff is private, and I get to choose who knows what about me. It's that simple. I'll talk the intense stuff with the right person."

"Friends?"

"They were there, they don't need the recap." I take a drink.

"Family." She nods.

"You and I did our talking." I wave away.

"So you're saving all this to dump on your imaginary girlfriend? Counseling. Go to it. Embrace it. Learn to love it. I promise it helps." She half begs. "Really. It does. I wouldn't talk about it if I didn't think it would help."

"Maybe I don't need help. Maybe I'm good as is."

"What's the longest you've managed to sleep since you got back?" She counters.

"Six whole hours."

"Uninterrupted." When I don't answer she smirks. "I know a good office. I'll give them your number as soon as I check your wound."

"It's fine."

Before Daisy can argue with me, Ellie comes back out, glitter on her cheeks, pink lipstick on her lips, and her fingers covered in colors. I turn and see Sofia coming slowly towards us wearing purple and pink eyeshadow, glitter everywhere, and bright red lips and pink cheeks.

She's pouting hard, but the gleam in her eyes is a dead giveaway that she enjoyed her time with Ellie. I don't know why that makes me happy, but it does. I wrap my arm around her waist and jerk her onto my lap. She gasps and pushes against my chest. "Jasper!"

"Well, I can't help it. Ellie, where did you find a princess?"

Ellie giggles. "It's Kat, silly! Isn't she pretty?"

"So pretty." I give Sofia a wide smile. She glowers at me, but her face softens when I tip her chin up. "I mean, just look at all that glitter. You really are a princess."

Ellie giggles. Daisy compliments Ellie's makeup, and she says that Sofia did it. Sofia tries to get up, and I tighten my grip on her. She wiggles, and her ass brushes my cock, sending a tingle up my spine. I huff against her shoulder and dig my fingers into her side.

"Settle down. There's a kid present," I whisper in her ear.

She blushes and shoots me another look. It's only at half-venom. When she glances at my lap, I nod once. "Yeah. That's a thing."

I can practically see the lightbulb go off in her head. She turns her attention to Daisy while leaning on the table, triggering an image of her riding me reverse cowgirl style. I can feel the blood flowing to my cock. Fuck. Wrong place, wrong time for an erection.

"So, Daisy, tell me something about your brother no one else knows."

"Hey!" I call out.

She rolls her hips, and I grit my teeth. Daisy smirks, and I hope she doesn't notice what Sofia's doing to me.

"He's crazy about holidays," she begins. "Always wants to decorate as much as possible – inside and out. Makes treats, hangs lights, all of it. He doesn't even care if no one else does."

"Aww... that's cute," Sofia says, looking around at me.

My brain short circuits. Was that an actual compliment? I just look at the back of Sofia 's head and try to keep myself under control.

"As a kid, he'd draw a bunch of pictures and hang them up. I swear, I have some of them. I'll dig them up for you."

"Don't you dare," I growl at her.

Sofia rolls her body against mine again, effectively shutting me up as I try to picture naked old ladies to keep my dick in check. She chuckles. "I'd love to see them. Tell me more."

"Every year, Uncle Jazz gets more deer," Ellie yells. "Another one this year?"

"Another reindeer. Yeah," I promise. "Sofia, we should go."

"Oh no. We're staying for dinner." She looks over her shoulder, shooting me a devilish smile. "Aren't we, Pookie?"

Now is not the time to switch up the dynamic. She's not supposed to be interested in my life, teasing me to shut me up or calling me pet names. She's not supposed to be indulging Ellie or bonding with Daisy. She's supposed to be angry, frustrated, begging me to leave so she can get away from me.

I curse under my breath as she adjusts again, nearly bouncing on my lap.

"So, he's the opposite of a grinch," she continues, getting a taste of victory and running with it.

"Halloween is actually his favorite. He's never met a prop he doesn't like. I think there's a whole storage unit full of decorations," Daisy answers.

"Well, Halloween is the second-best holiday. I love New Years. The promise of things changing and getting better." Sofia softly sighs. "Plus, everyone – for one day – is hopeful and ready to be more than they were before."

Daisy gives me a look I hate, one that's curious. Her eyes flick between us, and she jerks her head in Sofia's direction as if telling me she's the one. All because of that answer? Ridiculous.

Sofia rubs herself on me again, then leans back against me. She leans up to whisper in my ear. "Now I know how to shut you up."

"You're playing a dangerous game," I growl.

"But you're all about protection." She pats my thigh, then drags her fingers down towards my bad knee until I catch her hand. "So I have nothing to worry about."

"Pushing your luck," I answer, then I point at Daisy. "You too."

We make it through dinner with actual conversation, and Sofia seems to forget about her makeup until we're about to leave. Daisy reminds me that she can help with physical therapy if I need it, and I roll my eyes.

"Think about it," she says as we get into the rental. "And stop being a hard you-know-what!"

I ignore her, giving my attention to Ellie who's waving us goodbye. "Bye, Uncle Jazz! Bye, Aunt Kat!"

Sofia tenses, but then she smiles and waves, then gets extra busy searching for a napkin. She starts wiping at her face until I reach over to help her. She laughs, then falls quiet as I wipe over her lips.

"You're putting a lot of trust in me to not make this worse," I say.

"I do trust you, Jasper," she whispers. "Even if I don't show it sometimes."

To say I'm shocked would be putting it lightly. I would have dreamed of Sofia saying these words to me. "You never show it, Sofia. That's the problem."

"Well, I'm sorry you feel that way. But I do. I trust you with my life. Literally."

For the first time, I'm speechless. I just concentrate on wiping the makeup from her face.

"Thanks for today," she says.

The napkin falls from my hand. The makeup is softer, not terrible at all. And she's so beautiful with that smile softening her face, warming her eyes, making her approachable, and ... I swallow hard. No. I've already built a wall around my heart to protect it from my feelings for her. I can't afford to fall again.

"I mean it. It was fun." She sits back, then dabs at her lips with another napkin. "Maybe a life like that wouldn't be terrible."

"Doesn't actually work with a skyscraper ambition, though," I remind her.

"True, but it's nicer than coming home to an empty house."

"Messy is better than empty?"

She thinks on that, then wrinkles her nose. "Maybe a little cleaner."

"Carissa said you don't date. Why?"

She rolls her eyes, and immediately that smile falls. "I don't like talking about it."

"Come on. You owe me after that stunt."

"You put me on your lap!"

"That doesn't mean I needed a lap dance."

"You didn't see your face."

"Sofia." I sigh while starting the car.

She bites her lip and is quiet for half the drive before she finally says anything. "My ex nearly derailed my career. He wanted a shadow, but I wanted to be the light. I couldn't settle for being the second-class citizen he wanted me to be, so I left him. He retaliated by trying to ruin my career."

"I'm sorry that happened to you." I reach over to pat her hand, careful to return it quickly to my lap.

"It's fine. His antics all failed. He's no longer around to put hurdles before my efforts to help the less fortunate. All's well that ends well."

"I'm glad. But is that dipshit the only reason you don't date? Aren't you giving him more power than he deserves?"

She shakes her head. "That's only part of it. I don't date because it's a distraction I don't need right now. The last thing I want is to get caught up in a relationship, and before I know it, I'm getting married and having kids and putting my dreams on the back burner."

"You don't want to be your mom."

She looks at me, surprise filling her face. "You remembered."

"I remember a lot. Like I said, more than stuffing in here." I tap my head.

She glances away – the red brake lights of the car before us, highlighting the confusion on her face. She clears her throat. "Yeah. We'll see tomorrow."

TOMORROW COMES FASTER than I'd like. I haven't had time to process yesterday. How gentle and honest and ... wholesome Sofia was, how well she fit in with my family and the fact that we actually had a good time together.

Cash had called us last night when we got back in, giving us the green light to proceed today. It had been a week since the attack, and there's been no sign of anything amiss. We're still on a tight leash; nothing but from the safehouse to work. But I'm relieved to get out of the house. It's easier being around Sofia when there are a dozen other people sharing the space.

When we get to work, Sofia back in her slacks and button-up combo, I'm sure the moment we shared on Sunday is already gone. Whatever was there ... it was fake, right? Just to make things easier on me.

I take my mind off her and instead focus on the job I'm being paid to do. Moving to the windows, I scan the street. About an hour into the day, my attention narrows on a tall, tattooed guy who's walked by about three times and glanced in the office windows each time. It could be a coincidence, but I won't leave it to chance. I take a few pics of him and send them to Cash. Hopefully, he's just a random guy who's lost or something.

As I walk towards Sofia, I spot my sister coming down the hallway towards us, bringing me up short. Detouring, I move towards her, and her face brightens when she sees me.

"Daisy? What are you doing here?"

"I came into the city to handle an emergency close by, and I didn't want to leave without checking in."

"What kind of an emergency?"

"Nothing serious. Don't worry about it." But her eyes immediately fall to her feet, the way it usually does when she's lying.

"Daisy."

Her eyes flick up to me, and she smiles, reaching to stroke my arm. "It's nothing, I swear. I'll tell you about it when the time is right."

Before I can push her further, the stationery room door beside us opens, and Carissa steps out. I move to introduce them, but they are already squealing and running towards each other.

"Carissa!"

"Daisy!"

"What are you doing here?"

"Oh, my God, how long has it been?"

My eyes flick to my right as Sofia comes up to us, looking just as befuddled as I am. Carissa and Daisy break apart, and they both turn to me. For some reason, it feels like I'm caught under a microscope.

"I see you two already know each other," I say, and Daisy nods.

"Carissa and I go way back, since high school. It's been years, though. Oh wow, what a small world, huh?"

"I know, right?" Carissa says, gesturing to Sofia. "I want you to meet my best friend, Sofia."

"We've already met," Daisy says, and I feel my chest tighten. There's an urge to clamp my hand over her big mouth, but it's too late anyway. She's already spewing details I wanted to keep from Carissa. "Jasper brought her to meet me yesterday."

"Oh, that's... nice." Carissa's response sounds empty, although there's a smile on her face.

"It was just a simple dinner, nothing else," Sofia speaks up, the alarm clear on her face.

"Was it, though?" Daisy says with a sly grin, and I facepalm in my head. She soon notices the tension on my face, and her smile diminishes. Her eyes shift between us, and her brain starts connecting the dots. "Oh... um... yeah, it was just dinner. Sofia played with my daughter the entire afternoon while Jasper and I talked about family stuff—okay, I think I'm going to shut up now."

We stand there for an awkward beat until an office door opens, and I'm never more relieved to see Sofia's boss emerge. He gives me a cool stare like he's been doing since I started accompanying Sofia to work, then he beckons to her.

"I need a minute, Sofia," he says.

Sofia seems just as relieved to get called away. Without saying a word, she dashes towards her boss. I watch the office door close before turning to Carissa. I feel like shit. Why the hell did I give in to Sofia's prodding and ask her out? I should have left her alone. Now, I'm faced with dealing with a woman I unintentionally hurt.

"Look, Carissa—"

Her palm shoots out to stop me. "It's fine. There's no need to explain."

Again, there's the smile that doesn't reach her eyes, making me feel even worse. I need to get a handle on today before I lose complete control. Daisy being here, Sofia running off at the first chance given, Carissa, the stranger outside ... one more distraction, and I'm going to be fucked.

My cell phone vibrates, and I swipe at the screen while moving away from the two ladies. "Cash, talk to me. What have you got?" I say.

"A problem," he replies, his voice serious, filling me with concern. "A huge one, too."

Chapter 15

Sofia

"Nick, I'm sorry. I wish I could tell you more of what's going on, but I can't." I sigh as I rub my forehead.

It's not the conversation with my boss that's making me feel so stressed, although it's a close second. Nick wants to know why Jasper's still here, and I can't lie to him anymore. But he can't know the truth, either. I'm caught between a rock and a hard place, and I'm sick of it. This situation needs to end. Now.

But I wish this was my only problem. Dealing with the anxiety of knowing someone's trying to kill me is so much easier than facing my best friend. I don't know what to say to her. Nothing happened between Jasper and me, but I would be lying if I didn't admit how much I wanted it to. I'm attracted to him. I'm hungry for his touch. I want him inside me so bad it hurts. But how do I say that to her, knowing how much she's into him, knowing I'm the one who pushed him her way?

Fuck. This is a mess. I hate messes. God, I don't know what to do.

"Look, I just want to ensure you're okay, that's all. Jasper doesn't seem like the average reporter. I mean, I've seen him observing how we do things around here, but I don't understand why he's here so long. Plus, the way he follows you around, one would think he's your bodyguard or something."

I reply with a dry snicker. Nick has no clue how close he is to home.

"Whatever it is, Sofia, if you need more time off for anything, just let me know."

"Time off, now?" I snort. "Very funny. We have way too much to do. Plus, I've been away for a week, almost. Maybe after the holidays."

Nick walks to me, taking my hands. "Sofia, no one appreciates your work ethic more than I do. But you have to understand that you – a burnt-out version of you – isn't going to do much to help."

"Yeah." I sigh, slumping down.

Nick rubs my shoulder. "And if that's the way you have to think of it instead of doing it for yourself, then think of it that way."

"Right now, I'm fine, okay. Maybe in a week or two, I'll take a few days off once I know everything is set, I promise."

Nick sighs. "Alright. I guess I shouldn't be complaining that you want to work. The opposite of a problem for a boss."

"And I shouldn't be upset that you want me to take more time off." I give an inch.

Nick chuckles, his beautiful eyes sparkling. "Did you just compromise?"

"Maybe. It's a work in progress," I reply with a shrug.

I slowly exit his office, hoping Carissa had already gone back to her desk. I need more time to create a plausible explanation for hanging out with Jasper outside of 'work'. But she's still standing in the hallway and talking with Daisy. She sees me and gives me a we-need-to-talk glare. Oh, boy. Guess I'll have to wing it. I hope Daisy hasn't told her about the subtle lap dance I gave Jasper or that she thought there were sparks between us.

I move towards her, but Jasper intercepts me before I get there. He takes my hand, his expression grave. "We need to talk."

"Not right now, Jasper," I hiss, brushing him off. I take another step towards Carissa but gasp as his powerful arms tighten around my waist. He pushes me into the supply closet and closes the door. He switches on the light, and I push against his chest, trying to get past him, but he doesn't budge.

"Get out of my way, Jasper! You just made things a hundred times worse!" What the hell must Carissa be thinking right now?

"Sofia, stop and fucking listen," he growls. "Someone's been casing your office all day, and from what Cash told me, there may be others on the way. We need to leave. Now." His voice is low, careful. There's not a trace of panic even though every muscle of his body is spring-loaded.

"What? That's not ... I still have work to do," I whisper, then glance at the door. "Jasper, if you're not one hundred percent sure about this ..."

He takes a step closer to me, and I wonder how he even fits in the door. He's so huge. I don't know how I forget when I only come up to his chest, but he has a way of making me feel inches taller than I am. But now, he's overwhelming me with his presence, pushing my panic to the back burner. All I'm feeling now is a white-hot, burning lust. Being trapped in this enclosed space isn't helping at all.

"I'm sure enough, Sofia." He keeps his voice low, controlled. "Trust me."

"They would hurt everyone here, wouldn't they?" It comes out shaky. "Carissa and Nick and the volunteers and ..."

"To get to you, yes." He nods.

"Oh, fuck."

"Just relax. And I don't want you to alarm anyone, either. Just tell your boss you need to go, then grab your bags and let's leave as quietly as possible."

"What will I tell Carissa? And what about Daisy? She's still here. Jasper—"

"Sofia, breathe."

"No! I can't do this. I—"

Jasper grunts, gripping the back of my head and seizing my mouth. My thoughts pause for a beat. My body stills. This isn't real. There's no way Jasper's kissing me right now. But when he parts my lips with his tongue and deepens the kiss, it sends a teasing shiver up my spine that confirms how real it is. How amazing. Fuck, this man can kiss. His big hand spreads over my back, then clutches at my shirt, fire following in the wake of his fingers.

He licks into my mouth, changing the angle to get deeper, and my whole body ignites. I shiver, rubbing the nape of his neck as his body presses to mine. Groaning, he drags me closer, nearly sweeping me off my feet to kiss me deeper, harder.

The sudden knock on the door makes me pull back, breathing hard. The lust on Jasper's face makes me want to finish what we started, but the door's already opening, revealing a concerned-looking Nick.

"Is everything okay?" he asks, glancing from me to Jasper.

I nod, hoping my expression gives nothing away. But my body's still on fire. I'm sure my face is crimson red right now. "Jasper and I were just discussing an angle for his story."

"In the supply closet?"

"Yeah, I wanted total privacy," Jasper replies. "Do you mind?"

I shoot him a hard glare before giving Nick my attention once more. "Do you need me for something?"

"Yes. I need the monthly budget. Since the latest proposal got rejected, we may need to make several adjustments if we're going to stay on track."

"Okay, I'll email it to you. I'm also going to take a few days off like you suggested. You were right. I need to rest for a while."

His expression flickers with surprise, but he just nods. "Of course. Take all the time you need."

I move past him, leaving him in a stare-down with Jasper. I hurry to my computer and email the budget, then apply for a week-long departmental leave. I'm almost done packing my bags when Carissa appears at my desk.

"We need to talk," she says, her tone cold as ice.

"I know, and I'll explain everything to you later, okay? But I need to go." I drop my cell phone inside, then zip it closed. "But it's not what you think."

Except I just locked lips with Jasper in the supply closet, and I didn't want to stop. It was the best kiss of my life, hands down. My life is in danger, and all I can think of is Jasper's arms around me, his cock pressing against my belly. This is wrong. So, so wrong. But I can't help myself. I want more.

I take a deep breath, knowing I'm about to hurt my best friend for the first time. "Okay, so I'm lying. But Carissa, please don't hate me. I never meant to—"

"Sofia. We need to go. Now!"

The urgency in Jasper's tone makes me grab my bags, giving Carissa another pleading glance. Her expression's half hurt, half curious as she watches us walk away. Jasper's hand braces the middle of my back, pushing me forward. The elevator sounds before we get there. Jasper pauses, one arm now around my shoulder, the other on his hip. He shoves me to the side when the doors open, revealing a tall, spiky-haired guy with a rifle in his hand.

Holy shit.

I land on the floor sideways, my face hitting the tiles. An overwhelming terror threatens to take over, but I shake it off along with my bags and scuffle under a desk. The sound of explosions reminds me of fireworks on the Fourth of July, but there's no excitement. Only fear. Is Jasper okay? My coworkers, are any of them hurt?

There's a sudden break, and I fall to a tabletop position, listening for movements. My entire body's shaking. My mouth feels dry. There's this sudden urge to pee that's getting worse by the minute. Oh, God. I can't die like this.

A sudden sound to my right makes me tense, and I relax when Carissa comes into view, shuffling on all fours. I quickly beckon to her, and she hurries over, joining me under the desk.

"Are you fucking crazy?" I whisper. "What the hell are you doing moving around?"

"Looking for you," she whispers. "I heard the shots and thought—" She huffs, and her eyes fill with tears. "I'm just glad you're okay."

"Oh, Carissa. I don't deserve your tears," I reply, wiping her face. "I kissed Jasper."

"Yeah... I figured. You were both in that supply closet for a minute."

I chance a glance outside, but there's no activity. It makes me even more worried than if there were still bullets flying around. The anticipation makes my body tight with tension.

"You're in trouble, aren't you?" Carissa says.

I nod. "Courtesy of daddy dearest. His sins are coming back to haunt me, too."

"And Jasper?"

"He's somewhat of a bodyguard, I guess. We've been living in a safehouse for a few weeks." But nothing happened between us," I quickly say when she frowns. "Not until today."

The sudden blaring of gunshots cuts Carissa's reply, and she grabs my shirt. "I don't want to die, Sofia!"

"I promise you won't," I reply, sounding way more confident than I feel. Where the hell is Jasper?"

As if on cue, he suddenly appears in front of us, making us both gasp. "Come on," he says, taking my arm. "I got him, but there's more coming."

"No, no, no! You can't leave us here like this!" Carissa says, panting. "They'll kill us all!"

"No. They want her, not you guys. They won't bother you once she's gone. But you still need to clear out, just in case," Jasper says. "Got it?"

Carissa nods, and Jasper pulls me out a second later. I glimpse a body on the floor, the blond, spiked hair filling me with relief as Jasper guides me down the stairs, one hand clutching his gun.

"Where's Daisy?" I ask, almost tripping on the first landing.

"I left her in an office. Told her to leave when the smoke gets cleared."

"What?" Alarmed, I twist to face him. His expression seems calm, which adds confusion to the list of emotions I'm facing right now. "Why would you leave her there?"

He twists me around again, guiding me forward. "Because it's safer in there than with us. They're after you, remember?"

Of course, it makes perfect sense. But I'm not thinking straight right now. So much has happened in half an hour, leaving me whirling from it all. Jasper's kiss. Carissa's hurt. The bullets that would have taken my life if Jasper wasn't there. It makes me sick to my stomach, yet I'm so grateful.

"Thank you," I say to him when we reach the ground floor. All seems quiet. Please, God, let it stay that way.

"Don't thank me yet," Jasper mumbles, pulling me out the back door behind him.

His head swivels as he leads me to a pickup truck, caging me against it. Again, he scans the area, his arms positioned forward. His body tenses, then he crouches down to face me and cocks his head towards the front wheel. Understanding right away, I shift down to it, careful to keep low. Jasper edges around to the front, his hands curled around the gun. I hear a crack and a thud, then Jasper returns for my hand, and we start running.

After half a block, he picks me up, throws me over his shoulder and sprints the rest of the way. I clutch his torso to keep my upper body from banging against his back, my eyes dazzling as the buildings zip by. Damn, he's fast. And he's barely blowing a breath.

Jasper slows down and soon lets me down beside an SUV. Using his elbow, he quickly breaks the glass on the passenger side. I hear the crack of a gunshot as he opens the front door, and he chucks me in so hard my body sails over to the driver's side. I hurry to reposition myself as he joins me, taking off with such speed the tires screech.

I pant as I look out the back window. "Fucking hell."

"Don't worry. I'll lose them soon enough."

I drop my head on the back of the seat with an anguished whimper. "Oh, my God. The guys at work. What if they got hurt? How will I face any of them again?"

"The guys are fine, Sofia," he grunts. "Keep your head down, and don't look out the windows."

For the first time, I don't feel like arguing. I obediently sink down and curl into a ball. Holy fuck, it's sinking in. Someone is actually trying to kill me. Me, not just my dad. And all this time ... I could have gotten Carissa hurt. I could have gotten so many people ... A sob pulls from my throat.

Jasper jerks off the highway and soon pulls up at a motel that looks like its seen better days. I ease up on the seat, looking around as Jasper reverses into a parking spot at the back of the building. "Why are we here?"

"The safehouse has been compromised. We can't go back there," Jasper says.

"What—how? We've been careful all this time, haven't we?"

He shrugs. "Cash is still trying to figure out what happened. For now, this is where we'll stay."

My body trembles as understanding finally rips through me. This entire time, every moment out of the safehouse, it hasn't just been Jasper or me in danger, it's been every single person I've talked to, every place I've gone ... all of them.

"Sofia."

Another sob echoes from my chest. All I've ever wanted to do is help, especially if it meant helping those who were forgotten by others, and those are the exact same people I've put at risk because I was too selfish to take even a short break.

"Come on, darling." Jasper pulls me across the seat and sweeps me into his arms, honeymoon style. I turn to hide my face in his chest. "You're okay. We're safe."

"I'm estupida."

"No, you're not." He adjusts me in his arms until my breathing normalizes. "I'm going to get us a room. So be as quiet as you can for me."

"No." I grip his shirt. "You're not leaving me here by myself."

"Sofia—"

"I feel safer around you, Jasper. Please, take me with you."

Jasper sighs, his chest bouncing as he breathes. "Fine. Stay close to me, okay?"

My hand grips the tail of his shirt as we hurry along the asphalt-covered path that leads to the front desk. Still clinging to him, I scan the dingy-looking lobby as he books us a room with cash from his wallet. The clerk hands us a key, and we take the stairs to the second floor, and I hurry inside the second Jasper opens the door. The smell of fresh linen hits me, filling me with relief. The room is definitely an upgrade from the lobby. A queen-sized bed stands in the center, with two night tables on each side. There's a dresser in the corner, a small closet and an open door that leads to an ensuite bathroom.

Jasper locks the door, makes a few phone calls and checks the windows, but he seems so far away. I release my hair from the barrette that's been keeping my hair in a ponytail, kick my shoes off and pull my feet up onto the bed. After a moment, I fix my shoes, making sure they're in a straight line. But what I really want is to fix this situation, to get back to that night when I had nothing to worry about but my lesson plans and the donors I needed to charm. God, I would give anything to have my old life back.

Jasper stops in front of me, and I remove my hand from my jaw to look up at him. "How are you doing?"

I shake my head and rub my face. "I think I'm still in shock."

"Yeah, you definitely are. Perfect explanation for why you just put your shoes by the bed. As long as I've known you, you're a stickler for putting them right against the wall right next to the door." His hands turn mine over, and my fingers wrap in his.

"It's where they belong," I murmur.

"I think they look fine right where they are." He tightens his hold on me. "We need to keep our heads low from now on, you understand that?"

"No more work?"

"No more work. No phone calls. You can't talk to Carissa or your boss or anyone else." His eyes hold mine. "Until the coast is clear, you need to trust me, okay?"

"This is how it was supposed to be the whole time, yes?" I ask.

"Yes, but you were so stubborn, hell-bent on having your own way. I'm not trying to blame you for what's happening right now. These guys are resilient. They would have found us anyway. But this time, you're going to follow my rules, no questions asked. Let me do the job your father paid me to do."

I nod. "Okay."

He smiles slightly. "Look, we'll have fun in this hell hole, I promise. Plenty of bad movies, junk food, and the best stories we can make up."

I sniff and nod. "Yeah, definitely sounds like hell."

Chapter 16

Jasper

Sofia's watery eyes remind me of Ellie after she's taken a fall, and just like with my niece, I want to take her in my arms and console her until the pain disappears. I brush her hair back from her face with a sigh. I need to distract her. But right now, my brain is coming up blank. All I can think about is ensuring we're protected. For right now, we're quite safe and sound. I'm hoping it lasts, at least until I hear from Cash once more. I pick up the remote and scan through the options on the screen. "Sofia, you ever watch spy movies?"

"A few, not by choice."

"What do you like to watch?"

"Documentaries. True crime. Sometimes, the um ... how do you say ..."

"You can say it in Spanish," I murmur. I feel her eyes on me then. Glancing back at her, I give an apologetic smile. "I speak Spanish."

"Campy movies." She says finally, not bothering to argue with me. She rubs her foot. "How about you? Are you just interested in rom coms?"

"Honestly, I like movies that make me feel something. It sounds like a low bar, but that's what I go for."

She nods, not commenting. This isn't easy for her, I can tell. I've been there. I remember what it was like the first time I realized that situations could really be life or death when I learned how much every decision mattered. No matter how small, no matter how insignificant. If I hadn't been in combat, it would have taken weeks to process. For Sofia, I don't know how long it will be.

"Pizza?"

"Yeah."

I order, promising to pay in cash, then sit with Sofia. She's still in a daze, her fingers running through her hair. "I should have known my dad would have gotten to this point."

"What do you mean?" I hesitate again, not sure how to comfort her. I should wrap an arm around her or something, right? I should hug her or tell her she's safe.

She dabs at her eyes. "The people he's gotten off. The things they've done ... been accused of doing. Whatever. I mean, I questioned his morals plenty, but in the last few years, it seems he's gone from bad to worse. First, he got hired by people who claimed they were innocent, but as the years went by, his clientele was nothing but obvious criminals, even guys who were in the FBI's most wanted list."

Standing, Sofia chuckles, then circles the room. "I knew he had crossed over to the dark side, but I wanted to believe some of my dad was still in there. But now, there's a hit placed on him because he didn't get someone off, and they're where they belong. It proves he's as bad as I didn't want to believe."

"No one is all bad, Sofia. Even when it's easier to think that," I say, moving up to her.

She sniffs and faces me, shaking her head. "A lot of *bad* people got away and got to hurt more people because of my dad."

I pull her close to me, palming her hips. "What's a good memory you have of him?"

Sofia exhales slowly. "Those memories don't matter. Him, doing this kind of work, that's why we're here, stuck."

Of course, she doesn't want to share. We're hitting personal spots, and if I know anything about Sofia, it's that she's not the type who likes personal, vulnerable conversations. Not that I can blame her.

"Let's lay down." I pat the bed.

She looks at it, at me, then sighs and climbs on the bed, pulling a pillow under her even though she's on her belly. I lay on my side next to her. Sofia sucks her bottom lip and rolls her eyes.

"I'm sorry," she whispers.

"For?"

"Being a mess. You're used to this kind of hard stuff, so I'm sure it's annoying if your client just ... loses it."

"You're entitled to losing it," I assure her. After a slow breath, I rub my face. "My dad is a bastard too. I have a good frame of reference."

"Yeah?" She says, turning on her side to face me.

"He's a stubborn son of a bitch who wants things done his way, the military way, and no other way." I nod. "Makes yours look like a walk in the park."

She rolls her eyes. "I doubt that very much. Was he ever good?"

"With my sister, yeah. He could be gentle with her, but my brother and me ... it was military discipline all day, every day. The only time I got a pat on the back was when I took out my brother's bully, and then I was grounded for getting in trouble at school."

"Damn." She moves an inch closer to me.

"He was always nice on Christmas, though. Made an effort, probably because our aunt and her family would come over. Aunt Val is my mom's sister. She'd bring presents for all of us, she'd make cookies and let us drink chocolate milk until we were sick of it."

Sofia wiggles a little closer. After a long moment, she lifts her head. "My dad took my brother and me to see Spiderman when it came out in theaters. He acted like we were going to school, but we took the whole day off. We saw the movie, hung out at the mall, and when my brother tried to say I'd never be a hero because I was a girl ... my dad said anyone could be as long as they always looked out for people."

I smile and brush her hair from her face. "So, all this time, you just wanted to be Spiderman?"

"Don't tease."

"No, I see it now." I lean towards her. "In this light, absolutely. Friendly neighborhood hero protecting and caring for people when others don't."

She leans into my hand, closing her eyes as I brush my thumb over her cheek. She exhales slowly. "You can be charming when you want to be."

"You don't sound half as surprised as I expected."

"Two truths and a lie?" She offers.

I nod.

"I think you're likeable without the lies. Alcohol would help right now. I left my phone at work." She lists.

"Hmm. Normally, I'd say the first one." But she blushes slightly, and I know it's true. "No way you left your phone."

She laughs softly and nods. "Yeah, it's in my purse. Your turn."

"I'm excited for pizza." I stroke her hair again. "You have very soft hair. I think we should put on ESPN."

Sofia shakes her head at me. "ESPN."

"Your turn."

She licks across her bottom lip. "How about a confession instead?"

I lean closer. "What do you mean?"

"I know about your leg." When I start to pull away, she follows. "Why didn't you tell me, Jasper? Daisy thought I already knew, but you could have said something."

"Why? So you could give me shit about being able to protect you? So you could call me broken or-"

"I wouldn't have."

"Come on, Sofia -"

"Just listen for a second." She catches my hand, then adjusts so she's on her knees. "The way you've been protecting me since we met, there's no way I could doubt how capable you are. Besides, you know what I do for a living, you know the people I work with. Have you ever seen me look down on them?"

"No."

"I won't ask how it happened." She says it with the seal of a promise. "It's not my business. But you don't have to hide it from me. Okay? That's all."

I watch as she sits back on her heels. Groaning, I sit up. "Damaged it in combat. Worthy of discharge. That's all."

"That's all," she repeats, then bites her lip.

"One, I had no idea about your leg until Daisy told me. Two, it doesn't change how I see you or my trust in you. Three, I know you said we need to keep low, but I can't survive being locked in a motel while sober. We need alcohol."

"Sofia—"

"Pretty please..."

Sighing, I shake my head at her. I'm either already whipped after our first kiss or my common sense has fled out the door. "Can I trust you to stay here while I run to the liquor store?"

"Can't you take me with you?" she asks.

I shake my head. "It's easier if I go alone. Faster."

"You don't have to go, then," she replies. "Pizza is good enough-"

"You'll want something to drink anyway. Plus, it's the perfect time to grab a few items of clothing. We won't get by with just the clothes on our backs."

"Fine. I'll stay. But hurry back, or I'll kick your butt," she says, giving me a look that tells me she's trying to sound braver than she feels. I force myself out of the motel. If I stayed a second longer, I would give in to my stupid impulse and take her with me. No way would it rest well on my conscience if something were to happen to her. For now, she's safer inside.

Thankfully, there's a strip mall across the road, so I don't need to go very far. Pulling the cap low on my head, I jog the short distance, then head to the closest clothing store. I grab a few pieces of clothing for her and me, soap, a twelve-pack of beer, and a few other things we might need. By the time I get back, the pizza man has arrived. I pay him with cash, then knock on the door three times. She knocks twice back, and I knock once.

She's wearing a relieved expression when she unlocks the door, and I slide in, holding up the bags. She goes right for the beer, turns, then returns to hug me, her body clinging to mine. Closing my eyes, I savor how she feels against me. Real, warm, sweet.

"You're okay," I assure.

She nods and lets me go. "I'm ... I'll shower."

Ten minutes later, she walks out in a thigh-length t-shirt, her hair still damp hair from the shower. She sits on the couch cross-legged, giving me a peek of her upper thighs. I avert my eyes and join her, placing the pizza box on the center table. We eat in silence while watching a rom com on TV.

Sofia leans back, and her hand brushes mine. I glance over at her, expecting her to pull away, but she smiles and pats her stomach with her other hand. "I'm so full."

"Feeling comfy?" I ask.

She nods and rubs her fingers over mine. I toss the empty box to the floor, watch her glance at it, then steal her attention before she can go after it. Leaning towards her with our bodies brushing, I smile.

"Jasper." She points at me. "What's that look?"

"I want to talk about that kiss earlier."

"What about it?"

"You kissed me back."

"And?"

I sigh, realizing I may have to pry the truth from her mouth. "Be honest with me. Why did you kiss me back?"

Exhaling slowly, she meets my gaze. "Because I wanted to. It felt good." Her expression brightens with mischief. "But who knows? It probably was a fluke."

I chuckle and nod. "Want me to prove it wasn't?"

"Okay, enough teasing," she says, blushing.

"I've never teased you, kitten," I whisper. "I've been nothing but true to you."

She straightens on the couch, narrowing her eyes at me. "Be honest. What do you think of me?"

"You're fierce, smart, determined, and a little bit crazy."

"I am not -"

"And it's damn attractive," I finish. "And I'd be an idiot not to respect the hell out of you."

She looks me over and shakes her head. "I can't figure you out, Jasper."

"Keep trying. I'm sure you'll get somewhere."

"Not without your help." She curls up against my chest, pulling my arm around her. "Tell me something else that's true."

"You'll be back to your normal life soon." I kiss the top of her head.

She sighs softly, but I hate the countdown. As stupid as it is, I can't imagine going a day without her. I can't imagine her being cuddled up with anyone else. I clear my throat and rub down her back.

"Are you comfortable?" she asks, her voice drowsy.

"For now. Go to sleep," I murmur. "I'll take the first watch."

I kiss the top of her head again and feel her hand clutch the shirt at my side.

"I trust you, Jasper," she whispers before drifting off to sleep.

Chapter 17

Sofia

Waking up in the morning feels normal until I realize I'm snuggled against Jasper. His gentle snores bathe my ear, his face pressed against the back of my head. I shift my body a bit, only to feel something hard against my back.

He groans softly and pulls me tighter against him, and I surrender to his arms around me. Memories of yesterday start coming back, and I push the horror aside and focus on the pleasant parts, like the kiss that sizzled my whole body and last night when we just talked. There's no denying how real it was, more real than anything I've experienced in a long time with any other man. But I don't know what to do about it.

Jasper's heavy sigh makes me open my eyes once more. "Good morning."

"Buenas Dias."

"You feel good," he greets in a low, husky voice as he rubs his nose over my neck.

A shiver teases my spine, and I rub his hip slowly. "Teasing again?"

"Never." He hums. "One second."

He rolls over for a beat; then he waves a breath strip in front of me. Scoffing, I roll over to face him as he pops one in his mouth. I follow suit as he presses his forehead to mine, making my chest squeeze. I run my fingers along his jaw.

As soon as this job is over, he's going to leave me. I'm not silly enough to think he will stick around just for my shitty personality. He'll take the money and run away to his happily ever after with someone else, but I can't pretend I don't want him. Not when we're this close when he's watching me like I'm the only reason he bothered to wake up today.

But I don't have any clue what to do with him. Do I forget my reservations and kiss him? Because once I make a move, there's no going back.

Jasper tucks my hair behind my ear and brushes his thumb over my cheek. "How do you feel?"

"I'm okay."

His thumb traces just under my bottom lip, sending a buzzing through my skin that makes me ache for more than his touch. I suck my lip, and Jasper takes a harsh breath. His forehead brushes mine, and I feel that tension in his body again, spring-loaded, ready to attack.

"What do you want to do with your first day off?"

How is he having a normal conversation with me when I'm fighting my arousal for him? It would be so easy to wrap my leg around him, pull him close, kiss him and spend the morning like any other sane woman, considering this sexy man in my bed.

And I'm so damn tempted to do just that. He's right here, touching me, holding me ... but what if all his teasing really has just been teasing? "It's not a real day off."

"No. I guess not." His hand strokes along my neck, then he follows my spine. "Is this okay?"

I nod.

"You can tell me to stop. I know you know that; I just ... want to put that out there," he whispers.

"I'm good at saying 'no.'"

"Yeah." He nods, his lips so close I swear I can taste him already. "It's your favorite word."

"What would you do if I told you yes instead?" I meet his eyes.

His hand tightens in my shirt, and a shaky breath fans over my face. "That's dangerous."

"So is your job."

"And this position."

"What position?" I slide my leg over his hip. "This one?"

"Sofia." He closes his eyes a moment, and dread fills my stomach.

"I ... I'm sorry, I read it wrong. I thought-" I start to untangle myself.

"No, you're right." His hand clings to my thigh, holding it in place. "I just don't want to push you too far or-"

Kissing him seems to be the right response. If we keep talking, we won't make progress. I kiss him again as he holds still, like he's debating whether to kiss me back. I suck his bottom lip and draw back to kiss him one more time.

Huffing, I shake my head. "Look, if you don't kiss me back, this is going to get really awkward."

"Sorry. Shock's worn off. I'm good."

To prove it, he kisses me, licking into my mouth and greedily pulling me close. I cup the back of his head. I want to feel every bit of him under my hands, to memorize him.

Jasper groans and rolls on top of me, holding himself above me as he devours my mouth. His tongue pushes between my lips again, and I suck it while dragging my nails down his back. We can't seem to talk about this shit, but we're plenty good at doing this.

I gasp as his hard on presses between my thighs, right where I need him. The lust makes me dizzy and stupid because I've never been this kind of girl. I don't go from making out to sex in the same day. I don't put out without a few dates in the bank, but here I am, tugging Jasper's shirt off his body, wanting to claim him as mine, even if it's just right now.

"No rush." Jasper pants even as he tosses his shirt to the side. "No pressure."

I hear him, but I'm too busy taking in his chest, finally touching the hard planes of muscle and tracing the tattoos that litter his skin. I sit up to kiss a jagged mark just under his right pec, then grab his ass.

He chuckles and cups my face between his hands. "Someone's getting handsy."

"Leading by example," I pant before squeezing his ass again.

Jasper shakes his head and kisses me, feasting on my mouth like he needs me to live. And I believe it. I feel it. I don't need oxygen. I don't need food. I don't need anything but his mouth on mine. But every brush of his lips makes me hungrier for more of him.

He strokes up my thigh, fingers brushing the underwear he bought me. When he finally grabs my ass, we both moan. I tighten my arms around his neck, and Jasper jerks me against his hips.

Oh, I definitely needed that. I definitely need his cock, need him filling me and fucking me. Jasper kisses down my neck, then back up, nibbling on my ear until my body rolls against his. The foreplay alone is going to kill me if it's as hot as this.

"Touch me," I pant. "Please, Jasper."

He slowly pulls the large shirt over my hips, his fingers teasing my skin and triggering dizzying little sparks from each touch. I moan softly as I lift my arms, so he can pull my shirt over my head.

Jasper looks me over, his eyes filled with lust. He strokes over my breast, cupping one and licking over my nipple. He groans and takes it between his lips, making my toes curl as he sucks and flicks his tongue across the sensitive peak.

"You're beautiful, Sofia," he groans before switching to the other breast.

Panting, I hold still for as long as I can, letting him explore with his hands and mouth until I can't stand it. I'm so wet I'm uncomfortable, and I need more than this slow, soft moment. I roll on top of Jasper and pull his mouth back to mine.

I rub myself on his hardness and swallow his moan as his hands tighten on my ass. I lick into his mouth and tug on his button and zipper. Jasper catches my wrists. "Are you sure?"

"I think I'm pretty clear." I pant. "I want you."

He lifts his hips, so I can jerk his pants down, then he tugs on my underwear. I get them off clumsily, nearly falling over as the panties catch on one ankle. Jasper chuckles and catches me. I blush but laugh once before kissing him again.

"So eager."

"I blame you."

"I happily accept the blame." His hands stroke down my back, and he kisses along my throat and the inside of my shoulder. "Condoms in the bag."

I pause and arch an eyebrow. "You planned this?"

"I'm a boy scout. Always prepared."

I roll my eyes, but something squeezes my stomach. I lay next to Jasper, kissing his chest but also catching my breath. What am I doing? Jasper rolls onto his side, then hovers over me, stealing my mouth until I forget everything but his name.

He strokes down my belly and pushes my thighs apart. "Yes?"

Nodding, I lick my bottom lip. "Yes."

He strokes over my clit, and my back arches. I gasp and dig my nails into his shoulder. Jasper kisses me softly and presses his forehead to mine. "Tell me how to please you."

Fuck, that may be the sexiest thing I've ever heard. I guide his fingers right where I need them and nod. He circles my clit, then rubs his fingers up and down. My hips roll against his hand, and I gasp, my head falling back.

"Just like that."

"Yeah?"

"Yes! Yes!"

He groans and kisses down my throat, gently nibbling the skin above my cleavage before picking up the speed. I squirm as my body rolls into his hand, grinding down on his fingers until I feel the familiar build up in my belly, threatening to explode.

Fuck, he's good.

"Faster. Harder," I pant.

He groans, and I feel his cock brush my hip as he moves to do exactly as I ask. His muscular arm flexes with each brush of his fingers across my clit, and when his fierce blue eyes turn on me, all I can do is kiss him.

Jasper groans and pushes two fingers inside me. A moan tears me away from him, and I lose myself in the climax as he hits the perfect spot deep inside me. My legs shake, my body tightens, and I grab his wrist, not sure if I want to stop him or hold him right there where I need his fingers.

My body rolls against him again before I go limp. He kisses me hungrily. "Again."

"Again?"

"I'm happy to make you come all morning." He purrs in my ear. "Again."

His fingers move with slow, steady thrusts, then he tries a few different techniques, quickening the pace, curling them deep inside me until I come again.

"Fuck!" I bite his shoulder, my body quivering from the onslaught of pleasure filling every crevice of my being, leaving me undoubtedly addicted to this man.

Jasper removes his fingers and reaches for the box with condoms, opens it, then tears the condom wrapper open with his teeth. There's something so primal and hot about it, just like watching him roll the condom over every impressive inch of his thick cock.

I lick my lips, promising myself that I'm going to blow him before we part ways. Jasper moans and tightens his hold on his cock for a moment before his searing eyes flick back to mine. "Still yes?"

"Hell, yes."

I climb on top of him and slowly slide down his cock. His lips part, and his eyes close as a low moan bubbles up from his chest. I brace myself on his abdomen, and I take every inch of him deep in my pussy.

"Fuck." I pant. "You feel good."

"Jesus Christ, Sofia." He groans, his hands on my hips. "Fuck, you're tight."

I roll my body as a test, and his hips flex, thrusting into me. Fire dances on my nerves, and I roll my hips again, taking him deep once more. Jasper fills me perfectly, stretching my pussy around his cock like I belong to him alone. Pleasure spreads through my body, making my head hazy.

He kisses across my breasts, thrusting up every time I come down on him as the bed shakes and thuds against the wall. Sweat beads on his forehead as I ride him hard and fast, no control or restraint possible when he's buried inside me, touching me, kissing me.

It's too much. It's nearly impossible to keep from coming again. Jasper gasps. "Fuck, I'm already close."

"Yes." I nod. "Yes!"

Jasper groans and rolls on top of me, holding the back of my head in one hand as he fucks me hard and deep. His body moves so beautifully on mine, even as his arms shake. I wrap my legs around him and drag my nails down his back as I get closer and closer to release.

"Fuck! Fuck!" I whimper, biting his neck hard.

"Sofia! I'm going to come."

"Come with me," I beg.

And he does. We find release together as the orgasm rips through me, blackening my vision and filling me with ecstasy until I feel like I'm flying. All that exists is Jasper and me. And fuck, I don't want to drift back to reality.

Chapter 18

Jasper

Sofia's heart thuds under my ear as I lay against her chest. I should feel better, finally getting all this horniness out of my system, but instead, I feel like my brain is setting itself on fire. Something about Sofia, about what we just did has etched itself on my soul. I rub her sides and kiss her chest as she plays with my hair.

"That was ... fun," she murmurs.

So we're going for understatement? I swallow. "Yeah. Fun."

She keeps petting me as I stroke her soft skin. I'd love to stay like this all day. But how am I supposed to categorize this? It feels like a huge thing, completely changing our relationship, altering everything about us, but Sofia being quiet and reducing it to 'fun' is throwing me for a loop.

Is it really just sex for her? Just a way to get off? To kill time?

An experiment based on the obvious chemistry we had last night?

I clear my throat and lift my head to look at Sofia. She smiles slightly, but it doesn't reach her eyes. I kiss her softly before pulling to a sitting position. "Want to join me for a shower?"

"I ... I should actually reach out to my dad." She pushes her hair back. "Let him know we're safe, and we survived and—"

"I already spoke to the guys from my team. Your father knows we're safe."

"Still, I'd like to talk to him myself," she replies, stretching her palm to me. "May I borrow your phone?"

"Sure." I nod.

The second I'm not touching her, I feel her walls come back up. So I give her the distance she needs. Once in the bathroom, I rest my back against the door and shake my head. "That was fucking stupid."

I'm stupid for assuming sex would evoke emotions in Sofia when she has been so aloof since we first met. The shower helps wash away those fucking expectations and leaves me with a world of questions. How should I handle being around her from here on out?

Sofia looks me over when I come out in just a towel, and I see that flair of lust in her eyes. She licks across her bottom lip and then looks away, holding the sheet over her breasts. "I spoke to Dad. He seems okay, him and Scarlett."

"Your stepmom, right?"

"Yeah." She nods. "I'll get a shower and be right out."

I pull out some animal crackers I got from the store and leave the Danish for Sofia. She's all the way in the bathroom, but I can still feel the awkward tension between us. Damn it, we shouldn't have fucked. I don't know what to think or do right now, and I definitely don't know what's going on in her head.

She soon emerges, wearing a long-sleeved shirt cinched at the waist with a broad belt. I sit on the couch as she comes towards me. "Food's on the table," I say.

"Okay."

Her tone is dry as chips, frustrating me. I feel like a fucking chick, and she's the guy trying to shut me out after a one-night stand.

"Are we?" I ask. "Tell me, babe, because I'm confused as fuck. You've been so closed off since we—"

"We're fine, Jasper. This has nothing to do with you or what we just did. I wanted to make love to you. And in case my multiple orgasms weren't enough to convince you, it was really fucking good."

"Good." I've never been in need of an ego booster, but her words are doing just that. Still, it changes nothing between us. We had sex because we were caught in a forced proximity situation. As soon as this is over, so will whatever that's going on between us. I need to remember that before I get attached.

Sofia turns on the TV and starts watching a crime series while I idly work out until I flop back out of a crunch and groan. Sofia jumps up, rushing to me and checking my side. "Are you okay?"

"Your concern is making me feel awkward as hell," I huff.

She eases back. "It was a lot easier giving you hell."

"I miss it. Where's your sass and cutthroat attitude? You haven't complained about not being at work or not being allowed to leave or anything like that." I sit up and rub her shoulder. "Tell me honestly ... did those orgasms finally break you?"

She shoves me. "Smart-ass."

"It's a fair question. You told me it had been a while."

"That doesn't mean it broke me!" She shoves me down. "As if your dick would have any effect on-"

In one move, I wrap my hand around the back of her neck and kiss her. Her lips soften, and then she melts against me, her tongue curling with mine until she gently pushes against my chest. "We shouldn't do this."

"Why?"

"Choose your reason. There are plenty." Her eyes search mine, dark, nervous. "We can say it was a mistake."

My stomach dips. "I can't say that."

"Come on," she huffs.

"I don't normally want to repeat mistakes." I keep her eyes with mine. "And I won't lie to you even if it makes things easier."

She swallows and nods. "I get that."

"Good." I rub the back of her neck. "What's going on in that stuffing-free head of yours?"

She laughs softly and shakes her head before biting her lip. "About a million different things."

"Sharing is caring." I shrug.

"Who says any of it is related to you?"

"Hence the question."

She picks at the carpet before her lips turn up, and she wipes her hand on my shorts. "Just figuring things out. You are a lot to take in."

"Is now the time for a dick joke or..."

"Jasper, be serious for five seconds."

I sigh and adjust, so I can press my forehead to hers. "It's not ideal. I could lose my job over what we just did. Being emotionally involved in any way is grounds for removal. If you wanted someone else to take over, you could request it."

"I don't want to screw you over."

"I know." I nod. "We can pretend like it didn't happen."

"I don't think that will work either." She bites her lip and looks away while blushing. "But we could do something else to keep busy."

"I didn't bring Scrabble, darling. Did you pack something in your purse for us to play?"

"You could teach me some self-defense since I'm so terrible at it. Hand-to-hand stuff since we're stuck in a room." She shrugs. "That would kill some time."

"True." I nod. "Keep us busy in a good, positive way."

"And you're all about positive."

"You know me." I flash her a smile. "Always trying to find the sunshine on a rainy day."

I get her in a good stance, promise not to hurt her, then teach her basic self-defense. She can't flip me or anything, but after the third hesitation to hurt me and how light she's going, I pick her up and pin her on the floor. She squirms and actually fights against me.

"Jasper! Let me up!"

"When we're doing this, I'm not Jasper. I'm someone who's trying to hurt you. Are you going to lightly tap their instep? Are you going to hold back when you elbow? You know I can take a shot and keep going. Don't. Hold. Back." I growl.

I let her up, and she glares at me before throwing her hair in a bun. "I was trying to be nice."

"I like you mean and determined," I remind.

She shakes her head. "If I hurt you, and you can't do your job ..."

"Then I must be shit at my job, to begin with. No holding back."

"You're going to be on your ass."

I grin. When I grab her from behind, she jabs her elbow into my side but then switches it up, kicking my inner leg. Unfortunately for her, she chose the wrong leg to do that with. I end up falling forward and taking her with me.

She groans, then laughs. "Well, that wasn't your ass."

I roll her over and pin her arms above her head. "Now what, hellcat?"

She kicks at me but can't get anywhere. I straddle her, which pisses her off even more. "Where's all that bite?"

"Come closer, and I'll show you," she threatens.

I chuckle, and we keep going until we're panting, sweating, and I have at least six bruises from her. She manages to get away the last time, turns like she's still expecting me to come at her, then she laughs.

"I did it."

"Mmhmm." I rub my shin. "You did."

Sofia does a little happy dance that's so fucking cute and terrible I can't help but smile. She sticks her tongue out at me, then tries to tackle me. I catch her and pin her to the floor. She groans as her body relaxes in surrender.

"No points for being cocky."

"Well, obviously, if it were a real situation, I would have kicked him while he was down and run away."

"Don't go in for the kick," I murmur, hovering above her. "Anyone conscious is going to grab your leg and pull you down. Take the extra seconds to run and get a weapon."

"What weapons are in this room?" She looks around as if it's obvious.

"Besides the ones I brought? Two lamps with cords that can be used to strangle. The chair. The very heavy TV. A pillow over their face. You can wrap a towel and use it to choke someone. The vase, one of the paintings."

She blinks at me a few times. "Seriously?"

"Everything is a weapon if you know how to use it. And you can throw plenty, even as a distraction." I brush my fingers across her cheek. "Use *everything* to keep yourself safe."

"Okay."

"I like you in one piece, and if you have to defend yourself, the goal is to stay alive. No matter the cost to the other person."

"Until you can save me?"

"No matter what," I say seriously. "Fight until you can't ... or until they're dead."

She swallows hard and vigorously nods. "I can do that."

"Promise?" I let her up, but Sofia moves onto my lap and hugs me. My arms tighten around her. "Promise me."

"I'll keep myself alive, Jasper."

When she draws back, my mouth molds to hers. I don't even think about it, it just feels right. I suck her bottom lip, then lick deeper into her mouth. Our lives can change at a moment's notice. I know that better than most. And I know I'm going to take advantage of every moment I have her.

Sofia's arm tightens around my neck, and a soft whimper slips from her mouth. I hold her tighter against me as electricity buzzes through me. I can't get enough of her. Of her determination to do what's right, her stories, her playfulness, or her mouth hungrily clinging to mine like it's the first and last time we'll be able to do this.

My fingers knot in her shirt, and I pull up until I can stroke the soft skin of her lower back. She shivers but pushes into my touch while renewing the kiss. Groaning, I let my hands wander, memorizing every line of her body.

"Again?" she asks against my mouth.

I chuckle and shrug. I'm already hard for her, dying to have her under me, on top of me, wherever she wants to be, but I'd be happy to just keep kissing her. To feel that addictive heat spreading from my chest, the sparks threatening to burn through me until there's nothing left.

Sofia tugs at my shirt, her fingers spreading across my abdomen. "Again."

Groaning, I pull my shirt off for her. I'd have to be a fucking idiot to say no to her. "I still have a to-do list with you."

"Yeah?" She asks as she kisses across my chest. "Me too."

Groaning, I pull her face back to mine so I can kiss her. "This is the best game."

Chapter 19

Sofia

I bite Jasper's bottom lip and roll my hips on his lap. He steadies me and presses his forehead to mine. "No more of that in public. I'm still recovering from that lap dance at Daisy's."

"Maybe. I won't make any promises," I reply, grinding down on him, satisfied when he releases a moan. "Depends on if I need you to shut up."

He grins and kisses down my neck softly, too softly. Shivers spread through me, and I don't know if it tickles or feels good, if I want him to stop or continue. It's torture. I moan and clutch at his shoulders. "Jasper."

"Two can tease. Remember that later," he breathes in my ear before biting my bottom lip.

Before I can give him a smart-ass reply, he jerks off the belt, then my shirt and licks across my collarbone. I bite my lip and nip his neck. Jasper pushes to his feet, bringing me with him.

"Jasper!"

"Not the first time I've carried you." he reminds me. "It won't be the last."

I wrap my legs around him and cling to him like I'm going to fall anyway, which apparently leaves his hands free to tug on my panties. He drops me on the bed and looks me over after freeing me of the silky underwear.

His eyes make me sizzle, and I squirm under his sharp gaze, especially as his jaw tightens. I slowly stroke between my breasts and circle my belly button, enjoying the way his gaze follows my touch.

"Are you just going to watch?"

"Depends on what you plan on doing, gorgeous." He licks across his bottom lip. "Or what you want me to do."

I spread my legs and see his throat bob as my fingers slip between my thighs to stroke my clit. I shiver and do it again, letting a soft moan escape as I tease him. His hands curl into fists, the hunger clear in his eyes as he watches me finger my pussy.

"I think you feel better than my fingers," I pant.

Jasper licks his lips. "Yeah?"

I nod quickly while trying to bite back another moan as I rub my clit in slow circles. "And you have a to-do list."

"I do."

"You should get started on it ..." I gasp as I push one finger into my wet pussy. "Before I finish."

A feral groan leaves his throat, and then he's on the bed between my legs. His calloused hands stroke up my calves, my outer thighs, then his arms press against my thighs and pry them apart.

"Fucking hell, Sofia," he breathes, his eyes locked down there. I shiver and pull my hand back, tasting myself on my finger. He groans and kisses my hip. "You drive me insane."

Jasper lets out another ragged breath, then licks over my slit. My lips part with a moan, and I push up on my elbows to watch him as he licks again, brushing my clit with his wicked tongue. He jerks me tighter against his mouth as his eyes meet mine.

I pinch my nipple, rolling it between my fingers. Jasper laps at my clit, using his tongue in ways I've never experienced before. He freezes, looks up at me again, and I swear I see a victorious smile in his eyes.

Like he just figured out exactly how to make me crazy.

And when he flicks his tongue over my clit again and again, I know he has. I writhe against his mouth, gripping his head in one hand while trying to watch him and make the most of the pleasure at the same time.

My head falls back as my legs twitch and try to close around his head. Oh fuck, he's so good. He sucks my clit hard and teases me with his tongue until I can't tell where one moan ends and the next begins.

I fist the sheets on the bed and roll my hips against his mouth until the floodgates open, and I'm drowning in pleasure. I nearly scream into the pillow as I come, white spots flitting over my closed eyes.

But Jasper doesn't stop. He ups the game, pushing two fingers inside me as he devours me. I can hear how wet I am, hear his panting breaths, and then I'm moaning and cursing again, so overwhelmed by Jasper and his sinful mouth that nothing else matters.

After my second orgasm, he goes faster, fucking me hard with his fingers until sanity is a word and nothing else. I'd do anything to keep him right where he is, tongue flicking back and forth like he'll never get tired, fingers pumping into me and hitting that perfect spot over and over.

I come a third time with a loud, relieved groan, trying to escape the little licks he's still giving me. I'm too sensitive, too overwhelmed.

"Ah!" I gasp as he flattens his tongue and licks from my entrance to my clit and back slowly. "Jas ..."

"There's one thing off my list." He kisses up my belly, licks over my nipple before sucking it hard and gently biting, then he feasts on my mouth. He tastes like me, and the way he kisses should be fucking illegal.

When he draws back, he smirks. "Ready for the second thing?"

"Fuck, yes," I nod, my whole body humming with pleasure. "You're too good at that."

"Then I'll have to do it more often," he growls against my ear. "You choose. On your knees or on top?"

I lick my bottom lip, then roll over onto my hands and knees. Glancing over my shoulder, I see Jasper get up, shuck his pants, revealing his damaged leg and every other amazing inch of him.

He glances up at me, and a flash of vulnerability crosses his face. "What?"

"You're so fucking sexy," I pant.

Jasper grins, his expression lighting up. "You don't know what that means to me."

"To me, it means you need to get your fine ass over here before I jump you," I reply.

He kisses me again, then reaches for a condom. I groan as he rips it with his teeth, eyes on me the whole time. Fuck, this is definitely a better way to be locked up. He gets on the bed behind me and guides my hips where he wants them before slowly sliding into me.

"Fuck, you're so wet." He groans.

"Your fault."

"Absolutely." His chest presses to my back, and his hands rest over mine as he kisses my neck. "I don't regret a damn thing."

When he thrusts into me, I groan and rub myself back against him. He's everywhere. Panting in my ear, kissing my neck, his fingers lacing through mine. He thrusts again and again, filling me over and over with his cock just like I need.

"You feel perfect, Sofia." He groans. "So warm and tight."

I whimper and cling to his fingers. "Fuck, don't stop."

"Not until you come," he promises, slamming into me harder.

Jasper growls as I fuck him back, meeting every thrust as I pant. He lifts one hand to cup my breast as he drives into me harder and harder. I'm going to overheat from his body wrapped around me, but it feels so good. He's too good.

Feral but not painful. Passionate without being ridiculously romantic. He's the fucking perfect balance of everything I need.

Jasper grunts with each thrust and nibbles the back of my neck as we fuck.

With a whimper, I guide his hand to my throat. "Choke me."

"Yeah?"

I curl his fingers around my neck. "Yes!"

He does as I ask, holding my throat in his thick hand until all that exists, him and the pleasure that's weighing my body down, making it impossible to move, impossible to do anything but take what he gives.

A shiver tears down my spine, then I fall over the edge. I nearly scream his name as I collapse into the pillow, clinging to his hands tightly. Jasper groans and sits up, stroking down my back while fucking me even harder, faster, so deep.

My eyes roll back, and one orgasm rolls into another as I moan and beg him to keep going. He loses his pace, then groans loudly, slamming into me twice before gripping my hips and panting.

"Jesus Christ, Sofia." He pulls me with him as he lays on his side.

My legs tremble, and my body rocks against him, even as he plants teasing kisses on my shoulder. I roll, feeling him slip out of me. He cuddles me against his chest and strokes my hair.

"That's not everything on my list, but it's progress," he murmurs.

I turn to him, running my fingers over his abs. "And I haven't even scratched the surface of mine."

His brows shoot up, and a wicked gleam fills his eyes. "Sounds dirty. Care to share?"

"Well... I've been fantasizing about sucking your cock, for starters," I admit.

Jasper swears, throwing his head back. "Give me ten minutes to recuperate. That's all I need."

I kiss his chest softly and listen to his breathing slowing down as we relax. My mind travels back to work, and I wonder how everyone's doing. I hope to God they are physically okay, at least.

There's no doubt they are all traumatized after what happened. Hopefully, they don't hold the attack against me.

I think of Carissa, and the guilt hits again. I chew my bottom lip and close my eyes. Yeah, they only had one date, but I can't forget that hurt in her eyes when I came out of the supply closet. She likes him, and here I am, sleeping with him.

And I can't even blame him. He didn't start this. I did. I swallow and press my forehead against his chest. How the hell did this happen? Sure, I stopped disliking him a while ago, and I enjoyed being around him. I liked how we could talk in circles, give each other hell, and still be fine, but should I have crossed the line?

I clear my throat, easing up from him. "I'm going to clean up."

"Okay." He pulls my chin up and kisses me again. "Everything good in here?"

"Yeah." I manage a smile.

Yeah, I feel like a shitty friend, but at the same time, I can't deny how right this feels with Jasper. Being with him. Making love to him. It feels right. Nothing has ever felt *right* with a man before. It had always been an uphill battle with my exes, but with Jasper ... with Jasper, it's shockingly, suspiciously simple.

The shower washes the sweat and sex off me, but it doesn't change how much I want to be curled up with Jasper, feeling his fingers stroking my back as he makes bad puns and makes sure I'm okay.

I sit on the shower floor and try to focus. Because Jasper's going to leave, isn't he? There will be no reason for him to stay once this is over, and I need to remember that. For now, I'm going to focus on staying alive and leave the rest to destiny. Whatever should be, will be.

When I get out of the shower, I see Jasper on the phone. I hesitate, clutching the towel tighter against me, but he smiles. "Yes.

The sushi platter, please." He hangs up and smiles at my questioning stare. "I think we need more than a snack."

"Good idea."

He grabs his towel, kisses me softly and winks. "Maybe one day, you'll be comfortable showering with me."

"Maybe."

"Let's eat and talk about our next step," he says, kissing my temple. "All the ways we're going to keep you alive."

"I sense an ulterior motive now."

"Yeah." He pinches my ass. "More of you."

He leaves the door open when he goes into the shower, and I drop on the bed with a sigh. Why do I feel like this will all change the second we leave the motel room? I shake my head. No. I can't think like that. We'll survive this terrible situation, overcome whoever is trying to hurt me and my dad, then we'll see where our relationship goes afterwards.

Glancing at the bathroom where Jasper's singing off key, I can't help longing for more, much more of this.

Chapter 20

Jasper

I spend the rest of the day teaching Sofia how to use a knife. She slashes at the air uselessly at first, but slowly she gets better. I still manage to disarm her and tug her against me. She shoves at my chest with an impatient sound.

"You're not Jasper right now."

"No, I'm not." I grin, giving her a hefty shove. "And what happens if someone other than Jasper touches you?"

She scratches me, kicks my shin, and gets away with the knife firmly in her grasp. With her hair in her face, her panting breaths, the way she watches me with murder in her eyes... fuck, it's sexy. I come at her a few more times, and she actually cuts me.

She drops the knife, covers her face, then immediately puts her hands over the cut. "I'm so sorry, Jasper."

"Good job." I praise.

"I hurt you, pendejo! That's not worthy of praise!" She holds my arm tightly and guides me to the uncomfortable little sofa. She looks at the slight wound and bites her lip, shaking her head. "I meant to come at you, but I thought you'd move and—"

I cup her face between my hands and press my forehead to hers. "You did everything right. I just wasn't fast enough."

"Shut up," she grumbles.

"So you get to choose what we have for dinner." I rub her cheek.

She pushes my hands away and walks to the bed. There's the wall again. Sighing, I twist on the couch to look at her. "My hand is fine, Sofia. It's barely a cut. Give it a day, and it will start healing again."

"I know," she replies, pulling back the covers, her voice sounding as glum as her expression.

"Okay, so, why that look on your face?"

"What look?"

"I don't know... like someone just stole your fundraising idea or something."

She shrugs. "I don't know what you're talking about."

"Truth or dare?" I ask.

"What?"

"Me oiste."

She sighs. "I keep forgetting you speak Spanish. Truth."

"Why do you keep pulling away from me like that?"

"I'm not."

"Sofia."

She releases another deep exhale. "I don't realize I am. Not really."

"Then you should come back over here, where I can touch you."

"You don't like touch."

"You do," I whisper.

"What was that?"

"You like being touched. You don't like questions or deep conversation. But you like being touched."

Sophia stares at me for a beat, then smooths over the pillow and comes to stand in front of me. "How did you know?"

"You don't pull away when I touch you. But you don't like when I ask questions about you. Your tells are pretty obvious, dumpling."

Sofia smiles slightly. "Truth or dare?"

"Truth."

Her chin jerks towards the wound on my hand. "How much does it hurt?"

I chuckle. "Not at all. I barely feel it. Now get over here."

Sofia squeals as I grab her and pull her onto my lap. She rubs my chest with a gentle sigh. "Am I really that easy to read?"

"No. But I'm invested. You're an interesting novel. Plenty of twists and turns," I say in her ear. "I'm captivated."

"You're sappy." She rolls her eyes. "Are words easier for you?"

"Yeah. I'm a words of affirmation guy. I like to say what I feel, and I feel reassured when I'm told what others think about me."

"I think you're a dummy." She sticks her tongue out. "Does that help?"

Scoffing, I drop my arms from around her. She pulls them back and cuddles against me. She sighs, her breath tickling my skin. "Words are ... flimsy. People can say anything. It's their actions that mean something."

I smile and kiss her. Sofia eases back, looking at me with confusion. "I just insulted your love language."

"By telling me how to *show* you I care." I run my nose over hers. "Action. Quality time. Doing things for you."

She shivers. "God, you're impossible."

"And you like it, or you wouldn't be in my lap."

"I'm catching your stupid," she huffs, her cheeks going pink.

I kiss along her jaw, then press my lips to her ear. "Once we're done with this, I'll cook for you. We'll have dinner with wine, and I'll rub your feet."

She shivers.

"Just what you need after a long day saving the world." I kiss just below her ear. Then again, along her neck.

"Jasper." Her voice is huskier.

"I can get us wine tonight. With whatever you want to eat. As long as it can be delivered, it's yours."

She turns to face me, our lips so close. She takes a hesitant breath. "What are we doing?"

"Making the best of an otherwise bad situation."

"I should be worried about getting back to the real world. To work. Making sure the guys at work are safe."

"But?"

"No buts. I should."

I rub her cheek slowly. "My sister said 'should' is a bad word. Because it implies an impossible ideal."

"That's a lot of big words for you."

"Hey. I kicked your ass in Scrabble. I'm qualified to use them. Don't say should. I know you're worried about everything you're going back to, but why does that mean you can't enjoy right now?"

"Because right now is temporary."

"So is life." I kiss her softly. "Wouldn't you rather have regrets than wonder 'What if'? I know I would."

She stares at me for a long moment, then whispers, "fuck it" and kisses me hard and hungry. Her tongue rolls in my mouth, and my heart squeezes in my chest. I tease her tongue with mine as I rub her back.

Sofia draws back, then ducks her head, nuzzling my neck. "You're going to mess everything up, aren't you?"

"Or I could make things better," I offer hopefully.

We end up getting Italian delivered. Sofia seems restless after dinner, and she confirms it when she starts pacing the room. I encourage her to enjoy a hot shower and relax. Thankfully, she does, and I check in with Cash and Kingston after she disappears into the bathroom.

Cash and I have a heated argument over my decision-making skills, and he starts questioning whether I'm the right choice for protecting Sofia. It pisses me off, and I tell him so. After all that I've done to keep her safe, there should be no doubt how capable I am. Ending the call, I crash in bed, turning on the TV while waiting for Sofia to return. She soon comes out in a towel, looking from me to the TV and biting her lip as she looks at the bed.

"Are we ... are we sharing again?"

"Do you want me to make a wall of pillows between us?" I tease. "To protect your honor?"

"No." She pulls a big shirt from the bag of clothes I got her and pulls it on before putting her hair up in the towel. Her eyes flick to me again, and she rolls them. "Stop staring. I know I look half-human without my makeup."

"That's not why I'm staring." I adjust myself openly, and she scoffs.

"Always about sex?"

"No. But you have an effect on me," I reply, sliding one arm behind my head, trying to focus on the TV as she climbs into bed. "How does the towel thing work – on your head."

"My hair is wrapped up in it." She pats it with a smile. "Helps it dry."

We lay with a canyon of space between us. I have a feeling that's how we're going to sleep too. She settles on her side and stares at the TV, obviously pretending I'm not here. I decide to leave her alone to her thoughts. She's wrestling with something. Hopefully, my silence will allow her to overcome whatever it is. Eventually, I flop over and get comfortable, letting sleep take me.

I have a shit night of sleep. I wake up at every unfamiliar sound and jump up twice with my knife ready. The third time, Sofia puts her hand on my arm. "Stop."

"What is it?"

"There's no one trying to break in. It's just people getting it on next door." She pulls me back into bed. "Cuddle me."

After double-checking that she's right, I return to bed, wrapping myself around her. She pulls the knife from my hand, welcoming me to spoon her. I nuzzle her neck and smile. "You're warm."

"Sleep."

It's an order I'm happy to obey. Until I wake up to an empty bed and start to panic. I fly out of bed as Sofia peeks over from the sofa. I sigh with relief. "Fuck. You're okay."

"Yup. Looks like you're stuck with me," she says.

"Want me to fix that sour puss face, love bug?"

"Jasper." She gives me a warning glare.

"I'll brush my teeth, and I'll make you come until you're smiling," I reply, turning to head to the bathroom.

"At least we agree about morning breath being awful," she says after me.

I brush my teeth and change my pants, not bothering to put on a shirt. I've seen how she looks at me when I'm topless. And when I stand in front of the TV, her eyes drink me in. She's still in that big t-shirt, and I can't help but wonder if she has anything under it.

Leaning closer to her, I pull at the hem of her shirt, and she swats me while giggling. "Behave."

"Eye fuck me again, and I can't promise I will," I threaten.

She bites her bottom lip. "Well, if you didn't look so delicious..."

"Me?"

She adjusts on her knees and puts her finger over my lips. "Keep your mouth shut, and I might just make today interesting."

I cock an eyebrow but reply with a brief nod. She kisses across my abdomen, her fingers hooking in the top of my jeans. She licks my hip, and I groan. "Fuck that feels good."

"You opened your mouth. No blow job for you." She rocks back, sitting on her heels.

Shaking my head, I join her on the couch, kissing her hard and deep as my hand tangles in her hair. She pulls away, letting out a shaky breath and licks her bottom lip. "You're not pissed?"

"Tell me no all you want. I'm in it for you, not the sex."

A flash of tenderness crosses her face, and she palms my cheek. "Take off your pants," she whispers.

Chapter 21

Sofia

I'm in it for you, not the sex.

Jasper's words run deep, touching something inside me that leaves me smiling yet feeling terrified. What should I do with this information? Do I lean into it or run the hell away?

God, I'm confused, yet so damn turned on. It's easier to submit to my carnal side than to get entangled in these emotions. I leave the couch and get on my knees as Jasper undoes his button, then his zipper, standing back up. I watch his face, the obvious anticipation in his eyes, the softness of his lips. I drag his jeans down and find him already half hard.

"Number one on my to-do list," I murmur, gripping his cock.

"Fuck, yes," he pants, running his fingers through my hair. "I like your list."

I answer by licking from the base of his cock to the tip. Jasper hisses, his grip tightening in my hair. I like that he's shaved and how clean he smells. I like how soft the skin of his shaft is. I like how quickly he gets hard for me.

I wrap my lips around the head of his cock while watching his face. His cheeks go red as I slide my hand up to meet my mouth, then he moans as I lick over the tip. I take him deeper, testing myself.

He's thick and long. I don't know how much is going to fit. I drag my tongue over the base of his cock, savoring the salty taste of him. Jasper's eyes close, and he moans softly, his other hand fisting tightly in my hair.

I sink lower and lower, taking him in my throat until I gag. I pull back and mark the place with my hand. I'm going to need it. I bob up and down, hollowing my cheeks with every suck, teasing him with flicks of my tongue, and then I moan as he hits the back of my throat again.

All at once, Jasper slips from my mouth and my hands. Dipping, he pulls my shirt up and over my head and lays me back on the couch. I swallow, slightly disappointed. "You didn't like my oral skills?"

"Without a doubt, baby. But I need to feel your pussy around my cock."

I moan.

Jasper hurries to get a condom and comes back as he rolls it on. He curses and pulls it off before flipping it. "These fucking things."

"Someone's *too* eager," I tease.

"Listen, they look the same from both directions." He tugs one of my ankles towards him. "And this is a small couch."

"If only we had a bed," I reply, sarcasm dripping in my voice.

"I'd fuck you on the floor." He comes down on top of me and pulls my thigh up and over his hip. "Or in a van."

"Going to start rhyming for me?" I accept one kiss and another and another. "On a train and a plane?"

"Not a plane." He teases me, rubbing his cock against my pussy without dipping in. "The bathroom is too small."

I laugh and pull him down to kiss me again. I've never laughed during sex before. It had always been a serious affair. Jasper grins and kisses me again, wrapping his hand around the back of my head before rolling his body with mine.

"Do you want this ... me?"

I suspect he's talking about more than sex, but I nod anyway. "Yes. I want you inside me. Now."

"I love when you give me orders," he growls, thrusting into me.

My lips part, and I cling to his shoulders, dragging my nails over his thick arms. "You're so fucking huge."

He groans and presses his forehead to mine, grabbing my hand and pinning it above my head, lacing our fingers. He thrusts again, filling me with his cock as pleasure sparks in my stomach. I wrap my leg around him, wanting to be as close as possible.

"Jasper." I gasp as he fills me again, and my hips roll to meet his. "Fuck."

"You feel so good." He breathes in my ear. "So fucking good, Sofia."

I moan and roll my hips against his, meeting his thrusts as I jerk my hand from his to wrap around his neck. I kiss him hard and hungry, pushing him back until I'm on his lap. I bounce on his cock, riding him hard as my climax builds in my stomach. God, he feels so amazing. The spots he's hitting are driving me insane.

"Fuck!" I gasp, kissing him again, swallowing his moan.

Jasper thrusts up and into me, pushing me higher and higher. My toes tingle, and I can't hold out. He's just too good. He kisses across my chest, squeezes my ass and thrusts again and again.

A long scream escapes my lips as I come, biting his shoulder hard as my body slumps against his. My hips roll slowly, still humming with the pleasure of the orgasm. I gently kiss the bite mark I left. "Your turn."

"You're edging me already, baby." He kisses across my temple, his arms wrapped around my waist. "You are so fucking amazing."

I roll my hips, and he grunts. Nodding, he licks his bottom lip. "Just like that."

Groaning, I bounce on his cock. My soft panting accelerates to a loud, continuous moan as I get closer and closer to the edge once more. He just gives nonstop orgasms, and I take them with no complaints. My body shivers as another one rocks my core. I lean back, bracing myself on his knees as I roll my body, jerking back and forth to take his cock over and over again.

"Yes, Sofia! Yes!" He grips my hips tight, squeezing as he pumps up and into me.

I fall over the edge again, panting and groaning. "Fuck!"

We come down together. Jasper holds me against his chest, shaking. He chuckles. "We do this a few more times, and we'll have knocked out a whole day."

I laugh and push myself up, and Jasper steadies me. "Easy."

"I don't think you could go that many rounds." Leaning in, I kiss him softly.

Jasper pauses, then holds the back of my head as he kisses me back. Our tongues stroke and tease, but there's no rush. Every kiss is drawn out, savored, slow, like waking up on a Sunday morning.

When I draw back, I feel the butterflies. They stir my stomach until I'm half nauseous, half convinced I need to kiss him again. I touch his face, slowly stroking his jaw. He turns to kiss across my fingertips.

Shivers follow in the wake of his mouth, and I know I'm damned. I'm damned for wanting him. Damned for having him. Damned for not wanting to leave this horrible motel room as long as he's here with me.

I brush my thumb over his bottom lip, lean in and kiss him again. His hands tighten on my hips. "Don't pull away this time."

I swallow hard.

"Let me in, querida."

I melt at the Spanish on his tongue, the way he knows me, protects me, treats me like I'm gold. "You terrify me, Jasper. Your life terrifies me."

"The violence?"

"The chaos." I whisper. "The way you just ... do what you do because your heart tells you to. There's no reason. No plan. No ... no steps to one goal."

"I have steps. I have goals."

"Tell me about them?"

"I want to keep you alive." He kisses my neck. "I want to take you on a date once this is over – and I plan to finish it as soon as possible." A kiss to the other side of my neck. "I want to settle down and live happily ever after, maybe in my sister's neighborhood, so I can be a better uncle and brother."

"And the steps?"

"Convince you that we can be good together. Teach you all about survival. Deal with the threat. Absolve it by whatever means necessary. Get you back in your apartment and fix the door. Take you on a real date with flowers, kick your ass in Scrabble, make you moan, and see you kick ass in congress."

"That simple?"

"That simple," he replies, his nose brushing mine. "Not everything requires ten steps and weekly updates. I want to be spontaneous, want to go with the flow."

"But you're military."

"I *was* military, babe. I was discharged. I spent years hating it, trying to find ways back in, and then accepted that I can do different things."

"How?" I want to know what turned him from predictable, straightforward, understandable to this tempting, infuriating ... annoyingly impossible-to-ignore man.

He lifts me up and grumbles about how this isn't a conversation to have while he's inside me. We get dressed and sit together on the couch. He picks at his fingernails until I catch his hands. "I can't stand the sound."

"Sorry." He clears his throat. "I accepted it after working with Daisy on physical therapy. After helping her through losing her husband, Ashton, while she helped me with my leg ... we lost my brother. He died overseas. His first deployment. His first ... time with the enemy."

"Fuck. Jasper, I didn't mean to bring that up, I ..." I take his hand in mine.

He squeezes it. "I talked to my dad, and he gave me hell. Said I wasn't a man since I failed my psych eval. Said that my brother was more of a hero than me because he never stopped fighting and didn't take the easy out. I realized then that nothing I did would be enough for him. Not until I died for my country. It wouldn't matter who I saved. It wouldn't matter because I was broken."

"You're not broken and fuck him," I exclaim.

Jasper smiles and pulls me close. "You're sexy when that viper strike is aimed at someone else."

"I mean it." I hold his face in my hands. "You are whole and good, and you've saved me twice. You've protected me and treated me so well and made this so much easier than it could be. You are amazing, Jasper."

He swallows and looks to the side. "That's a lot to hear, dearest."

"And you're a lot to take in." I grumble, starting to pull back. "Too much sometimes. Overwhelming."

"And that's what scares you?"

I swallow. It scares me that he makes me feel so much when I haven't known him long. He's unpredictable. He could leave at any moment. He's so ruled by his emotions. I don't know how to handle all that.

Jasper brushes his hands over my arms. "Let me in, Sofia."

"You're unpredictable, and you make me rethink everything," I whisper slowly. "It's terrifying."

Jasper smiles and shakes his head. "You are much too strong to be afraid of me."

I swallow and nod, then kiss him again, and again, and again. He groans and adjusts me in his arms. "You are one hell of a woman, and my favorite thought is of you conquering the world."

"And what about you?" I ask.

"I'm a bit big for a Spiderman suit, but ... I know I want to do something without guns or violence."

"Gentle?" I verify. I smile when he nods and fit myself into his arms. "A gentle protector. I could see it."

"Just let me be the knight in shining armor occasionally. Just once in a while," he murmurs against my ear. "And you can be the dragon ripping through the big issues."

How am I supposed to hold onto my heart when he says things like that? When he knows me well enough to know that I'm not a princess waiting on someone to save me? I bite my bottom lip and curl tighter against him.

I'll have time for words later, right? Once I figure out what I want to say, what I'm willing to follow through on. I chew my bottom lip as the TV plays out in front of us.

"How long do you think ... do you think we'll be here?"

"Complaining about your company?"

"No."

He freezes a moment, then smiles. "You like playing house with me, don't you?"

"It's not terrible." I grumble. "It's almost nice."

"That sounds like a half truth. Do we have to play another round of truth or dare to get it all?"

"Bring it on, bodyguard," I challenge.

He chuckles and rubs my side. "As you command, sweetheart."

Chapter 22

Jasper

The next two days are honestly amazing. I didn't think work could be pleasant. Not like this. Sofia and I talk constantly about movies and books and her plans after we leave our hiding place. We have sex every day, and each time, I feel her pull back a little less. And she opens up more, telling me about college and high school, playing sports, getting scholarships and meeting Carissa in college.

It feels like we're actually in a relationship. She hasn't fought with me since we got here, but she has plenty of sass, now mixed with a healthy dose of genuine answers. It's refreshing, sweet, real.

As she leans against my shoulder while watching a Hallmark movie, I check my phone. Cash checked in this morning, saying all's still clear at Ernesto's safehouse. He still gave me shit about not being able to keep my target where she belonged. I took his mouthing without arguing back this time because he's right. After taking the time to stew, I realized I had been careless. I should never have allowed Sofia to leave the safehouse in the first place. She was an unpredictable client, I knew that from the start, and I should have kept my feet down like I always did. But I was already weak to her the second she took my hand in her apartment.

I lean back on the couch with a sigh. There's been a thought that's been niggling at me since the attack on her workplace, and that thought has been getting stronger each day. What if I'm not enough to keep her safe? Maybe she needs someone who's more objective than I am, someone immune to her charms. Someone like Kingston, cool and disconnected, whose first priority is her safety, not her comfort. It had always been my goal on any assignment, but with Sofia, I failed.

There, I admit it. I failed to keep her safe because of my weakness to her. Now, what should I do about it? The bad guys are still out there, searching, trying to accomplish their goals. Am I enough to keep them at bay?

"Jasper."

"Mhm?"

"What are you thinking of?"

I kiss the top of her head with a forced smile. "Nothing, really. I'm just noticing how relaxed you look."

She puts her leg over my thigh, wrapping her arm around my middle. "This is the first time I've had more than a weekend off in over two years."

"How's it feel?"

"I don't know. I don't really like not being productive, and I'm worried about Carissa and the guys at work." She chews her bottom lip, then squeezes me. "But I know they're safer without me there."

I kiss her forehead and rub her back. "Only for a little bit longer. Then you'll be back to saving the world."

"And hopefully, I'll have some better ideas to put in place." Her finger circles my most recent injury, and she sighs. "What do you think we could do to better support the Veterans Administration?"

"You want my opinion?"

"You worked with me for a week and change," she reminds me. "And you're uniquely qualified."

"I'll let you know when something comes to me." I stroke through her hair.

"I can't wait to be back home. Not in a crampy motel room."

"We added to this uncleanness," I whisper in her ear. She shoves me, and I chuckle. "You weren't complaining at the time."

"Shush."

"In fact, I think you were begging me not to stop. Telling me to go harder. How good I felt. Something about me being amazing. I even think you called me-"

She covers my mouth with my hands, her cheeks red as an overripe tomato. "Cállate! Just shut up!"

Sofia is so fucking adorable; I can't stand it. I pull her hands off my mouth and kiss her palms. She's glancing around like someone's going to hear us. Then she sighs and slumps into my side.

"Just when I think you'll be a gentleman."

"I can be a gentleman and hilarious." I kiss her temple, then just in front of her ear, then down her jaw.

She squirms, and I squeeze her gently. "Does it bother you that I like you, baby doll?" I ask.

"No."

But she doesn't look at me when she says it. I roll my eyes. "Two truths and a lie. You first."

"I miss Scrabble. I'm worried about Carissa and the guys at work. We should get the cops involved so they can end this."

"You don't miss Scrabble?"

"No." She turns and huffs. "I want this to be done, Jasper. I'm tired of being holed up, even if it's been pleasant lately. And ... I don't like starting something or maybe starting something so far away from reality."

"Quiet is good. As for getting the cops involved, it's still not a good idea. As soon as Tiberon gets sentenced, we'll focus on the next step. We don't need to jump into-"

"Two truths and a lie." She faces me directly.

I sigh. "I like what we have. Your dad can handle this. We can get out of this intact, together."

She studies me for a long time. "See. We both know what this is going to come down to."

No way can her dad sweet talk himself out of this. If he could have, he never would have hired us. I pet Sofia's back and twirl her hair around my finger. It's tempting to want things to stay just like this, but I can feel her getting more restless.

I glance at my phone and see a timer set. Kingston clarifies.

Issued threat. Twenty-four hours to comply. Need rendezvous at SH1 in twelve.

Great. The whole gang together again.

For now, I want to focus on what's in front of me. I kiss Sofia's neck, gently pushing her hair to the side before doing it again. She shivers and welcomes more by leaning her head to the side. I'm getting more familiar with her love language.

Dragging her onto my lap, I rub her thighs and kiss across her neck until she rubs herself against me. "Jasper," she breathes, her voice thick with need.

"Tonight?"

"Now." She agrees.

I groan and pick her up, carrying her to bed. I devour her mouth as we strip each other. She's kissing me back with so much hunger, I wonder if she feels our time alone is winding down too. I kiss every inch of her, taking it slow, drawing it out. I don't want her to forget this. Once I'm inside her, our foreheads brushing as she digs her nails into my hips, the emptiness goes away. It's only temporary, but for now, I'll enjoy feeling whole again.

Sofia feels right against me. Like she belongs right here, nothing between us. She gasps as I sink deeper inside her. Her pussy pulses around my cock, and I groan, clutching her thigh as I fill her completely.

I hold the back of her head, wanting her to watch me, wanting to watch her as we do this. Only us.

"Gentle tonight." She whispers. "Slow."

I nod. I like when she gives me instructions when she tells me just how to please her. It means she wants me, means she wants this, and it's so fucking good to know how to give her what she wants.

Rolling my hips, I feel every bit of her as I slide in and out. She whimpers and clutches me harder. I swear I'm shaking already, undone by her.

"I like you, Sofia. Really like you." The words fly from my lips without warning, but I wouldn't have stopped them if I could, anyway. My feelings aren't influenced by the mind-blowing sex we're having just now. I have genuine feelings for her.

"Fuck, I like you too," she pants, stroking up my back. "So much."

It's the most I've gotten out of her, but as relieved as I am to hear the words, I'm greedy. I want more. I want her to tell me everything she likes, everything she wants. I want the constant reminder that my emotions aren't one way, and that she feels the same way, too. Our slow, gentle sex isn't enough, not here in this cramped motel room where we are hidden from the outside world. I want a lifetime with this woman.

Sofia gets on top of me and rides me hard. Her hair thrown back as she moans, her gorgeous tits bouncing as she rocks back and forth on me, using me for the pleasure she needs. She's a goddess. A woman that gets shit done by sheer will and effort.

And I'm hers. Hers entirely. I groan and thrust into her, holding her ass as she fucks me hard. "Christ, Sofia."

"Te sientes bien," she moans.

Fuck, I know she's close when she switches to Spanish. I don't think she even realizes it. Words pour out of her until I grab the back of her head and pull her towards me to devour her moans and dirty words.

"I'm yours." I pant as her thighs tighten around me.

"Shit." She groans.

"Come for me," I beg. "Please, baby."

She kisses me hard and guides my hand to her clit. I rub in quick circles and feel her pussy tighten around me, sucking me deeper until I can't hold out. When she comes, yelling my name and biting my shoulder hard, she takes me with her.

I groan and hold her down even as she keeps grinding on me. Our sweaty bodies flop back onto the couch, and she rubs my chest as we descend from the high of our climax. I rub her back, and she sighs contentedly.

My phone chirps again. I read the message from Cash, my chest tightening as my brain registers each word. He's taking me off the mission. My final task is to reunite Sofia with her father, and then I'm done.

Fuck.

"Something's happening, yeah?" she murmurs.

"Yeah. We're leaving in the morning." There's a lump in my throat, but I try to keep my voice calm. I can't let Sofia know I'm about to renege on my promise to her. Not right now. Tomorrow, I'll face the music and deal with her reaction, whatever it may be. Tonight, I just want to savor the last hours with her.

Silence stretches between us for a moment as she processes what I just said. I brush my fingers through her hair and try to get my heart to stop beating a thousand miles a minute, praying she doesn't ask where we're going. Sofia's smart; I have no doubt she would connect the dots in a minute.

"Okay," she finally says, kissing my chest. "Can I get some decent clothes, at least? These oversized shirts are killing me."

Forcing a small chuckle, I nod. I'm certain Cash will have someone take care of her every need. In a few hours, it will all be out of my hands.

We clean up and get into bed for one more night in the motel. After a fitful night, I wake with the sun and watch it spread over Sofia's back. The sheet is bunched over her ass, but the sight pales in comparison to the way the sun makes her glow like bronze. I slowly stroke her back, looking at the difference in our skin tone before kissing her forehead.

"Time to go?" she asks, groggy, still half asleep.

"I'll pack up. Get some more sleep."

"You'll pack wrong," she murmurs, pulling herself up and wrapping the sheet around her as if I haven't licked almost every inch of her delicious body.

"How am I going to pack wrong?"

"You'll find a way." She kisses my neck quickly. "But it would be cute."

I roll my eyes and get dressed. Sofia pulls on the first outfit she had on when we got here, the only one that fits. She looks at the rest of the clothes and only saves one shirt. The rest gets put in a plastic bag.

Within forty minutes, we're gone with the keys turned in. We stop at a thrift store, and she throws an ugly Hawaiian shirt at me. When she giggles, I hold up a shirt with a shark and a tiger about to battle underwater.

She laughs and shakes her head. I roll my eyes and buy both, just to spite her, and a pair of jeans. She gets a cute dress that brushes her thighs.

With that, we get changed in the car and head over to the safehouse. I keep under the speed limit, constantly checking my mirrors for anything amiss. But my reason for going slow isn't just to keep an eye out for the bad guys. I'm trying to prolong our final moments together. I take her hand, giving it a gentle squeeze. I clear my throat. "When we get there, I'm going in first."

"Jasper, come on," she huffs. "I already told you; I don't want to leave your side."

Oh, fuck my life. She definitely won't handle the news well. "It's my job to protect you, Sofia. That means you're getting in the back seat and staying low until I come get you."

"That's fucking stupid. Give me a knife, and let me have your back, Jasper. I'm not helpless."

"I didn't say you were." I pull her hand up to my mouth, but she pulls away before I can kiss her palm.

"I can protect myself. You made sure of that."

"It'll depend on what it looks like when we get there." I try for compromise. "If I don't trust it, I'm going to expect you to do what I say."

"So nothing over the last few days matters?"

"Of course, it fucking matters." I face her at a red light. "Of course, it does. If anything, I'm more determined to protect you and keep you in one piece. Whatever it takes."

She glares at me for a long moment, then crosses her arms over her chest. I sigh. "You can be mad about my decisions, cupcake. That's fine. As long as you're alive."

"I don't like this," she grumbles.

Oh, Sofia, you won't like what's coming, either. I contemplate telling her the truth instead of trying to prep her like I've been doing for the last few minutes. But I'd rather face another mission than her anger.

"Sofia, I don't want to lose you. Please understand that." Even though I know she won't ... not considering what will happen once we arrive.

She snorts. "So, you'd rather rush in and take the bullets yourself and leave me to pick up the pieces? Why is your life worth less than mine?"

I roll my eyes and shake my head. "You really think we'd be called there for that type of scenario?"

"I know my dad would rather lose you or your buddies than get a scratch. I wouldn't be surprised if they're surrounded, and you're nothing more than a sacrifice... a distraction."

"He can't be that bad. My dad is a jackass, but I know he cares, even if he can't show it. Your dad is just the same. He wouldn't have hired me to protect you if he would just turn you over to keep himself safe," I insist.

"You don't know shit about him. Plus, he hired you. You're biased!" She points at me. "You don't have a single clue."

"I'm just willing to give a little doubt. I can't see him as some evil cartoon villain."

"He's not! He's plenty fucking real," she replies. "And he's done things that have caused others to get hurt. The reoffenders. The people he's gotten off on technicalities when they all but admitted to murder. What's another body on his conscience?"

"I never said his conscience was clear; I'm just saying that he has limits."

"Oh yeah. Speaking of, how is your conscience, Jasper?"

"What?"

Chapter 23

Sofia

"Carissa? You know, the girl who was crazy about you? How do you feel knowing you're fucking her best friend? Huh?"

Jasper looks to the road, then back at me. I can't control the anger sizzling through me. I'm frustrated that he's forcing me to be a damsel in distress. I'm pissed that we're just doing whatever my dad says and trusting him when he's capable of anything. I've seen who he's let go. I've seen the kind of men he keeps company with.

And Jasper trying to say that Dad isn't that man has me questioning his morals. And mine for sleeping with him at all. For caring about him and not wanting to watch him get hurt for me ... again.

"Are you going to answer me, or what?"

"Fucking hell, Sofia," he bites out. "Carissa and I went on one date! Why are you throwing that into this argument? It's not about her."

"You want us to have a relationship when this is done, and you haven't even considered how she's going to feel. How will she feel seeing you with me when she was over the moon for you? Knowing we slept together."

"Yeah, *we*. If it were wrong – which I don't think it was because she and I weren't together – then we're both in the wrong. It's not like I forced you."

"I didn't say you did!"

"Then why the fuck are we arguing, Sofia ?!" He comes to a stop on the side of a road. "Why are you picking this *now*?"

"Because it's like the last few days didn't even happen! If they did, you should trust me and treat me like a partner. If they didn't, then-"

"We don't have time for this right now."

"Make time!" I demand. "This is important. I need to know where we stand because right now, I feel like I betrayed my best friend and myself for nothing."

He glowers at me, panting hard. "This is not *nothing.* And I know that you know that. *I* like you. I want you alive. And right now, I'd like it a lot if you'd do what I'm asking you to do."

"You're full of shit."

He groans and then takes a slow breath. "Fine. I can't argue with you right now. Get in the back seat."

"Make me." I hiss.

"Do I need to remind you about all the innocent people around?"

I grind my teeth but climb into the back seat. Of course. Back to me being the danger. Me being the reason I can't do anything. Because it's clearly my fault, not my dad's. It's on me for wanting to have my own life and not wanting to give up who I am and what I do because my dad can't just keep his nose clean.

"Give me two minutes, and I'll come get you," Jasper says.

He gets out of the car and takes my anger with him. I dig my nails into the seat of the car to avoid popping up to keep my eyes on him. I bite my lip and prepare to hear gunshots, my body tightening with tension as the silence progresses.

The longer I wait, the more active my thoughts become. Should I be pissed, or did I just overreact? I'm not sure where that hot fury came from, if it's just about Jasper not trusting me to protect myself despite the time we've spent together.

Or maybe it's something else...

A sudden cracking sound makes me curl up on the backseat, waiting to get dragged out and beaten or killed. After a few minutes of tense-filled silence, I start imagining the worst. I'm picturing Jasper on the ground, holding his guts as the life disappears from his eyes, gone forever, all because I stayed in the car and didn't listen to my instinct.

I take a slow breath, psyching myself to get out. But just as I reach for the door handle, it flies open. The fear calms, but only for a moment when I spot the graveness on Jasper's face. He offers me his hand, but I get out on my own. He reaches for me when I am on my feet, pulling me close.

"Something's wrong, isn't it?" I ask, but he shakes his head, quickly guiding me to a narrow pathway, where we are sandwiched between two high walls. I hate the clustered feeling it gives me, but I know I'm safe. Jasper's here. I'm protected as long as he's around.

A rush of guilt fills me, and I look up at him, taking in the tension in his jaw, the focus in his eyes, the tightness on his lips. He's been doing nothing but protect me all this time. Or at least trying to. I haven't made it easy for him, have I? Especially with the way I behaved earlier.

"Jasper, I'm—"

"This is where your dad and stepmother are staying. They're waiting for you," he interrupts as we approach a wrought-iron gate. There are two men in black with machine guns standing outside and another one coming up the long driveway towards us. I recognize him as one of the guys from that first night.

It takes a moment for Jasper's words to sink in. "Waiting for me? You mean us, right?"

Jasper sighs as the gate slowly opens, and we enter. "No, Sofia. Just you."

I look up at him again as dread fills my chest. What the hell is he talking about? He seems distant now, his eyes looking everywhere but at me. There's nothing of the man I just spent a week with left in him. I take a step back. "What's going on?"

"Sofia ..." His eyes soften for a second, and he looks at me.

He opens his mouth to say something, but the biggest guy comes over and puts a package in Jasper's hand. The guy pats my shoulder and nods to Jasper. "Brookes, you're dismissed. Miss Wilson, you can come with me."

But I don't move right away. Instead, I look at Jasper. "Dismissed? What the fuck is he talking about, Jasper?"

"My job was to keep you safe as long as you weren't here. You are now here," he replies, his tone empty as the expression on his face.

"So, what, we're done?" I ask, the flare of panic making it hard to breathe.

Jasper's eyes fall to his hands, and I choke back a sob. It's just like I thought it would be, physical, no emotions. I should have known I'd regret being with him. That I'd regret letting him in. Laughing over TV shows as we ate sushi, pretending to be a functioning couple when the world couldn't touch us... it was all bullshit, wasn't it?

Was that all to keep me compliant? No. He wanted to have sex with me. I knew that. He'd been flirting since we met, but to break down my wall just to let me down like this, God, it's downright cruel.

"You're safe here," he whispers.

I close my eyes a moment and rub my forehead as my commonsense chips in. This isn't all Jasper's fault. I knew about the risks, so I'm as much to blame for my own heartache as he is. I clear my throat and nod. "Sure. You got what you wanted."

"Don't say it like that when you know how I feel," he murmurs. He reaches for me, but I pull my hand away. He sighs. "Sofia, come on."

"Fuck your feelings. You fucking betrayed me. You knew there was no plan for us to stick together, and you didn't tell me."

"Because I know you by now, Sofia. You would have flipped and given me a hard time. This isn't personal. I'm just doing my job."

"Because that's all I am to you, right? An assignment."

"That's not fair, and you know it." He closes the space between us and runs his hand down my side. I close my eyes, needing his touch, yet hating it, too. "Once you're safe, we can get in touch."

"No wonder you were so eager to get me here," I hiss, jerking away from him. "You got to fuck me, and now you got paid for it. What else could you possibly want?"

He flinches. "It wasn't like that."

"Then please, explain. I'm all ears." God, I sound like a teenager, but I just can't shut up. "Explicame!"

"Just because you're focused on how to move up in the world doesn't mean everyone else is. Some of us want to enjoy what we have." His eyes rake over me. "Or had."

I blink a few times and take a step back. As I open my mouth, Jasper puts his finger over my lips. "Think about it. When it's done, Sofia, if this is what you want, I promise, I'll come back for you."

"Yeah, right, like you promised to always be here. Screw you, Jasper. You will never touch me again."

"Miss Wilson," the big guy says. "Let's go inside."

"Keep a close eye on her, Cash. She's a flight risk," Jasper murmurs.

"Understood."

I shake my head at him, more disgusted with myself than anything and turn to go inside. I think I hear Jasper give another order, but it has to be my own heart talking to me. "If she gets hurt, we'll have a problem. Understand?"

Walking through the house, I hear my dad talking to someone. I stay just out of view after peeking through the doorway. He sighs. "Tiberon isn't going to stop. It doesn't matter how long we try to hide. His men are going to find us eventually."

"Mr. Hernandez, don't talk like that."

"It would be easier to just let them have me if I was sure that it would keep my family safe." He sighs. "I don't see any other way to deal with this. Maybe I just need to give them what they want."

"You've been holding hard and fast all along, which is the right thing to do. Just give it time. Sentencing's in a few days. As soon he's locked down for life, or worse, you will be free."

"We don't have time, Kingston. And a man like Tiberon won't stop just because he's trapped behind bars. In fact, he'll be more ruthless than ever. I can't afford for anything to happen to my kids, Scarlett, even my ex-wife. I couldn't live with myself if they were harmed because of me. All because I decided to do the right thing."

"Then you need to consider Cash's plan," Kingston says. "That's the only way you and your family will be safe."

Kingston's words send a chill over me, and I wrap my arms around myself and enter the living room. Dad's sitting on the section couch, looking older than when I last saw him, a lifetime ago, it seems. His hair is a little greyer in some areas, with more wrinkles lining his face, especially on his forehead. I sit next to him, more to get answers than to be near him. "Dad, what's really going on?"

"El Tiberon. The ex-client who's sending men after us—"

"I know who he is, Dad. What do you mean by doing the right thing?"

Dad sighs, shifting his body and staring directly at me. "I've done some crazy things, Sofia, all in the name of building my legacy. I'm not proud of what I've done, but back then, I didn't care as long as I remained on top. But lately, it's been eating me alive, especially when I realized how broken you and I were. I know my career choice is the main cause of our rift."

I'm itching to correct him and remind him that our estrangement began when he divorced my mom, but I don't want to break his flow.

"When I took this last case, Tiberon wanted me to bribe the cops to make the evidence go away. But I couldn't. Tiberon's case wasn't like the others. Those were regular possession and dealing charges. Never murder. Tiberon's a killer. He organized a drive-by on his enemies, and a few kids got harmed in the mix. I took his case, thinking I would do everything in my power to get him off, but my conscience wouldn't allow me to follow through. I had to let justice prevail." He gestures around the room. "But instead of firing me, Tiberon tried to force my hand."

To say I'm shocked would be an understatement, not at hearing Dad's dirty deeds from his lips but learning of his change of heart. Is it permanent? Is my father turning over a new leaf?

The clicking of heels precedes my stepmother's appearance and interrupts the moment. She enters from the kitchen, her hands bearing a tray with drinks. She gives me a smile, and I return a stiff one. We've come a long way from when I found out she was Daddy's mistress, but our relationship is still a work in progress.

She places the tray on the center table and sits beside my father, placing his hand on her lap. Her thick caramel hair falls over her shoulders. Even in a safehouse, she looks like she's ready for a movie set. She's wearing a one-sleeved cocktail dress and full makeup. Very trophy wife.

Scarlett's only six years older than me, which makes it hard to grasp their relationship. But if my dad can change his evil ways, the least I can do is meet him halfway.

I avert my gaze as she kisses his temple. "You have enough stress on your shoulders, honey, don't add to it."

He takes a drink of water and sighs. "I'm not, baby. I need to tell Sofia the entire truth."

"And no talk about giving up to Tiberon. It won't change a thing. He'll just kill us all, anyway." She leans her head on his shoulder. "I don't want to lose you, Ernesto."

I shift impatiently on the couch. "What truth do you need to tell me, Dad? What did Tiberon do?"

Dad eases Scarlett off him with a weary sigh. "He has some information on me, on places I've been, things that ... out of context, would be very bad for my career and very embarrassing for Scarlett, you and the family. I pretended to back down, but I didn't. I purposely lost the case."

"A gangster tried to blackmail you? Why didn't you say anything?"

"Talk about being blackmailed? By Tiberon? No. I know you, Sofia. You would have gotten way over your head trying to get involved." He shakes his head. "I love you, but you don't really think things through when you're heated."

"Dad."

"It's true, and you know it. You're passionate, but when your emotions get involved, you don't have a sense for the long game." He pats my knee. "But there's something I need to confess. Tiberon's not just after me because I didn't get him off. It's much more than that."

The seriousness on his face triggers a sudden drop in my stomach. "What do you mean?"

"We're going to get this straight. I'm ready to tell you everything right now."

Chapter 24

Jasper

My palm slams against the steering wheel, and I drop my forehead to the center, taking a deep inhale. Seeing the tears in Sofia's eyes, knowing I was the cause... man, it was like a dagger to my heart. All I wanted—what I still want to do is to make her smile every single day of her life. I hope to God I get a chance someday.

I didn't *want* to leave her. I wanted to stay, even on perimeter duty. But I don't call the shots. I'm still desperate enough to text Cash, making sure he doesn't want a man watching the boundary with three people – including a flight risk – and potential bogies on their way.

He insists that I take at least a twelve-hour break. That I'm on call and nothing else. I drive by the house, checking the road out front until Cash sends me another text to go home and get rest. Reluctantly, I continue on.

I don't want to leave Sofia there. I especially don't want to leave her based on that last conversation or the fight we had. I'm not ready to be done with her. I want everything I told her I wanted before.

I remember us curled up in bed, her lying in my lap as I played with her hair. She rubbed my damaged leg and then turned to look at me. "You really think you'll be happy with a white picket fence? After all the excitement in your life?"

I brushed her hair away from her face and bent down to kiss her forehead. Her eyes never left me, and I give her a nod when I straighten again. "Excitement like I've seen is nothing to enjoy. I want a schedule I can rely on, one that gets me home for dinner. I want a woman like you yelling at me about not moving the laundry from the washer or forgetting to take out the garbage. I want to wake up next to you each morning, and I want your face to be the last thing I see before I sleep at night."

"That's your dream?"

"Why wouldn't I want to marry a successful woman and spend my free time making both of us happy?" I pulled her up, so she was seated on my lap, and I cupped her face in my hand. "Do you think you could manage life in congress with a devoted man, eager to take care of the house, who can take being yelled at and laugh it off ... or make you laugh?"

She swallowed hard and brushed her hand over my chest. She kissed me then and distracted me by kissing down my body before giving me the best blow job I've ever gotten.

But I'd meant what I implied. Which was stupid. I see that now.

And since I don't have a home to go to, no hotel room comfortable enough to allow me to lick my wounds, I drive the forty-five minutes to Daisy's. I knock on the door and hear her talking to someone before Ellie opens the door, squealing when she sees me.

My constant best friend. She looks at me, her smile disappearing, then she reaches out for me. I pick her up in a hug, and she squeezes my neck. "What's wrong, Uncle Jaz?"

"My princess is gone, and I'm sad."

"Are you going to turn into a frog?" she asks seriously, squishing my face between her hands.

I laugh once. "I certainly hope not."

"Ellie!" Daisy comes up behind her, then looks at me, eyes worried. "Where's Sofia?"

"She's safe," I promise. "With her father. Where she needs to be." I step inside, adding, "I need a place to crash for a while."

"You don't need to ask, Jasper. You're welcome to stay as long as you like. Are you hungry? I have leftovers from dinner." Daisy shuts the door behind me. "Oh, before you take another step, I have company."

"Oh. I'm sorry."

She shakes her head. "It's fine. Just giving you a heads up."

Before I get to ask her what she means, I round the corner to the kitchen and spot Carissa leaning against the counter. She jumps when she sees me, then arranges a smile on her face. I rub the back of my head. This is what Sofia was worried about. This exact awkwardness.

"Hi, Carissa. How have you been?"

She shrugs. "Um... still a little shaken up, but I'm fine, I guess. Where's Sofia? Is she okay? I've been calling her cell phone for days."

"Hey, Ellie. Why don't you come with me? Let's get a bath," Daisy jumps in before I reply.

"But Uncle Jasper lost his princess," Ellie says with a pout.

"He'll be okay," Daisy assures, looking at Carissa and me over her shoulder.

Once she's out of earshot, I sit down around the counter and rest my elbows on top. "Sofia's fine. She's with her Dad and a few guys who will ensure she remains safe and sound."

"Oh, thank God," Carissa breathes, plopping down on the stool across from me. "I've been so worried. I came to Daisy's, hoping she'd heard from you. But when she didn't, I thought the worst. I'm so glad she's okay."

"You're a good person, Carissa. You know that, right?"

"Yep. I know," Carissa smiles, then offers me a cookie from the jar. I return her smile and take it.

"I'm sorry about... you know."

She nods. "I'm a little hurt, but I understand, Jasper. The heart wants what it wants, isn't that what they always say? I get why you chose Sofia. A lot of people like her. It's just so rare for her to like them back, so I know you must be something special to her." She takes a shuttering breath. "And we knew there wasn't any chemistry from the first date. I knew."

I'm sorry for hurting you," I insist. "I never meant to."

She shrugs. "When you wear your heart on your sleeve, it gets broken. I'm always prepared for the worst."

I shake my head and take her hand, squeezing it a little. "You're too good for me, anyway. You deserve a real prince. One with a whole country to offer you."

"You're speaking my language. You know anyone?"

I laugh and shake my head. "I'll definitely keep my eye out for your prince charming, how about that?"

"Sounds good." She sticks out her hand. "Friends?"

"Friends."

She squeezes my hand, and I give an exaggerated wince. "Ouch!"

"There's more where that came from if you ever break my best friend's heart. You got that?"

"Loud and clear, ma'am."

We sit in silence for a moment while I send Sofia a text, hoping she had already turned on her phone. But there's no response. I'm not surprised if I never hear from her again.

"So, are you guys a thing now?" Carissa asks, and I lift my eyes from the phone to meet her curious stare.

"I don't know what we are right now. She's furious with me."

Carissa frowns. "What did you do?"

"Nothing but try to protect her. She's mad at me for leaving her behind. But I had no choice, plus it's what's best for her." I lean back with a sigh. "It's one of the hardest things to let her go. But her safety is more important than my love for her."

"Wait. Rewind. You're in love with her?"

I nod, closing my eyes. It doesn't matter what I feel. Sofia isn't the forgive and forget type. She won't let go of the last fight, so it doesn't matter that I got the best week of my life because losing her is going to hurt so much more.

Every touch. Every kiss. Every soft look and smile. It's etched in my brain, and I can't shake it free. Just like I can't forget how she looked at me when I left her at the safehouse. The hurt, the fury... knowing Sofia, she won't let go of those emotions anytime soon.

"I got this, Carissa. You want to start the movie?" Daisy interrupts, coming into the room.

"Yeah, sure thing," Carissa replies.

Daisy turns my head as she drags a chair to sit next to me. "Hey."

"Hi."

"Your face reminds me of when Dad gave away your puppy when we were kids. What's this about?"

"Sofia."

Daisy sighs. "You did your job, Jasper. No one else can ask more from you. You kept her safe. You are a hero; do you hear me?"

"Then why do I feel like a fucking idiot?"

"Little ears in this house. Watch your mouth." She points at me but then softens. "Talk to me."

I swallow and rub my face. "I don't know what to say. You know how easily my emotions run away from me. You know how easily I get ... caught up."

"Oh, I know. You like to save people. You like to be the one people go to." She smiles. "You've been that person for me."

"Yeah, but I fu-screwed up."

"Good thing this will be your last assignment, right?"

I nod and shake my head. "That's the plan. Then I'll find a regular job."

"Like what? Talk to me about that."

But I can't. Because I don't know what I want to do. Maybe get involved in the Veterans Administration? Maybe focus on what I can do for those who come back? Be an advocate for them? But that would mean using my in ... maybe working alongside Sofia. Watching her drift further away from me.

"I don't know," I whisper.

"That's not the Jasper I know."

"I'll start babysitting or something." I throw my hands up. "I hear it's easy to become a substitute teacher."

Daisy keeps watching me, and I sigh. "I betrayed her, Daisy."

"What happened between you two after you left here? After it was obvious you were both crazy about each other?"

"We talked. Just talked the first night. She told me about her dad. I told her about ours."

Daisy holds up her hand. "You what? You don't even talk about Dad with me."

"She needed it. She was shaken up after the gunfire. Worried about Carissa. Felt guilty. To get someone to open up, you have to open up. You taught me that."

She bites her lip. "And?"

"And we slept together. Often. When I wasn't teaching her combat. When we weren't talking about the future, the past, her work, my experience. Somewhere in all that, I ... I don't know. I started thinking that we'd make it through the job. Like, we would have a life together."

Daisy squeezes my hand and shakes her head. "It's not like you to make a mess of things, Jasper. So, what really happened?"

"I left her there. I didn't even explain. And we had a fight about her dad. And ... then I fucked it all up."

"What's that mean?" comes a tiny voice behind me.

We all turn to look at Ellie. She stands there in her pajamas, then pads over to me, climbing onto my lap. I rub her sides. "I messed up."

"With Sofia?"

"Yup."

"So she won't come play dress up with me?"

"Missy, your bedtime is quickly approaching," Daisy says.

"I've got that," Carissa chips in. "Let's go read a story, Ellie."

"Okay, Sister."

Carissa takes her hand and smiles at Ellie as they disappear down the hallway. Daisy's phone chirps, and she swipes the screen, her cheeks reddening as she reads. I clear my throat, and her head shoots up, a guilty expression on her face.

"What's that about?" I ask, my chin jerking towards her phone.

She smiles, her expression clearing. "I don't want you to judge me, but... I met someone."

"Why would I judge you for that?"

"Because, you know... Ashton."

I take her hand, giving it a squeeze like she did earlier. "It's time to move on, Daisy. You've been alone for a long time. I don't think you should feel guilty for wanting to be with someone else."

She chuckles. "Oh, that's such a relief. I hate lying to you about it. Remember when I showed up at Sofia's office, when everything went down? I lied about the emergency. I was actually coming back from our date."

"Oh, you sneaky little minx. Who is he, anyway?"

"His name is Trent, and he's an investment banker. We met when Ellie and I went to the playground a few months ago. He has a son her age, and we hit it off almost at once." She palms her cheeks, her face reddening again. "He's such a dream, Jasper."

"I'm not the only one in love, am I right?" I tease.

"Shush. That's a big word for me." She shakes her head. "Especially considering I haven't really spoken to Ellie about her dad. Having people come in and out of her life isn't going to do her any good."

"Seeing you happy will do a world of good for her," I assure.

"Just like seeing *you* with someone will show her how a man should treat a woman," Daisy redirects. "Also, you *can* fix this. You can. Don't count yourself out."

"You don't know Sofia. Her trust is next to impossible to earn, and I broke it. I broke it by leaving her there, by not telling her."

"By doing your job." She pats my cheek. "From what Carissa says, that's something Sofia will definitely understand."

"She hates me."

"Give it two days. If she doesn't call by then, prepare to spend some serious money and get familiar with being on your knee."

"Oh, I have no problem with that," I tease.

She smacks my cheek lightly. "To grovel! Get your head out of the gutter. Keep being honest. Really honest. Be uncomfortably honest."

"Dating advice from my little sister. This is what it's come to?"

"*Valuable* dating advice," she corrects me. "Next time, please have your money upfront. My services aren't free."

I chuckle and ruffle her hair. She shoves me off; then we're bickering like we should be. I feel better, just having talked to her. But I'll feel best when I have Sofia back in my arms. Safe. Whole. With a smile on her face.

Chapter 25

Sofia

I rub my face. This is too much to take in. Way too much. Too much to the tenth degree. Scarlett gets me some tea, and I stare at it stupidly. "Why do I feel like whiskey would be better?"

Dad chuckles, and Scarlett smiles. "She's definitely your daughter."

"Her ambition says that more than anything." Dad flashes a smile, but it dies as I take a sip of the tea. "I know this is a lot, Princesa."

"More than a lot, Papa. You're holding evidence that could get Tiberon a death sentence if you hand them over to the authorities! Why didn't you tell me?"

I should have known something didn't add up. Why would Tiberon want to kill us because my father lost the case? Now, this makes perfect sense.

"The less you knew, the better, Sofia," Dad calmly replies.

I wildly gesture around the room. "Better for who? I'm stuck here with you, aren't I? And based on what you just told me, I'll probably always be on the run like a fucking criminal. Oh, my God. I think I'm going to be sick."

"I'm sorry, Sofia. I wish you didn't need to endure this with me."

"Sorry fixes nothing, Dad. It never does." I argue. "Only a change in behavior fixes things. Apologies ... they're words."

And words are thin as fucking air. Like Jasper telling me that we could get through this together. Like him telling me he'd be there for me. Like the hint of us having a future. A future that started to sound like a pleasant dream, almost like a life I could have. Like I could take on the world and come home to a warm body instead of a quiet house with the lights off and premade food in the fridge. But instead, all I have is this... what is this? A lifetime of living in fear?

I adjust the hem of my dress and shake my head. "This is so much. Too much. How the hell are we going to survive this?"

Dad glances at Kingston, then back at me. "There's a plan, but I need you to trust me, keep your head low and wait for Tiberon's sentencing. That's all I ask."

"Just give him the evidence, and he'll leave us alone, Dad. We could get back to our lives in a heartbeat."

My father scoffs. "Tiberon's a cold-blooded criminal. Do you really think he'll allow us to live?"

"Dad—"

"Trust me, Sofia. Please. I've done a poor job of taking care of you all these years. Give me a chance to make it right."

I nod in response, but I hate it. I hate that there's nothing I can do to fix our situation, to help keep us alive. Dad hugs me, and I don't flinch. I pat his back. He takes a slow breath as his familiar smell washes over me. He always smells like fresh laundry, clean and warm.

"Te amo."

"Papa." I sigh. But I'm not good at reconciliation, especially after all these years. I need to think about how me and Dad will move forward before I say a word. "I ... I should sleep. It's been a long day."

"Yes. Get some sleep. You're safe here. I'm sure it's been hard the last few weeks. Not being sure." He rubs my shoulder. "Not to mention dealing with a stranger."

I shrug. "It was okay." Better than okay while it lasted. Now, it feels like a little like regret. Not for the intimate moments Jasper and I shared but the way I behaved afterwards. I wasn't fair to Jasper. He was just doing his job.

"You're exhausted," Dad says, squeezing my hand when my eyes drift close. "Your bedroom's upstairs. First room off the landing.

You can rest without worrying about someone breaking in. We have multiple layers of protection. Cashton and Kingston are the best of the best."

Cash nods at me, but Kingston watches me carefully. I bid my Dad goodnight and head towards my bedroom. I'm halfway up the stairs when I notice Kingston following me. Turning to face him, I cross my arms. "Kingston, right?"

His brows slightly lift, and there's a ghost of a smile on his face. "Yes."

"Why are you following me, Kingston?"

"Is that a rhetorical question?"

"Of course, it is. I'm here, safe inside. Your men are stationed outside. You don't need to tag along wherever I'm going."

"Jasper told Cash you're a flight risk, so we're keeping all our bases sealed."

"There's no need. I do things my own way, okay?"

Kingston frowns. "That won't work here, little girl. I'm not as lenient as Jasper. Cash doesn't have his kindness. So, for your sake, I'm telling you to behave."

"Whatever." I turn and continue up the stairs as his cell phone rings. Hopefully, the call is enough to stop him from following me.

But I'm taken by surprise when he pushes me inside my bedroom and closes the door. "What the fuck, Kingston? You can't be in here—"

"Shut up and listen," he hisses, his voice low and dangerous. "Tiberon's men have found the safe house, got that? We just got word they are on the way."

"Then why the hell aren't we moving? Why are we locked in the goddamn room?" I attempt to push past him to the door, but he effortlessly holds me back.

"There's nowhere to go, Sofia. We have no choice to take but to take them down." He motions to the floor. "I need you to stay put until the coast is clear, okay?"

"So why isn't Jasper here?"

"I think that's fairly obvious." Kingston glances towards the door. "Objectivity is a terrible thing to lose."

"But he's another person. Trained. He's kept me alive. He kept me in one piece."

"He did. It's quite obvious," Kingston replies, quickly looking me over. "It's his methods that are in question right now."

I narrow my eyes at him. "I don't know what you're saying or accusing him of. He took a bullet for me. He's done *everything* to keep me and others safe."

"No argument from me. I don't give two shits about method as long as the job gets done. But that spat you had with him outside the house. It said plenty, Sofia. You should learn to lower your voice."

"Son of a bitch! You don't know anything. Not a damn thing." I fight the urge to shove him. "And I promise that you'll wish he was here. If this is as bad as you keep saying it is."

"We're perfectly qualified-"

"Bullshit." I hiss. "If you were confident, you wouldn't have said a thing."

"I'm just keeping you in the loop in case you do something stupid like try to run. Our hands will be full in a few minutes. We can't afford any other distractions, so for the last time, please behave. Do not leave this room until I return for you."

He doesn't wait for my reply. I stare at his broad back as he hustles out the door, taking my bravado with him. The direness of our situation feels even more real now that I'm alone. I plop down on the bed and pull my phone from my purse. Jasper's incoming texts light up the screen the minute I turn it on. I start to type a response, then delete it. I'll give him my reply face-to-face. He deserves that, at least.

Sliding down to the carpet, I pull my knees up to my chest and rest my chin on top, listening, waiting, hoping Kingston was wrong. I want to go home. I need my life back. I need Jasper here to keep me safe. But I've been nothing but a selfish, insufferable bitch; do I deserve to get what I want?

A sudden loud boom makes me whimper. I push up from the floor as a barrage of gunshots sounds outside the window. Or is it coming from inside?

Oh, shit, it's both!

"Fuck, we're surrounded!" I heard someone yell outside the door. "Kingston, get the-"

Another echoing boom. A gunshot.

Fuck.

I grab my phone and hide on the other side of the bed. I don't know where is safest. I manage to get under the bed, despite the claustrophobia that comes with it. The space is too small, making the stifling feeling even worse. But when the bedroom door flies open, I immediately forget that fear. There's someone in the room with me, someone more threatening than my fear of confined spaces.

A hand pulls my ankle, and my reflexes chip in. I give a hard kick with my free foot and hear a responding whimper.

"It's me, Sofia!" Scarlett whispers.

Pushing myself from under the bed, I meet my stepmother's anxious face. She's paler than normal, lips trembling. "They're here. They're everywhere!"

Another round of gunshots goes off, sounding closer than the ones before. Scarlett screams. I push her into the closet and shut the door. Taking a deep breath, I fight the queasiness in my system. This isn't the time to give in to terror. I need to remain focused to make it out alive.

"They're in the house, Sofia!" Scarlett grabs my arms, her nails catching on my skin. "They're wearing masks, and their guns are bigger— oh, Sofia, I don't want to die!"

I give her a rough shake, hoping she'll snap out of her hysteria. But she's still a shaking, blubbering mess. "Scarlett, I need you to relax, okay. Losing control won't help us one bit. Where's my dad?"

Scarlett huffs, still sniffling. "Your dad said ... he said he has to end it."

"What the hell does that mean?"

When she shakes her head, I open the closet door and peek out. The house sounds quiet. There's either death or victory beyond these doors, but either way, I need to find out what's going on and ensure my father's okay. I get out of the closet and tell Scarlett to call 911. She grabs at me again, her nails digging into my skin, but I shake her off.

"Stay here. Keep the door locked. Don't come out until it's safe."

"Stay with me! I need you here," she whispers.

I shut the door as she bursts into a fitful of sobs. I ignore the anxiety it triggers, then push away from the closet. I stumble over my own feet in my hurry to get to the door.

Come on, Sofia. Come on.

I make it to the door and realize exactly how useless I am. 911 will take too long. Calling anyone will take too long. I hear someone curse in Spanish, then there's a splintering sound, like a door is being kicked down.

What was it Jasper said?

Everything is a weapon if you know how to use it? Well, I don't know how to use shit. But I bite. I scratch. And I had a good arm once. I played softball in high school. That has to come in handy. Right?

I move along the wall, trying not to make a sound. Spotting a velvet rope used to tie back the curtains on the landing, I reach for it and wrap it around my hand. It's something. Not much against a gun, but I don't have a knife. I grab a hanger, too, then I pause and listen for footsteps.

"Here! Aqui! Aqui!"

My bowels loosen at the sound. Fuck. They found Dad. They found him. God, I can't let them hurt him!

I sink to the floor and crawl to the banister, looking downstairs. I see my dad thrown on the ground in front of the fireplace. Four guys stand around him. No sign of Kingston, but I see Cash's limp body on the ground, blood pouring out of him. Holy shit. We're definitely fucked. There's no victory, only death.

"I'm not giving him what he wants," Dad says. "You'll kill us anyway."

Thank goodness I'm behind the thugs, and that their attention is fixed on my father. I take the opportunity to crawl down the stairs, hiding behind the couch until I get to Cash. I pull his shirt open and see he has a bulletproof vest on. I drop my weapons and try to find where he's bleeding from.

His arm ... his leg. And his lower abdomen. I toss the hanger, and I push on him, just like Jasper showed me way back when. Cash gasps, then opens his eyes to stare at me. I put one bloody finger to my lips, telling him to shush. He looks past me, then reaches for his gun.

"Where's Kingston?" he whispers.

"No clue." I whisper back. "Scarlett is safe. They have my dad and-"

"Hide." He shoves me, and I force myself to fit under the side table.

Releasing soft breaths, and with pain stamped on his face, he pushes up on his knees, lifts his gun and gets two shots off. But his injury prevents him from ducking fast enough. I cover my mouth as he goes down in front of me and try to squirm away from the spreading blood.

"Donde está tu hija?" One man demands.

"I don't know where she is!" Dad yells.

My heart thuds in my ears. They're going to kill him if they don't find me. And when they find me because the house is only so big, they'll torture me to get what they want out of my dad. I swallow the growing lump in my throat and wrap the cord around my fist.

I'm vibrating, eyes swimming, but I have to stay alert. I have to do something right. Cash is dead. His open eyes stare at me like he's giving me away despite the blood that's creeping closer and closer.

"Find her!" Another man barks. "She's here. We know she's here."

I swallow hard. If I'm going to die, I'm going to do one thing right. I call Jasper. On the first try, I quickly hang up because of the pair of feet that appears in front of me. The guy kicks Cash, splashing me with blood. I cover my mouth and nose, trying not to breathe. Trying to stay quiet.

Once he moves on and they start trashing the house, I call again. Jasper picks up on the second ring. "Hey."

"They're here," I whisper.

He stops, I just hear him breathing. I whimper and then take a slow breath. "They're looking for me."

"At the safehouse?"

"Yes."

"Sofia, if you're hidden, stay there. I'm on my way. I'll be there as fast as I can, baby."

I sniffle. "I'm so sorry I was mean to you."

"None of that," he mumbles, his voice carrying a tremor that tells me he's on the move. My knight in shining armor. How could I have been so blind?

"I started the fight. I was wrong."

"Sofia, focus. Where are the guys?"

"I wish we had more time." I look at the feet that turn to face me and close my eyes. The phone shakes so badly in my hand, I'm afraid I'm going to drop it. "I'll keep my promise."

"Don't say that. I'm going to be there," he says, and I hear an engine rev. "Stay alive for me."

"I won't stop fighting," I whisper, right before a hand wraps around my ankle.

Chapter 26

Jasper

Sofia screams, and the line goes dead, and so does the calmness I've been trying to keep alive for her sake. I press down as hard as I can on the gas pedal. The more police attention I get, the better. Let them track me at a hundred plus as long as I get to her. The ride is too long. Unless they torture her, I'm going to be too late. I know that, but I can't make the world move any faster. I can't jump time.

I never should have gone so far away.

Somehow, I make the forty-five-minute drive in half that time. The gates are wide open, and I sail right through. I consider running the car into the side of the house, but instead, I get out and start several car alarms on my way inside. I want them looking the other way.

Kingston is down, but there's no blood. I check his pulse. He'll survive. I walk past him, staying low. I come across three dead in masks. Not my concern. Then I see Cash in the living room.

There's enough blood to tell me he's gone if the bullet to the neck didn't. But there are streaks in his blood. There's a trail. Fuck no. Fuck no.

"The safe!" Ernesto yells. "The videos are in the safe, just stop. Stop!"

"Papa, no..." Sofia's voice is hoarse, weak.

Keeping on my knees, I peek around the couch and see her on the floor, her wrists tied. A masked thug comes close to her, cupping her face. "I think we have some time to enjoy you, sweetheart."

Oh, this is not going to end well. Not for him. I allow the anger to fill me up. I need every ounce to take out these motherfuckers.

Scanning the room, I see another guy slumped on the floor with a cord around his neck. Good girl. Two others are focused on Ernesto. I'd need two perfect shots, then I'd have to deal with Sofia's captor.

He screams suddenly, getting everyone's attention. Sofia's attached to his hand, and from the tension in her jaw, she's gotten a solid grip. Her captor shakes his hand, but she sinks deeper, pulling another scream from his throat.

I take the opportunity after clearing my mind. Two shots. That's all. The first man goes down easily, dropping to the ground, but it gets the second man's attention. He looks at me in surprise, a young face. A bull's eye.

I touch the trigger, and he's down. The last guy slaps Sofia at the back of her head with his gun, and she slumps to the side. I shoot him in the back and run to lift her in my arms. She gasps and then spits out blood. It's all over her.

Her face is bruising, and she's not breathing right. She looks up at me, mumbling, "You came," then turns and throws up beside me. I pull my knife and cut her wrists free. I see to Ernesto, telling him to find a place to hide.

His eyes widen, and he yells, "Look out!" But it's already too late.

Heat and pain race through my stomach, stealing my breath. I put a hand over the gunshot wound as another masked thug approaches me. Another shot jerks my body forward over Sofia. She pulls the gun from my hand and presses the trigger. A thud tells me she hit her mark. Looking around, she pants as the gun shakes in her hand.

I pull it from her fingers before she hurts someone and hear Ernesto calling 911. I already hear sirens. Good. This was a quiet neighborhood. We chose it for a reason. Any sound of gunfire would trigger multiple calls.

Sofia rolls me onto my back and pushes her hands on my abdomen, holding tight. She gasps, and I hear her gag. She turns her head to the side. Her shaking gets worse, and I have no doubt she's in shock and some.

Ernesto comes over and tries to push her hands away. "Sofia."

She doesn't respond. She keeps saying "sorry" repeatedly, her eyes wide, looking around as the word keeps leaving her lips. I hear a door open and try to grab for my gun. A scream echoes, and a pale, well-dressed woman comes running towards us. No blood. No bruises.

"Scarlett, mi amor." Ernesto sighs.

She fits herself to his side, hugging him. "I thought you were dead. I called the police, like Sofia said. They are on the way, honey. Everything will be okay."

"Sorry," Sofia says again to me.

"Hey," I put my hand over hers. She swallows and looks at me, blood still on her chin, splattered over her face. "You did so good."

"Well," she corrects me, her expression blank as a new notebook.

"So well." I chuckle, then groan, dropping back against the floor. "Did you choke the guy?"

"Everything's a weapon, right?" she whispers.

"That's right." I smile and cup her cheek. "You did so well, cupcake. I saw you ... saw you bite him."

"He touched me."

"Are you going to bite me too?" I brush her hair back from her face.

She shakes her head and leans forward, pressing her forehead to mine. "Stop saving me."

"I'm bad at it, aren't I?"

She whimpers and presses harder on my abdomen. I don't have the heart to tell her that it's not going to do any good this time.

Unless I get to a hospital soon, I'm fucked. Sofia shakes her head as my vision dims. I'm so fucking tired.

"No!" She slaps my face as the words tear from her voice, all ragged and hoarse. "No. I stayed alive. I stayed alive."

"You did. I'm proud."

"If you don't, I'll kick your ass. I swear to God."

"Hey. No threats right now." I rub her hand and force my eyes open again.

"Sofia, you need to let him go." Ernesto says. "Come here."

"No!" Are those tears on her face?

I brush my thumb across her wet cheek and smile. "You're crying for me? Since when are you sweet?"

"Remember the white picket fence?" She insists, leaning closer to me. "You have to fight for it. Right now. Fight."

"I'm tired." I sigh. "Ellie misses you."

"Yeah, well, I need you."

"You survived all on your own." I remind. "It's okay, Sofia."

"No." She shakes her head and presses her forehead to mine again. "I'm so sorry, Jasper. I'm sorry. I got scared. Fighting is easy. I'm sorry. I'm sorry."

"Shhh." I close my eyes. "Just stay."

The sudden rush of footsteps interrupts Sofia's sobs. Her screams make me open my eyes, ready to take on whoever is hurting her, but I relax when I realize it's the police and EMTs. A pair of cops are pulling her away from me, and she's screaming blue murder and fighting them off. They settle her on the couch as a paramedic gives her an injection in her arm, and she relaxes against the seat, closing her eyes with a sigh.

"Three gurneys," someone else orders.

Another paramedic comes up to me. "We're getting you out of here. It's going to hurt."

"I'm used to pain," I reply.

I grit my teeth, muscling through the pain as they load me up. Everything feels hazy until I give into whatever they give me, and the last thing on my mind is Sofia's face.

WAKING UP IS HELL. I feel gross, slimy, and everything is too bright. Pain rips through me, teasing every nerve, and all I want to do is escape. I try to move, but I can't. I need to get to Sofia. She was screaming. So much screaming. So much blood. An alarm goes off somewhere and then more pain. Someone shouting and then silence. Darkness.

I awake to find Sofia petting my hair, her eyes red and weary. She gives a gasp when I touch her hand. Her face brightens a little. But her mouth doesn't match her words though. There seems to be a lag.

"Never have I ever ... killed someone," she whispers.

"Cheap shot," I reply. I take a gulp of water from the glass he hands me. "Never have I ever ... gone to a frat party."

"Nope." She grins. "Too much work to do."

"We'll have to crash one to fix that. I want to see you dance. Carissa says you're good when you're drunk."

"I can't trust her with a single secret." She shakes her head, then laughs, but it's wrong. That's not how it happened.

"Once we can leave, let's go dancing. We can even get tipsy first. So we only remember the best of it."

"Are you asking me on a date?" she teases.

"Seems right after all this sex and TV time." I sit up, wincing from the pain, although it's not too bad this time around. "Never have I ever done things this backwards before."

Her eyes soften, and she brushes her fingers across my lips. "Me either."

"Aw. You're making me feel special. Keep it up, and I might catch feelings for you." I kiss her chin before flopping back in her lap.

Her fingers brush through my hair again, and she watches them instead of me. "You haven't already?"

"Have you?"

She swallows. "Two truths and lie."

"Tell me," I argue. "I just want the truth. No more lies between us."

Sofia opens her mouth to reply, but the smile suddenly leaves her lips, and she gasps, leaning closer, pressing on my stomach. "For God's sake, Jasper, stay with me. Stay!"

What the hell? "I'm right here, Sofia." I grab her hand. "Hey, look at me."

"Wake up," she sobs, tears filling her eyes, blood rolling down her chin. "Wake up!"

The sound of a gunshot pulls me awake. Gasping, I try to sit up, trying to get free, to get to her. Hands push me back to the bed and hold me down. "Let me go!"

"Relax," a deep, familiar voice orders.

I blink, staring up at Kingston. He looks like he hasn't slept in weeks. He hasn't shaved either, which is definitely unusual for him. I settle down on the bed and look around the hospital room. So, I wasn't entirely dreaming after all.

My heartbeat calms, so the alarm stops, and I swallow the cotton-like sensation in my throat. "What ..."

"Save your energy, brother." Kingston pats my hand.

He hands me a cup of water, and I drink like I've been in the desert for days. He nods. "That's progress. This is the longest you've been awake."

"How long?"

"Two weeks. You've been ... violent, delusional. I told them not to use the heavy drugs." He shrugs. "You're alive, though."

"Sofia." I start to sit up again, despite the pain exploding in my shoulder and abdomen. "Where is-"

Kingston's gaze shifts to the corner of the room, and I see Sofia curled up in one of the chairs. She's asleep, with fading bruises on her cheek. Dull scratches on her arm, a cut on her neck. But other than that, she's whole.

She's whole, she's alive.

I force myself to relax and then try to take in my own condition. My arm is in a sling. Since I have an ugly blue hospital gown on, I can't see my other wounds, but I can feel them. "What ... the report?"

"Ernesto and his wife are safe. Sofia is alive. Tiberon got sentenced to life in prison, but someone murdered him two nights ago."

"Holy fuck."

"Holy fuck is right."

I keep watching him. He sighs. "We lost Cash. The medics tried, but ... he's gone."

"Goddamnit."

"You took two. One to the upper arm. One to the stomach. Missed your spine by an inch and lodged in Sofia's thigh. But it was shallow. Ernesto took a beating, but he'll be fine. The wife is fine ... just shaken up."

"You?"

"Apparently, I wasn't worth killing, or they got sloppy. Thought I was dead." He shrugs. "I don't get it."

I glance over at Sofia again. A wave of exhaustion floods me. I clear my throat. Although I drank the entire glass of water, it still feels dry. "Daisy... how is she?"

"She's visited twice. Left you flowers." He motions to the wilted color blooms.

"Good." I nod.

"Ellie has gotten very frustrated with Sofia."

"I'm sure that's a whole story."

"It is. And I'll let Sofia tell it. Get some sleep, brother."

"I've gotten enough," I argue, despite how tired I am.

"You're on heavy meds. You need it. Don't fight. Just sleep. It's okay."

I shake my head. "I need to get up."

"Hey." He puts his hand on my chest. "You're with the medical professionals. You're safe. No more. Just sleep."

"You take first watch." I agree, laying back. "I'll ... I'll take second."

"Sure thing. I'll wake you up in seven."

"Five."

"Sure." He nods. "Knock out." He pats my chest. "Enough fighting, Jasper. Heal up."

"Just five." I insist as my eyes close. "A bit of shut eye, and I'll be right."

Chapter 27

Sofia

I sit by Jasper's side again, my legs folded under me. I'd argued with my father for a solid hour before I finally left the hospital to get a shower and a change of clothes. Not that I bothered to go the extra mile. Gray leggings and black tank top, and I barely ran a brush through my hair. Scarlett insisted that I take her white wrap, in case I get cold and now I'm glad I did.

Two hours of reading to Jasper, and I'm half hoarse and more exhausted that I'm trying to show. But I don't want to leave Jasper's side until he wakes again. I want my face to be the first thing he sees when he opens his eyes. I can't believe I almost lost him before telling him how I feel.

A nurse comes in to check his vitals and then nods with a smile that gives me hope. "Today's the day."

"He goes home?" I ask, setting the ereader to the side.

"No. He gets off the heavy pain meds." She takes off the empty IV bag and replaces it with a fresh one, checks his arm, then pulls the curtain, asking me to step out while she takes care of the other wound.

I'm sure she's doing more that I don't want to know about. I watch her shadow through the curtain massage his leg. He won't be allowed to walk or move for a while. The doctors said he was in surgery for a long time to make sure his insides would stay where they were.

The bullet missed his vital organs. They keep calling him lucky. But I don't feel it. He's not lucky until he wakes up. Really wakes up.

The nurse pulls the curtain back, smiles at me, and leaves the room, closing the door behind her.

I sit back down. "Ready for another chapter?" I ask, although I know he won't answer.

But I'm halfway through the chapter when he opens his eyes and looks around wildly. Kingston warned me he might panic when he wakes up. I take his hand, relief flooding me. "Hey. It's okay. We're safe."

He freezes, then slowly looks at me. "Sofia..."

"Hi." I stand up and move to dim the lights. When I turn around, I see him trying to sit up and push him back down. "No. Behave."

"You're here."

"I'm here." I brush his hair back from his face. "Just like you."

He shakes his head. "No. You're okay. One piece."

"Thanks to you." I take his hand again as an emotional wave runs over me. "You keep saving my life."

"It's my life's mission, I guess." He cracks a smile, and I roll my eyes, but I feel the tears threatening me once again. Jasper shakes his head, and a croak of a sound comes out of his throat. "No."

I wipe my eyes and force a smile. "It's okay."

"No crying." He lifts his hand to brush my cheek. "We're alive."

"You came for me. Even after I yelled at you."

I lean into his hand and close my eyes. Seeing him was like the cruelest dream. I was sure that the blow to my head had fucked with me. Had broken my brain. But then he was hurt, not just setting me free. Hurt, bleeding. Again. All because of me.

"You keep getting hurt because of me. I'm bad luck."

"No." His fingers brush over my cheek again. "No, darling. You're good luck. I'm alive. The bullet missed my spine."

A sob escapes my lips, and Jasper squeezes my hand.

"If it had hit, you would have lost your favorite part of me."

I open my eyes, but everything is blurry. I chuckle and wipe my eyes. "You're ridiculous."

"It's okay to only like me for my dick," he snickers.

I want to swat him, but I'm too afraid to hurt him. I rub his hand, leaning into it as he warms my face. I take a slow breath. Jasper looks me over again, like I'm a miracle.

"Tell me what happened."

"No. Let's ... let's never talk about it again."

"Once and then never again," he argues. "I'm trying to remember, but everything seems hazy."

I swallow. "I called you, and they found me."

"Before that. Everything I missed. I need to know it all. Including the fuzzy stuff," he insists. "I can handle it from you."

I tell him about Tiberon's men taking over the safehouse. About Cash. About the blood. I get stuck on the memory of Cash slumping to the floor, and my body starts shaking, and Jasper gently kneads my shoulder with his good hand. I continue, telling him about how I grabbed things to defend myself. How they found me on the phone.

I take a deep breath. "He didn't expect me to choke him. I gripped him tighter than I thought I could. He tried to throw me off, and I heard a snap that told me his neck was broken. I tried to run, but the others grabbed me and tied my wrists. They beat me when Dad wouldn't talk."

Jasper sucks in a breath, his face darkening. "I should have done more than shoot those fuckers."

"Yeah. They kept asking dad where to find the video, but he wouldn't budge, and I was so proud of him. But then they threatened ... to do a lot to me. To make him watch."

"Sofia, open your eyes." Jasper says, his voice tight.

I meet his eyes, and he nods. "Take a breath for me."

I take a slow breath, trying to hold onto it. I exhale just as shakily. He nods. "Only if you can."

"When the guy held the knife at my throat, Dad broke down and told them it was in his safe. Then the guy groped my breasts. I didn't give him permission. So I bit him. I didn't want to let go. If I were going to die, I wanted them to find out who did it. I wanted evidence. I'd take them down with me."

My stomach rolls again as I think about it. "So much blood, and I could ... I could taste it. I got tested for everything."

"Smart." Jasper sighs.

"And then you were there." I hold his hand tighter, our fingers lacing. "You were there, Jasper. And you... he tried to kill you. He came from nowhere. He aimed again."

"What?" This time, Jasper does sit up. He groans and puts his hand to his stomach, but then adjusts himself, taking a deep breath.

I nod slowly. "I took your gun. You ... I know you shot, so I just ... I aimed. I pulled the trigger. He dropped. Then I ... I tried to save you. Dad and Scarlett were okay. They tried to ... tried to take me away from you."

"You screamed."

I chuckle, despite my legs bouncing and shaking. I sniff. "Apparently, I tried to fight the police. They pulled me away from you. I was given some kind of tranquilizer."

"Tiger." He teases.

"You're awake now." I want to climb into bed with him. Want to feel how real he is. "You're alive."

"Yes, I am. So you can yell at me just like you want to." He smiles slowly. "Tell me what a dick I've been."

I shake my head and tighten my hold on him, afraid he'll slip away. "I was wrong. I never should have started that fight. If I didn't, maybe you would have been there. Cash would be alive. You wouldn't have—"

"Shh."

"I was scared, and I don't like being scared. It's so hard." I sniffle again. "But then I thought I'd never see you again, and all I wanted was to say how sorry I was."

Jasper takes a slow breath and looks over at the water pitcher. I pour him some, and he drinks it slowly. After a slow breath, he looks at the ceiling. "I know that you ... you and I don't always see things the same way."

"Jasper—"

"That week we spent in the hotel ... it changed things. I thought I ... I was so sure about my outlook on life, that my dad was impossible, that there was no point in talking to him. That it's my fault my brother died. That I couldn't really protect anyone, and I was just playing pretend like some kid."

"Hey." I rub his hand.

He pulls back and clears his throat. "What I'm trying to say is, I want us to look ahead, not behind. I have a lot to do once I get out of here. A lot of things to fix. A job to find. And I need to take you on a date. A real one."

I stand up and kiss his forehead. "We have a lot to figure out, but we have time."

"You should be at work, shouldn't you? It's got to be a weekday."

"I had a few weeks to burn through and consider everything ... I couldn't leave." I bite my lip. "I guess some things are more important than work."

Jasper smiles. "Me?"

"You." I nod. "I know that I'm argumentative. I'm a control freak. And I'm going to have an ass load of trauma because of all this. But I ... I realized things too. I have had so much backwards."

"Sofia." He reaches back out to me.

"About my dad. About you. About ... about life." I shake my head. "Thinking there was only one path to get to where I wanted to be."

"Is that a yes to the date?"

I laugh and nod. "Yes, dummy. I'm saying yes to the date."

"Well, now I have to think about that, considering how mean you've been." He adjusts and smiles. "I might need some buttering up, especially since I hear Ellie isn't happy with you."

"Yeah. She was mad I didn't kiss you awake like the story." She shrugs. "But there's this thing about consent."

"I consent to every kiss you ever want to give me. Asleep, awake. Angry, happy." He whispers.

"You're such a ..." But I bite my tongue.

Every time I've called him dumb, every time I've avoided an answer, every time he's asked me for the truth, and I found another way to answer the question... It was all hiding one thing.

"You're under my skin, Jasper. So deep."

He smiles gently. "Then I think I should tell you a secret."

"Oh, no. Not when you're on drugs. I don't want to hear a single thing until we're out of the hospital." I press my finger against his chest. "Which means you need to eat and focus on getting better."

"I love you," he says anyway.

I kiss his palm, the happy bubbles bouncing in my chest. "Shut up."

"Do you think you could love a dummy?" He continues as if I didn't just insult him. "Do you think you could like me, injured leg, broken pieces, unsure and messy?"

"Jasper."

"I'll never put pizza in the fridge. I leave dishes for later. I toss laundry in front of the washer."

"Well, that just ruins it." I can't help smiling. "The laundry is my breaking point."

He shrugs. "I could work on that."

"We should go slow."

"We lived with each other for nearly a month. We had sex before a date. Your boss saw us kissing. We're past slow." He adjusts again.

"You were shot twice because of me, and you still think this is a good idea."

He shrugs. "With enough wounds, I might become some kind of half robot. Then I could handle you properly."

I laugh and kiss him. His lips are warm against mine, and when he teases me with his tongue, I pull back. "Oh no, you don't. No tongue until you're walking."

"That's a good incentive." He sighs. "I love you, Sofia."

"We'll get there," I hedge.

"Come on. Give me the truth. Who knows when I'll have the balls to say it sober."

I laugh and bite my lip. My heart swells in my chest. I know it's true. I know he knows it too. It was obvious when I called him, thinking I was going to die. It was obvious when I had to be knocked out to leave his side. It was obvious when I killed to keep him alive.

"I love you, Jasper."

His grin stretches over his face even as his eyes start to close. "You'll have to tell me again. I'll think it was a dream."

"We have time," I assure. "And you'll have plenty of time to bug me into saying it again."

"Promise?"

I squeeze his hand even as he takes a half-snoring breath. "I promise."

Chapter 28

Jasper

Sofia ends up going to work the next week while I recover. I'm finally told I can go home as long as I have family to help out. Of course, Sofia's there and insists I'll be coming with her.

The nurse doesn't argue. A part of me wonders if they're afraid of her. I wouldn't blame them. My vicious Sofia now has a body count. Unfortunately, before we can go anywhere, the police pay me a visit.

Sofia watches them with sharp eyes. She demands to know if I need a lawyer, but once I take her hand and let her know I can handle it, she calms down. She takes a slow breath and sits there, holding my hand while they ask questions.

When they leave, I move to the wheelchair, and Sofia takes a trip down the hall with me, pushing me slowly until I lean back to tease her. "Is there only one speed on this thing?"

She pops a wheelie and rushes with me down the almost empty hallway. I laugh, and when we come to the stop in front of a very unhappy nurse, Sofia bursts into giggles after apologizing. We return to the room, and she waves nurses away when it's time for me to get changed.

"Someone's protective," I tease.

"You might realize you can do better if some sexy nurse gets her hands on you."

"Let's get you a nurse costume." I tug on her shirt.

I undo the ties on my gown and lean back, resting for a second. Sofia helps me into underwear holding onto my damaged leg as she does so. Not one hesitation, not one pitying look. Fuck, could I be more in love with her?

She looks at the gauze on my stomach and chews her bottom lip. "I feel like I'm constantly in your debt."

"You are. Now stop looking at my sexy body and dress me, woman," I order.

She arches an eyebrow at me. "Really, smart-ass? You're going to be *that* kind of man?"

My smile gets me out of trouble enough that she pulls my pants on and reaches for the shirt. She laughs when she sees it. "The shark?"

"And tiger. Can't forget that." I sigh.

It takes us more time to get the shirt on, but Sofia doesn't rush, doesn't get frustrated; she just helps. Once I'm done, I catch her hand. She meets my eyes and shakes her head. "You're the most ridiculous person I've ever met."

She kisses my forehead though and works on packing up for me. Injured or not, seeing her bend over in that skirt as it drags up her thighs gives me a very healthy, doctor approved reaction.

"What a view."

She stands, looks around, then swats me playfully. "You're going to be impossible to live with."

"So much for going slow."

Her eyes flick to me and then away as she blushes. Oh yeah, I remember that whole conversation. I remember her telling me she loves me. I remember her holding my hand, her not wanting to leave at the end of visiting hours. I remember her arguing with a nurse outside my room before coming back in, flipping her hair, and sitting on my bed, asking me what I wanted to watch.

Just like I remember inviting her to lay down with me and her being afraid she'd hurt me.

"One bed at your place, right?" I push.

"And a whole lot of stairs." She grumbles. "The elevator had better be working or-"

"Take it easy, Tiger." I rub her hand. "We can handle it. I'm not helpless and neither are you."

It does take work to get to her place. Moving from the wheelchair to the car isn't easy. Sofia yells at the wheelchair since it doesn't want to fold, then does the same thing when we arrive at her place.

It's immaculate as expected, but I see that her shoes are now in a messy line instead of perfectly against the baseboard. She points out where the rooms are, and I nod, just watching her move around.

"Um, Kingston is going to get a bag from your place and bring it over. I bought some sweats and stuff that should be your size if Daisy's right about it. Do you want anything?"

"You, on my lap," I reply, not holding back my dirty grin.

She rolls her eyes and watches me move to the couch. I sigh as I sit down. I love not being in the hospital. I love not having nurses and doctors up my ass. A long recovery, probably, but being here is more than worth it.

Sofia sits next to me and turns my head to face her, kissing me softly. I kiss her back, running my hand over her cheek and into her hair. She pecks me a few more times and then leans against my shoulder.

The first few days are slow. Everything is exhausting. Moving from lying down to standing is a painful workout. So I do it more when Sofia isn't around. I look forward to Daisy coming every other day to check on me and help me with physical therapy. I love Sofia to death, but I can't stand when she treats me with kid gloves. She won't allow me to push through the pain.

But Daisy can't come over today, so I'm stuck with being handled like a five-year-old. I suffer through the ten-minute walk through the apartment where she insists on holding my hand all the way. Finally we're done, and I plop down on the couch, sweat running down my face like I had just gone for a 5k sprint.

"I think I'm ready for that bath now," I mumble, placing my feet on the coffee table. It takes me an instant to realize Sofia hasn't answered me at all. I twist in my seat to find her sitting at the breakfast counter typing on her laptop. "Cupcake?"

"The remote is right next to you," she says, her eyes still glued to the screen. "If not, it might have fallen between the cushions."

"I'd like to shower."

She freezes, swallows, then shuts her laptop. "I can call Daisy or-"

"Is there a reason you'd prefer she washes me?"

"Because we're not ready to shower together when you're still in pain." She blushes but sucks her bottom lip.

"Is that why I went to my last doctor appointment with Daisy too? Did you need to take care of yourself?" I tease.

She points at me. "You're going to regret that. Because I'm going to tell you no. No sex for six weeks. Minimum. That's what the doctor said."

"Don't remind me," I huff.

She gets me into the shower still wearing her underwear; sexy cotton panties and a bikini top. One fucking pull on a string, and she'd be topless. It's tempting as hell. I wash as much of myself as I can, namely my semi-hard cock, abdomen, and most of my chest, then all I can do is watch Sofia washing the rest of me.

She slowly rubs my shoulders, along my neck and sides, my arms. I lean down, pressing my forehead to hers. She breathes a deep sigh and hesitates before kissing me. I tease her with my tongue, and she groans. "Don't."

"I'm walking. You promised."

She hesitates again, holding my hips, then stands on her toes to kiss me harder. Her tongue strokes into my mouth, and I feel her moan as I answer her. We make out in the shower, her soapy hands on my hips, her tongue turning me to jelly. That little whimper she gives makes me hard.

Drawing back, she points to my cock. "That's not getting any attention."

"I'll jerk off later," I shrug.

She blinks at me, obviously not having put that together. I chuckle. "You think I could live with you and *not* jerk off?"

"It's ... it's hard on you, isn't it?"

"Oh yeah. Hard."

She rolls her eyes and works on my back while grumbling in Spanish. We rinse off together, and I motion to her. "Not going to save water with me?"

"You'd be naughty."

"Just a touch or two." I wink.

She shakes her head. "Sex isn't important right now."

"I'm still a man, Sofia," I huff, frustrated. "Not just some project or wounded bird."

"Jasper." She bites her lip, then hands me a towel. "Call me for help when you're done."

When I come out in the towel and amble to the bed, I expect her to yell at me for walking all the way on my own. But she doesn't. Maybe then things will go back to normal. I don't mind her doting, but she rarely sasses me anymore, and I've seen how she looks at me when I'm not watching. It's not loving. It's assessing. Trying to predict what I need before I need it, trying to keep an eye on me as if I can't do it myself.

I'm over it. She didn't see me as broken before.

Sofia pulls the t-shirt over her head and takes me in, her eyes lingering on my torso. I decided to ignore the gauze, so I imagine how she's cringing inside. But I'm healing well from the outside in, so I don't know what's her problem. Sex, off the table, absolutely, but having to beg for more than a peck?

"Jasper," she mumbles as I shuffle away.

"I can go stay with Daisy if this is too much," I murmur. "On our relationship or-"

"You are my boyfriend, and you are staying here." She takes a few steps closer to me. "I don't think you're broken, okay?"

"Don't lie to me."

"I'm not. I just have to remind myself of the limits, so I don't ... push them." She bites her lip, and her eyes rake over me again. "Sometimes, it's harder than others. I'm sorry for making you think that you're not ... you."

"What does that mean?" I want full clarity.

"It means I want everything we had in the hotel room. The kissing, the sex, the wrestling. I want to cuddle you, sit on your lap, make out in public with you." Another step towards me until our knees brush. "And if I don't remind myself that we have to wait another ... five and a half weeks, then I'll get greedy."

"So you do love me for my cock."

"It's not all the nicknames," she teases.

"Well, I don't think the doctor said anything about blow jobs, just to be clear. Or about fingering you with my good arm. I could probably eat you out too if we can figure out a position."

She laughs and sits next to me. "Your heart rate has to stay low."

"Impossible with you."

She kisses my shoulder, following my collar bone to my throat. My breath catches as her tongue flicks across my still damp skin. Her hand strokes down my chest, stopping just over my new scar.

"And I'm not good at restraint. Not with you. I'm an all or nothing type, Jasper."

I exhale slowly, trying to ignore the fact that I'm already tenting my towel. Sofia tosses it to the side. "But ... if you're already getting yourself excited, maybe I should do it."

Her hand wraps around my cock and strokes slowly. I groan and rub her thigh, pressing my forehead to hers. She kisses me hungrily as she jerks me off. Her hand is so much better than mine. Feeling her against me, her tongue teasing mine. It takes an embarrassingly short amount of time to get me off.

I come with my face pressed to her throat, moaning her name. She gasps, then turns to kiss me. "We can try blowjobs next week."

"Fuck, I love you." I kiss her again. I clean myself up with the towel and have her help me into boxers and sweatpants. I hold her hips in front of me, rubbing up her thighs. Spreading my legs, I pull her closer and kiss across her belly. "I do, Sofia. I love you."

She pets my hair and wraps her arms around my neck. "Once you're all healed up, I expect a full weekend of your attention."

"I'll put it in my calendar."

"So cheeky."

I squeeze her ass, and she giggles. "What do you want for dinner, cave man?"

"Other than you? Pizza."

She leans down to kiss me again, and just like that, everything is right in the world.

Chapter 29

Sofia

The weeks pass by, and work starts picking up again as we prepare for the gala. There's so much on my plate, it's hard to tell one day from the next. I've been tempted to give up my teaching time to be able to take better care of Jasper.

Not that he really wants it. He's getting more independent by the day, pushing his luck in a lot of ways, but the doctors are thrilled by how quickly he's healing.

I glance up from my laptop as Carissa walks by, her eyes buried in her phone. She's been a little distant since I got back. I haven't gotten a chance to talk to her about... everything. There's an overdue conversation that needs to happen, well, right now. I can blame work and Jasper's recuperation for not having the time to talk, sure, but I know it's more than that. I feel guilty, especially since I'm so happy with Jasper. Taking a deep breath, I approach her desk. She sees me coming and arranges a smile.

"Hey, you," she says, as I take the seat in front of her desk.

"Do you want to go out this Friday?" I ask.

She blinks at me. "Uh ... out? Like ... out, out?"

"Like going to a bar with music that's a little too loud. We have some catching up to do, and I'd really like to talk."

She sighs and looks down at her desk. "I don't know, Sofia. I kind of have a thing."

"Ok... how about Saturday?"

Another hesitation, and I wait for her to tell me I stole her man, that we can't be friends, that we're done. But she reaches over and rubs my hand. "Don't give me that look, Sofia. I still love you. That hasn't changed."

I put my free hand over hers. "I'm so sorry for how Jasper and I got together. I'm sorry about being distant since I've been back. I'm sorry for hiding behind work and every other excuse."

"I mean, yeah, it was kind of a bitch move to sleep with the guy I liked, but we weren't dating. I'm happier now anyway. How is Jasper?"

"Annoyingly determined to break doctor's rules." I roll my eyes. "How are you? How have you been?"

"I've been okay. I'm seeing someone, and things seem to be going well, but we don't really have a label which is ... new."

"Very new for you," I agree.

"Just like you going home on time?" She teases.

I roll my eyes. "I take plenty home, don't worry about that."

"You need a work-life balance, Sofia. I keep telling you that."

"I know. And I plan to, once this gala is over."

"I'm going to hold you to that. But I'm really tied up this weekend, so I can't hang out. How about tonight, though? You can bring Jasper if you want."

"And have him trying to dance and all that? No. He could probably use a night without me looking over his shoulder."

Carissa laughs, and just like that I get my old friend back.

When I get home, I find Jasper asleep on the couch with an office comedy playing on the TV. I hurry through a shower and get dressed in a mid-thigh black dress that clings to my body. I let my hair down and apply light makeup and a blood-red lipstick. I grab a pair of stilettos, then crouch down next to Jasper, kissing across his neck.

He squirms in his sleep. I grin and nip him softly. He sighs. "I like waking up to you, gorgeous."

I lean back as he looks me over, his long eyelashes fluttering. "Are we going somewhere?"

"*I'm* going out with Carissa."

"Fishing for a boyfriend?"

"Well, with all these medical bills, I need a sugar daddy," I say as seriously as I can, then giggle at his incredulous face. I kiss him quickly. "Try not to throw a wild party ... or burn the apartment down."

"It'll be hard." He hums in his throat. "So tempting."

I squeeze his hand. "I'll be home around midnight. We're just catching up ... maybe dancing."

He groans. "I'm up. I'll get dressed."

"*You* are not invited. Girls' night."

"But I want to see you dance." He pouts.

"Carissa will send you a video ... or I'll come dance for you after," I promise, kissing him again. "Text me if anything goes wrong."

"So you'll be checking your phone all night? Worrying about me?"

"Distance makes the heart grow fonder." I wink and head out.

Carissa and I meet at our favorite bar and order margaritas. We catch up about work and everything else, then she bites her bottom lip. I lean my head to the side. "What is it?"

"There's something I need to tell you. But I don't want you to judge me or anything, okay?"

"Okay..."

I'm dating Nick." She covers her face. "Oh, my God, it's been hell not telling you."

"Nick, as in our boss, Nick? I didn't know he was your type."

"I didn't either!" She shakes her head. "Not until that day when the gunmen stormed in. Oh, my God, Sofia, you should see how Nick took charge. You know I'm a sucker for guys who are in control."

I nod, thinking of Jasper. It's obvious Carissa has a type. But I'm not perturbed about it. I'm relieved, happy for my best friend. I rub her shoulder and tell her so.

"Thanks, Sofia. He's just so ... soft and sweet and deep," she gushes. "He says what he means and follows through. He's beautiful. It just kind of happened. We went on a date, then he invited me in for a nightcap. We were watching a movie and when they kissed on screen, I just couldn't not kiss him, and he kissed me back and ... Oh, my god. Fireworks."

I laugh and squeeze her hand. "I'm so happy for you."

"You don't think it's weird or wrong? I mean, he is our boss."

"No!" I shake my head. "Dios mio. Nick is amazing, and he's lucky to have you."

Carissa scoots closer. "Honestly, girl... best sex *ever*. I can't believe how good it is. How good everything is. The janitor almost caught us in the supply closet last Tuesday."

"Oh, my God. You're scandalous!"

We talk about all the fun she's having, then she looks at our hands. "How are you, though?"

"I'm ..." I try to find the right words, then ignore it. "It's different. Dad and I have had lunch a few times, and he's actually trying. It's good, but it's not easy to forget so many years of hating him. We're figuring it out."

"And you. Actually you?" She asks.

"I have nightmares where I wake up and see the floor covered with blood," I admit, something I haven't even told Jasper. "I wake up afraid that people are in the house. Loud noises are hard. I keep seeing bullets and hearing gunshots and screaming. I'm glad I survived, and I'm happy to have Jasper, but ... it was a lot."

"Well, I won't ask another thing about it," Carissa replies. "And we need to dance."

I take her hand and join her on the dance floor. I snap a video of us dancing and send it to Jasper, then have another round of drinks. We get tacos and laugh like old times, just making memories. Carissa gets hit on several times and when someone does approach me, my bitch face sends them away.

Carissa pulls her phone and take a photo of my face. I reach for it. "What are you doing?"

"Showing Jasper that his girlfriend's cold as ice."

When I get home, Jasper is still lounging on the couch. He motions me forward with a finger. "Your sexy ass needs to get over here."

"Oh yeah?"

"I love your bitch face." He groans when I sit across his thighs. He pushes my dress over my hips and slips his hand between my legs, teasing my clit. "And you, dancing."

"You're all kinds of horny for my mean side." I kiss him, wrapping an arm around his good shoulder. "My underwear is in the way."

"Are they?"

"Move them and touch me." I order as my nose brushes his.

He groans, and we get each other off on the couch before going to bed. I pull his arm around me and kiss his chest. Jasper rubs my side. "What is it, love?"

"I'm glad you're here." I meet his eyes. "I'm glad you're mine."

He blinks at me, then kisses me hard, licking into my mouth until I'm half convinced that he's going to try to fuck me. When he draws back, he studies my face. "I *love* you."

"I love you too. Everything we went through ... it was worth it."

"Sofia." His brow furrows.

I shake my head. "It is. I mean, I wish you hadn't been shot. I wish I didn't have nightmares, but we're here, together ... and I'm a better person than I was."

He kisses my forehead. "I'm seeing my dad tomorrow. Will you go with me? I don't think I can do it alone."

"You want me there? You always said ..."

"You're giving your dad another chance, and you're ... you're doing a lot of things differently. I want to try being better too." He kisses my forehead again. "Which means showing you shit."

"Like what?"

"Pictures from overseas. Telling you about shit I went through ... asking if you know any good therapists..."

I kiss him once, twice, a third time. "Give and take."

"Give and take," I agree.

I SLIP MY HANDS THROUGH the jacket sleeves and adjust the front over my dress. Glancing in the mirror, I give my reflection a satisfied smile. The outfit says innocent, cute. It's the kind a girl wears when a guy decides to take her home to meet his mom, or dad, in this instance. I'm a little nervous after what Jasper told me about his dad, but there's no way I'm not going. I need to be by Jasper's side.

He grins at me, and I straighten his collar before kissing him. "Do you want the cane?" I ask.

"No."

"Wheelchair?" He rolls his eyes, and I hug him. "I want this to be easy, but if he insults you, I can't promise my mouth won't run away with me."

Jasper kisses the top of my head. "This is one battle I'll fight on my own, Sofia. I just need your support."

"You have it," I promise.

We leave our apartment and head to the outskirts of town, soon pulling up to a little house. It's small and looks neglected. The blue paint job is faded and cracked, the gutters full, the screen door torn.

Jasper keeps a grip on my hand as he knocks on the door. A guy with a limp soon answers. He snarls at Jasper, then looks at me.

"Who's this?" he asks, his expression getting more curious by the second.

"This is my girlfriend, Sofia." Jasper pulls me closer to him. "You and I have some things to talk about."

"I don't talk to failures," he snaps.

I feel the reply on my tongue, but Jasper rubs my hand with his thumb. He meets his father's eye. "I'm not a failure. I'm alive. I'm your son."

His father shifts his gaze to the floor, his chest bouncing with a hefty sigh. "Why are you here?"

"I'm here to fix things between us. I don't want this rift between us anymore."

His father looks him over again and grunts, "Fine, but make it quick," then lets us into his dirty house. Daisy might be messy, but this is grime. The only thing that doesn't have dust on it is the bottles of alcohol. Jasper's father lights a cigarette as we sit on the old couch, and I start counting down the minutes until we leave.

Jasper rubs my knee and whispers in my ear. "I'll make you come for putting up with the dirt."

I pull out my phone, scrolling through my email while half listening as they talk, back and forth until Jasper's father hits the table, his hand shaking, his eyes threatening. He snarls. "You left the war. They needed you,; and you-"

"Daisy needed me too." Jasper glares. "She lost her husband. She lost the father of her child. She lost everything in one moment. You could have lost everything too. You rarely see Daisy. You never see me. If you want to be old and alone with your bottles, fine. But I'm here, and I'm not going anywhere."

His father sits back and shakes his head, but his expression softens a little.

"I'm a good man. I *was* a soldier, but I'm alive and here. I'm leaving the private sector. I'm going to work on behalf of other soldiers to help them when they get home. If you see that as failure, that's on you – not me."

His father scratches his neck and looks us over. "And this?"

"Sofia saved my life," Jasper says, his arm circling around me.

I blink at him and meet his eyes. What the hell is he talking about?

"I was dead inside before I met her. And now, I feel more alive than I've ever been."

"Oh, Jasper..." I lean against him with a delighted smile.

"It's true. You keep saying I saved your life, but it goes both ways, especially how you've been there after I got shot."

"Oh, so she's the one Daisy told me about. You got injured while protecting her." Jasper's father beams a little. "Good job with keeping her alive."

I hear Jasper's intake breath, then he sighs out loud. "Thanks. It means a lot coming from you."

His father fans him off, but he's still wearing a soft smile. "It's good to know you're still having a positive effect in the real world. I expect nothing less from my kids."

Jasper still appears in shock when we settle in the car half an hour later, after he spent the time reminiscing with his dad. He seems lighter, like a burden has been taken off his shoulders.

I lean over and give him a hard kiss on his lips. He sighs and kisses me back. "You did so well."

"I like your reward system."

"I love you." I say softly, clinging to him. "Not just words."

He grins and smiles. "So how are we going to tell people we met? That you stole my heart by being my sexy nurse? That you nearly destroyed me by swooping in and-"

"No." I shake my head and kiss him again. "The real one. Where you had to fight off gangsters and fight me until I couldn't help falling in love for you. So intensely, head over heels love that I even agreed to getting a dog in the future."

"A dog?" He chuckles then kisses me again. "Now I know it's true."

"And I'll remind you every day. I love you." I smile. "Te amo, estúpido."

Epilogue

Jasper

1 year later

Turning onto our street after leaving work at the VA, I smile at the sight of the white picket fence around our house. It's been three months since Sofia and I moved into our new home, but I'm still not used to the view. It feels surreal that everything I hoped for is now manifested in my life. I'm a lucky man. I thank the universe every day.

Sofia already told me she'll be late tonight, but I'm not surprised. She just got promoted and now that she has the entire company under her control, she's making changes that are improving the city.

She's even working with her dad to get new legislation passed to safeguard the welfare of young, homeless kids. Even with her softening for me, she's a fierce momma bear when it comes to making lives better for others. And it just makes me love her more.

I don't mind being the silent support at home, working a nine to five, keeping things clean, planning dates. Like tonight. She's not going to know what hit her. I take care of a few things around the house, namely picking up and doing my laundry.

Then I set some candles up on our little dining table, order Thai food, since she's been talking about how much she craves it. When I'm done with setting up, I remove the engagement ring I bought six months ago from its hiding spot. Life has been so busy, and Sofia is still hard to read when it comes to relationship points. But I'm sure she's ready for this next step.

Last month, she introduced me to her mother and her brother. She's met all my family. We've been living together since I got out of the hospital. We partner on work projects. And we have been doing well.

No major fights since she lost her shit with me for leaving plates out for a week. We've made efforts to share the important and unimportant stuff. We've balanced plans with spontaneity. It's been work, true work, but every morning I wake up and fall in love with her all over again. On the hard days, I choose to love her more than whatever's bothering me.

The sound of the front door opening makes me jam in the ring box in my back pocket. Shit. Why is Sofia already home?

"Hello!" Daisy calls, yelling into the house. "Anyone home? Anyone fucking?"

Damn it. I should have planned better when we moved. Living two streets away from my sister has led to more awkward moments than anything else. I walk into the dining room to find her staring at the setup, a tiny pout on her face. "What are you doing here?"

"Just wanted to check in on my favorite brother."

"I'm your only brother, and I can't watch Ellie tonight. I have plans." I motion to the table.

"Damn it."

"Looks like you're actually going to have to use a babysitter, aren't you?" I tease.

She sighs and rubs her hand over her forehead. "I just want things to go well with Trent. I think I'm ready."

"To give him boyfriend status, after dating for a year?" I smirk. "Wow. And I thought you were the romantic one."

"Shut up! And bullshit." She smacks me. "I move slow, for Ellie's sake."

"I know." I hug her. "Ashton would approve of him. He'd love him for you and Ellie."

She sniffs. "Now you're getting sappy. I didn't come over here to cry."

"I know why you came over here. But I mean it. I can't watch Ellie. It's a big night," I insist.

"Oh? You mean like that?" She motions to the outline of the box in my pants pocket. "It looks like you're about to change Sofia's title."

She lunges at me and pulls it out before I can stop her, dancing around the table as she stares at it. "Ooh, what a ring. I'm sure she'll say yes."

"Daisy!" I try to get it back from her.

She giggles and shoves it against my chest. "I guess I can find something to do ... that involves Ellie. Putt-putt or something."

"Good plan," I grumble, glaring at her after checking the ring. It's modest, the best I can do. "I'm so nervous. It's not good enough for her."

"It is." Daisy holds my shoulders in her hands. "More importantly *you* are. She loves you, and anyone can see it, even when she's calling you a dummy."

I smile slightly. "I swear, it means she loves me."

"Yeah, hold on to that ... and don't expect Sofia too soon. You're not injured anymore."

I roll my eyes. The woman hasn't been home on time since I was given the all-clear. We had sex, then it was back to overtime. Daisy finally leaves, and I finish prepping for the night. I practice two different proposals until I hear Sofia pull in.

It's five thirty, she still shouldn't be this early. I glance at everything already set up, at everything that she's not supposed to see until I'm ready to try and get down on one knee ... and hope I can get back up.

Fuck. I didn't think I would be so nervous.

I stow the ring in my pocket and watch her come in like a hurricane. She goes through her necessary routine, starting with kissing me. Then she's talking to herself, talking about her day in bursts that I only half hear. I agree to what I can hear without sounding ridiculous, open she stays away from the dining room until I'm ready to propose. She goes for a quick shower, and I rehearse my speech once more.

When she comes out of our bedroom, though, she's wearing a dress that has me drooling. Sofia should *always* wear red. Red, showing off delicious cleavage, her delectable thighs, all the places I want to touch and kiss and love forever.

"Wow," I breathe.

She walks up to me, suddenly shy. I notice both her hands are behind her back. "Jasper."

"What do you have there, sexy minx?" I lean to the side, trying to see. "Is it something naughty? Another crop?"

"No!" She gasps, blushing deep. "No. It's not a toy."

"You know I love you being a dominatrix. I think I'm even ready to tie you up, tigress," I tease, trying to distract her so she doesn't notice the very conspicuous set up.

"You know I love you." She breathes slowly. "And we do pretty well at this whole living together thing."

I tighten my hand in my pocket and smile as I close the distance between us. Is she doing what I think she's doing? "We do a damn good job of it."

"So I think ... I think we should um ..." She chews her bottom lip.

I brush my fingers over her cheek. "Should fuck more often? Call it quits while it's good? Finally get that dog you talked to me about?"

"No! Stop distracting me!" She shakes her head, then clears her throat. "I think we should make it official. We should ..."

She's never had trouble finding words before. Whatever she's saying is hard.

She swallows, takes a deep breath, and meets my eyes. "I love you, Jasper. Even when you drive me insane. And you're good at that. You're also good at calming me down. At making me feel alive. At making every day of my life better. Do you want to do that forever?"

"Of course, I do." I smirk. Now I know exactly what she's asking me. I know she's beating me to the punch, so I'm going to make her say it. I'm going to make sure that she says the words and sees it through.

She bites her bottom lip. "Do you ... want to get married? To me? Be my husband, even though I'm half-crazy and aggressive and have a million things to accomplish and-"

I pull her against me and kiss her hard, hungry, demanding. She melts against me and licks into my mouth, standing on my toes to be able to kiss me deeper. I swear, I can feel her heartbeat. When I draw back, I show her the box.

"You beat me to it."

She laughs and watches me pull out the simple ring. Her eyes water, and she nods. "Yes."

"Yes?"

She nods again. "Put it on my finger!"

I laugh and slide the ring on. She shows me the little gold band she got me. I hold out my hand, and she puts it on before laughing and fanning her watery eyes. "I said I wasn't going to cry."

The doorbell suddenly rings, and she jumps, her hand tightening on mine. I press my forehead to hers. "I had a whole plan, gorgeous. And you had to go and ruin it."

"Not my fault you were slow to the punch," she teases as I head to the front door.

"I was waiting for the perfect time," I grumble in reply. Truth is, I love how it happened just now.

I thank the delivery guy for the food, tip him, and place it on the table. Sofia takes my hand before I can open the bag and leads me to the bedroom.

"I thought we were going to eat."

"You are." She giggles.

I grab her ass and she squeals.

I learn she has nothing under her dress when I lift it over her head. She takes a step back, one, another, until she sits on the bed. I strip for her and join her. She keeps crawling backwards as I approach until she hits the pillows.

I kiss her hungrily, fisting her hair in my hand as I lick across her tongue and breathe her in. Mine. Sofia is mine, forever. A wild, sharp and prickly woman wanting to be a part of me. I smile and draw back.

"Do you really want to be mine?" I ask her.

"Oh no." She captures my lips. "You have it backwards."

I laugh and curl my lips around hers, jerking her against me. "You've had me since our first kiss, Sofia."

She moans and kisses me again. After a year of being with Sofia, I still feel the hum of electricity rip through me when she kisses me. I stroke down her side and over her thigh, that shallow wound from the bullet that tore through me.

"I love you." I say against her mouth. "Every inch of you."

"Even when I'm crazy?"

"Even with your wrong opinions about where things go." I kiss down her neck.

She pushes her body against mine, and I groan. She makes patience impossible. But she shakes her head. "I'm only wrong like ... ten percent of the time."

I rub her clit and push two fingers into her. She gasps. "Maybe twenty."

I chuckle and lick across the top of her breasts. "Maybe thirty?"

"Maybe." She groans and rubs herself down on my hand. "I need you, Jasper. Right now. Inside me."

"Condoms," I reply, then remember I didn't buy a box. Fuck.

"No." She strokes my hard cock. "We're forever. Nothing between us."

I groan and let her guide me into her. Fuck, it's so much better without the condom. I can feel how wet she is, how warm, everything amplified. I thrust deeper, and she claws down my back, grabbing my ass.

Sofia rolls her hips to meet mine and kisses me hard. "Just like that. So perfect."

"And all yours." I whisper in her ear. "Forever."

We go through at least three positions, and I make her come each time. I bask in her pleasure and enjoy every orgasm I know is mine. When I finally come, she holds me close and smiles.

We cuddle, and I see her admiring her ring. "You chose well."

"Thanks, picky pants." I kiss her forehead. "I can't believe we were going to propose on the same day."

"I realized last week that I was tired of waiting." She breathes. "That it was stupid since I can't see myself with anyone but you."

"I've had the ring for six months," I admit.

"Six ... You're crazy." She kisses me full on the mouth, then rubs over my chest. "Did you have to clear it with Lee?"

My counselor, no. I smile and shake my head. "Nope. I didn't bring it up. I just ... you're a meteor, Sofia. You changed my whole world."

"Don't credit me with that. I put you in the hospital."

"Nope. You make me a better person, and I like who I am with you. I like that you can enjoy my puns but also get me through the worst of my nightmares. That you never make me feel less than, that you've been there through the worst and ... and you're the only person I want to tell everything to."

She kisses my palm and nuzzles me. "I love you even when I don't like you. Plus, you just ... you make me laugh even when I'm furious, even when I don't want to. You challenge me a million ways but make me stronger and smarter."

"I fucking love you."

She opens her mouth, and her stomach growls, making us both laugh. I give her my shirt and slide into my jeans. She traces the scar on my back, then kisses just above it, following my spine up to my neck. "I love you. Every amazing part."

"Even the damaged parts?" I still can't believe she doesn't care about my leg, the things that are hard for me to do, the fact that I'm scarred and riddled with PTSD and nightmares.

"Yes." Another kiss before she bites my ear. "And you love me, even though I'm a terrible shot."

"You're a danger to everyone with a gun." I pat her thigh, then reach back and pull her into a piggyback ride. "But you can do the biting, I'll do the shooting."

"Hopefully never again." She sighs. "I want the fucking happily ever after."

"Until I'm your bodyguard when you're in congress."

She kisses my cheek. "Even then. Happily ever after. Fairytale shit only."

"Yes, ma'am. I can do that."

Pssst ... Like Fake Dating Romance stories? Great, you can get 5 of my fake dating novels for just **$2.99** or ***download it for free*** if you are a Kindle Unlimited or Prime Member? This amazing deal is ***over 1,500 pages***. Get this awesome deal below ^_^

[1]

CLICK HERE TO GET THE DEAL[2]

A STEAMY BOX SET OF FAKE DATING ROMANCE NOVELS.

List of novels inside are:

Fake Ex-Wife – A Enemies to Lovers Romance

Fake Boyfriend – A Bully Romance

Fake Stepdad – An age-Gap Romance

Fake Reverse Harem – A Forbidden Office Romance

Pretend Date: Grumpy Billionaire Stepdaddy – An Age-Gap Romance

All are standalones, contain no cheating and have happy-ever-after endings ♡

CLICK HERE[3] to download and enjoy!

LIKE ***secret*** bargains? If yes, then I have some great '*insiders' info*' just for you, but keep this on the hush. This deal is only for readers who have at least read one of my books to the end, ok? Did you know you

1. https://www.amazon.com/dp/B0C6737CSY
2. https://www.amazon.com/dp/B0C6737CSY
3. https://www.amazon.com/dp/B0C6737CSY

can have 8 of my full-length novels PLUS an extra steamy story from IZZIE VEE[4] included as a bonus, all for just **$2.99** or ***download it for free*** if you are a Kindle Unlimited or Prime Member? This amazing deal is ***over 2,100 pages***. Get this awesome deal below ^_^ ...

[5]

CLICK HERE TO GET THE DEAL[6]

A HOT, STEAMY COLLECTION OF AGE-GAP ROMANCE NOVELS.

List of novels inside are:

Heating Up the Kitchen - a reverse harem romance

Just Can't Behave - a forbidden, age-gap romance

Protection Details - a bodyguard, forbidden, age-gap romance

4. https://www.amazon.com/s?k=izzie+vee&i=digital-text&crid=31LQJTEQYT2EE&sprefix=izzie+vee%2Cdigital-text%2C121&ref=nb_sb_noss
5. https://www.amazon.com/dp/B0B1YTNCKQ
6. https://www.amazon.com/dp/B0B1YTNCKQ

Getting Through the Seasons - a stepbrother's best friend, enemies to lovers

Getting Through the Seasons 2

Getting Through the Seasons 3

A Dose of Sunshine - a rockstar, enemies to lovers romance

Mr. Grumpy's Fake Ex-wife - a boss, stalker, enemies to lovers romance

A Bonus Novella - My Roommate's Daddy - an instalove, OTT, age-gap romance

All are standalones, contain no cheating and have happy-ever-after endings ♡

Don't miss out on this fantastic offer, grab your copy today.

That's a completed 3 books series, 5 full length novels and a novella inside. CLICK HERE[7] to download and enjoy!

Let's connect.

Get this book for **FREE**[8] when you sign up for our newsletter.

WICKEDLY STEAMY & FILTHY!

7. https://www.amazon.com/dp/B0B1YTNCKQ

8. https://dl.bookfunnel.com/c4j8urik87

CLICK HERE TO GET FOR FREE[9]

SAMPLE

I thought my big, over-protective stepbrother was the biggest prick ever,

Until Thanksgiving, when he brought home an even cockier devil, Sawyer,

A tattooed rebel with jawlines of steel and dark piercing eyes glinting with danger.

I can tell he's the type to fight in public brawls, someone who would protect me if I'm his,

But I'm not his type, I am too young, too inexperienced, no experience.

He has every intention of being the wicked menace to his best friend's little sister,

Hell-bent on driving me up the wall, taunting me, teasing me, torturing me, leaving me in puddles,

9. https://dl.bookfunnel.com/c4j8urik87

Yes, leaving me in puddles has become a sick little game to him,
Loving to watch me squirm in need,
Knowing damn well he'll never cross the forbidden line between us,
And my stepbrother will never let him either,
He knows Sawyer only uses shy, nerdy girls like me for a one-night stands, I know it too,
Then why do I get so weak to his tease, his touch,
I vow to myself that I will never give in to him,
My V-card will be given to a gentleman who deserves it, not a bad-ass bad boy like Sawyer,
But then I made a mistake, our lips touched ... ***DOWNLOAD FOR FREE HERE***[10]***.***

10. https://dl.bookfunnel.com/c4j8urik87

Printed in Great Britain
by Amazon